PENGUIN MODERN CLASSICS

THE RECTOR'S DAUGHTER

Flora Macdonald Mayor was born in 1872 and died in 1932. *The Rector's Daughter* is not an autobiographical novel but her family had points in common with the family which the book describes. Her father was a Cambridge scholar clergyman of mid-Victorian vintage and her mother was a niece of George Grote, the historian of Greece. Flora went to Newnham when university education was still a rare adventure for a woman. Soon afterwards she wrote her first book, *Mrs Hammond's Children*, and published it under a pseudonym. The death of her fiancé from typhoid fever in India brought her back into the family circle, in which, with a naturally joyous temperament but an ever-increasing burden of ill-health, she spent the rest of her life. In 1913 she published a short novel, *The Third Miss Symons*, with a preface by John Masefield and in 1924 *The Rector's Daughter*, which won immediate acclaim from such critics as G. B. Stern and Rebecca West. Another novel, *The Squire's Daughter*, and a volume of short stories complete her published work.

The Rector's Daughter

F. M. MAYOR

PENGUIN BOOKS

Penguin Books Ltd, Harmondsworth, Middlesex, England
Viking Penguin Inc., 40 West 23rd Street, New York, New York 10010, U.S.A.
Penguin Books Australia Ltd, Ringwood, Victoria, Australia
Penguin Books Canada Ltd, 2801 John Street, Markham, Ontario, Canada L3R 1B4
Penguin Books (N.Z.) Ltd, 182–190 Wairau Road, Auckland 10, New Zealand

—

First published by Leonard and Virginia Woolf at the Hogarth Press 1924
Published in Penguin Books 1973
Reprinted 1978, 1980, 1981, 1985

—

Copyright 1924 by F. M. Mayor
All rights reserved

—

Made and printed in Great Britain by
Richard Clay (The Chaucer Press) Ltd.,
Bungay, Suffolk
Set in Monotype Times

I

DEDMAYNE is an insignificant village in the Eastern counties. There were no motor buses in the days of which I write, and Cayley, the nearest station, was six miles off. Dedmayne was ashamed of this, because without a station the most interesting feature for a picture post-card was not available. There was no great house with park or garden to give character to the village. Progress had laid hold of it fifty years before, and pulled down and rebuilt the church, the Rectory, and most of the cottages. Part of Dedmayne was even ugly; there was a bit of straight flat road near the church, with low dusty hedges, treeless turnip fields, and corrugated iron roofs of barns which might rank with Canada. Dedmayne was on the way to nowhere; it was not troubled by motors or bicycles, except native bicycles. The grimy 'Blue Boar' did not induce any one to stop for tea. Artists and weekend Londoners wanted something picturesque. Still, being damp, it was bound to have certain charms; the trunks were mossy, and the walls mouldy. There were also those tall bowery trees in the hedgerows, and little pleasant risings in the meadows, which are so common in England one forgets to notice them.

The social advantages of Dedmayne were on a par with the scenery. There were no gentry, not even the customary deceased clergyman's daughter or widow to help in the parish work. The late schoolmaster had been there thirty years, and had lost heart; Miss Gage, the new mistress struggled not to lose heart too. The late Rector had been at Dedmayne fifty years, and drank. The present, Canon Jocelyn with his daughter Mary of thirty-five, were the only outside influences, if they could be called outside, since he had lived there forty-three years and had seldom left the village, even when he was younger, and never in the last seven years. He was now eighty-two.

Mary was born at Dedmayne; she also had rarely gone outside its neighbourhood. She had charge of her imbecile sister Ruth,

5

who could not be left. When Mary was a young girl she had grumbled at the remoteness, and envied the Redlands from the next village, who moved to Southsea. But gradually she became attached to Dedmayne, and felt that the more isolated it was, the more it had its own flavour, unpolluted by towns. 'We just go mouldering along year after year,' she said to a friend, 'and it is always the same.' What has been known from childhood must be lovable, whether it is ugly or beautiful. Perhaps because its natural charms were not great she loved it the more, in case its feelings might be hurt.

Canon Jocelyn was conspicuous in the neighbourhood. His thin, stately figure, finely chiselled features, and eyes, severe, satirical, and melancholy by turns, would have made him noticeable in any society.

His daughter Mary was a decline. Her uninteresting hair, dragged severely back, displayed a forehead lined too early. Her complexion was a dullish hue, not much lighter than her hair. She had her father's beautiful eyes, and hid them with glasses. She was dowdily dressed, but she had many companions in the neighbourhood, from labourers' wives to the ladies of the big houses, to share her dowdiness. It was not observed; she was as much a part of her village as its homely hawthorns.

If Dedmayne Rectory, with its white stucco, outside shutters, and verandah, could not be called beautiful, it had a character of its own. The shutters and verandah were intended as a protection against the sun in summer. But what about the winter with its true country cold, the chill, chill dawns and twilights of January? The Rector before Canon Jocelyn planted laurels and deodars near the house to protect it against the wind. They made the study and dining-room as dark as a vault, and the wind rushed in all the same. Canon Jocelyn was fond of the dark, as his generation was, and fond of the laurels and deodars, giving them a special place in his heart with elms and oaks, because they had grown in his childhood's garden, and so he instinctively felt them to be extremely English.

A crumbling decay pervaded the whole place; it would have been the despair of energetic natures. There was a little black oblong pond in the garden, never full and never empty; it looked

6

like a monster slug. The hens were seldom killed off, they laid an egg a week, and the shrivelled, woody, herbaceous plants dwindled to the size of field flowers. The real field flowers came in unchecked and joined them; all was unweeded. There was a round bed in the front drive, supposed by the gardener to be Canon Jocelyn's favourite. But those geraniums, petunias, lobelias, calceolarias, and variegated plants, each in their crooked circle one within another, were never observed by him from one summer's end to another. He was indifferent to flowers; he sighed over the childish preoccupation of the clergy in their pergolas. Mary herself liked wild flowers best. There is a surfeit of neat bright gardens in the country; sometimes she felt she would be glad never to see a sweet-pea again. She could not stop muddle and decay, she had neither the money nor the capacity; she could not fight battles with her father, Cook, Emma, the gardener, and the pony. So she let things go, and came to like decay.

Not a new piece of furniture had been bought in the house within Mary's memory, not a room had been papered or painted, not a chintz renewed for thirty years. Everything had faded to mellowness. The walls were hidden by portraits of former Jocelyns: the men, handsome, mostly clergymen and soldiers; the women, plain and distinguished. The drawing-room with its straight-backed arm-chairs and striped chintz, had been getting old-fashioned forty years before, when Canon Jocelyn had wanted it to look like his mother's drawing-room. Now the circle was coming round, the new archdeacon's wife was enthusiastic about it. A charming drawing of the dead Mrs Jocelyn hung over the mantel-piece, lovely, graceful, and serene. Why could she not have given at least one of those attributes to her daughter?

Books streamed everwhere, all over the house, even up the attic stairs. They were on every subject imaginable. There was hardly any branch of knowledge which Canon Jocelyn's in-quiring mind had not investigated. He read many languages as easily as his own. His learning he considered simply what was suitable for a scholar and a gentleman. He was not elated by it, but he was aware that he knew far more than any one in the neighbourhood. He was gentle with the squires and with ladies, and from all below him in standing he expected ignorance. From

7

the clergy he did require something, and not getting it, he put them down as neither scholars nor gentlemen. He kept up his marvellous range of reading till about 1895. Then his mind closed to new ideas. Books published after that date he would not trouble to read: 'I have enough here to last me my few remaining years.' This weakness enabled the clergy to triumph over him sometimes, and even ladies, only they would much rather have his polite attentions than triumph, which he did not like.

Canon Jocelyn's study was filled with his own particular friends in literature. There was a bust of Socrates from civility to the Greeks, but, unlike most Englishmen, his passion was for the Romans. He really preferred Virgil to all Christian classics. Donne, Barrow, and Jeremy Taylor lay about on the floor, and early fathers were piled on the chairs. Engravings of Dante, Sir Thomas More, Dr Johnson, and Pascal were hung up the stairs.

There was a difficulty with Pascal. He was French, and Canon Jocelyn despised the French. The Revolution, Napoleon, and the Commune still rankled, so he always said of Pascal, 'He had a great mind, and I think, much as one respects the brilliance and lucidity of the French, one may say it was an English mind.'

He extended his patriotic antipathy to the French language. 'The French have a number of useful expressions; the turn of their phrases is often more subtle and delicate than ours. English is too noble a vehicle.' When there were subtle and delicate terms in Greek, he did not think English too noble a vehicle. He felt the French pronunciation of French was what was to be expected from them. He would not demean his English lips. If any English person, particularly any English *man*, tried to pronounce French correctly, Canon Jocelyn would say afterwards, 'There is a little affectation about him; I cannot tell precisely what it is.'

The *Monthly Packets* and Lives of missionaries were the taste of Mary's aunt, who had lived with them at one time. They were packed away in the large sunny spare-room, which had been hers. The sunniest and largest was the invalid's. Mary herself had kept always to a small dark chamber, which had been considered suitable for a schoolgirl. Some of the old lady visitors found the *Monthly Packets* a comfort; they blenched at the great leather backs and brown pages of most of the books, and at their s's made like f's.

As to Mary's room, it reflected her truly. There were childish animals and plush picture-frames on her mantelpiece, mixed with some precious china bequeathed to 'My own dear Miss Mary' from old village friends, and messy little pincushions made by their shaking fingers. There was rubbish she had bought at sales of work, all her children's books, her favourite Miss Yonge and Trollope, a large collection of Elizabethan dramatists, and books of medieval mystics.

Who that knows such households will wonder that every shelf and every drawer was crammed with papers and pamphlets? for Canon Jocelyn could not bear to throw away. There were, of course, Bibles in every room in the house, so that any one in a hurry to read the inspired Word should not waste a moment. There were six in the drawing-room and nine in the study. Honoured Jocelyn elders for generations had bequeathed them; some had their Bibles laid beside them in their coffins. These elders must have had wonderful eyes, for the print was often very fine. They were marked in several places; the marked texts shed a curious light on the markers. The favourites of the gentle great-aunt Eliza, a Calvinist, were, 'Many are called but *few* are chosen'; '*Strait* is the gate and *narrow* is the way.' The pugnacious bishop, Canon Jocelyn's father, chose 'Pray for them that *despitefully use* you'; 'I am *meek* and *lowly* of heart.' Each found in the rich treasure-house something contradictory, and therefore satisfying to their natures.

Shakespeare and the Prayer-book were in the same privileged position as Bibles. There were not more than three Miltons, because of undesirable views on kings, liberty, and divorce.

Such was Mary's home, the home of her whole life. She thought, as a child thinks, that most other homes were like it. But it was a frail, frail survival, lasting on out of its time, its companions vanished long since, and would fall at a touch when Canon Jocelyn died.

2

MARY's childhood had been happy. She had three brothers and a sister, all older than herself. There were families of children, too, who had come and played with them. She lost the sweet mother of the portrait early. At the time she did not mourn, only to long for her more intensely later. Her sister went away and did not return, she was not told why. Aunt Lottie, her mother's sister, came to live with them. Her brothers were sent to boarding-schools; she had dull governesses at home. As each brother grew up he went abroad, and became more or less lost to sight. By an unfortunate chance the families she had played with moved from the neighbourhood, and their places were taken by bachelors and childless couples.

Her aunt was no companion. She was puzzled by Mary, who was stormy, 'not like our family at all.' She managed by saying 'No' to everything Mary wanted. That seemed strange to look back to. Now she was the dear old lady, always saying 'Yes', and the role suited her better.

Canon Jocelyn was puzzled and alarmed with very young children, but from six onwards for two or three years he had found Mary a pleasant plaything. Then she passed to a less attractive stage. Faults showed themselves in stronger colours; Aunt Lottie grumbled about her. He withdrew himself; he was never a delightful playmate again. Besides, he became occupied with St Augustine, and had no leisure for her. From time to time his friends and their wives came to see him. Most of them took little notice of Mary, but some liked her. She liked them too, better than her own contemporaries, of whom she was afraid, she saw them so seldom. She fell back on reading, and got the reputation of being 'learned.'

She had longed for friends, and had cherished passions for two or three bright girls with pigtails, who never seemed shy. She had had some passions for elder ladies also, but they were impatient of uncouth adoration. She retired within herself, and fell in love instead with Mr Rochester, Hamlet, and Dr Johnson.

Sometimes even now when she did not sleep, she indulged in these delightful fantasies, more vivid than any incident of ordinary life, and would be suddenly startled by seeing it was dawn.

When she was eighteen, and should have come out, Aunt Lottie recollected that late hours were bad for rheumatism. Canon Jocelyn said that 'since things had been so different' (meaning his wife's death) 'he had not the heart for gaiety.' At nearly seventy the zest for parties was gone; he was absorbed in his literary work. What little contact he required with the outside world was satisfied by intimacy with one or two of the neighbouring clergy. So Mary was seldom asked to dances, for it was certain no return dance could be got out of the Rectory, and still seldomer went.

The Rectory tennis court was uneven and small. No one with pretensions to tennis could be expected to play on it. Mary and Will, her youngest brother, who was still at home, asked that it might be put in order. Canon Jocelyn answered, 'It is quite unnecessary.' He was at that moment helping a friend with almost more money than he could afford. Not a hint of this was given to his children. 'Stingy Jew,' said Will to Mary. Thus Mary got no practice in tennis. This, her short sight, and her learnedness made her a responsibility to hostesses, so she was not asked to afternoon parties either.

She became shyer, and from shyness awkward. Here was a source of annoyance for Canon Jocelyn. He had always been able to charm; he would have preferred a daughter who could continue the tradition. Mary accepted his decisions unquestioningly. She did not enjoy parties; it was no hardship to stay at home. Her bent was to work in the village. But here again she was crushed by the invincible force of her father's inaction.

He was glad she should carry on the old-established Sunday School, Bible Class, and Mothers' Meeting; it was different when she initiated something new. She had read Mill's *Political Economy*, and burned to impart her knowledge to the village. A class of girls was formed. It soon dropped away, even tea could not keep it alive, all but one stupid, silent girl, and a class could not be kept up for her.

From the first Canon Jocelyn had damped the undertaking with

11

his favourite 'I should hardly have thought it was worth while.'
He said it again when the class failed, and Mary was feeling very
sore.

For once she turned round on him. 'Whenever I do anything,
you say it's not worth while. It's unbearable.' She rushed out of the
room, and when she was alone she burst into tears. He followed
her and said stiffly, though he did not mean to be stiff, 'Mary,
why are you crying?'

'Never mind,' she said. 'It's useless telling you.'

He stood by her in silence; she went on sobbing.

'As nothing I do is any good, I wish I hadn't been born.'

Never had words stabbed him so much.

'My dear child,' he said earnestly. 'Never say that again. I did
not mean – let me explain myself.' He continued hesitatingly,
confused at the strange step he was taking. 'I do not consider
Mill's *Political Economy* a subject suited to your class. Political
economy is an interesting and by no means unprofitable branch
of study for trained minds, but it can never be an exact science.
The wild claims made for political economy by that inspector who
lunched with us yesterday are based on an erroneous conception
of what science can do.' (To see Canon Jocelyn's expression as he
pronounced the word 'wild'!) 'Sykes tells me there is a real danger of political economy taking the place of mathematics at
Cambridge. I can only say that will be the end of Cambridge.
Not that I think, Mary, it was possible you would have advanced
far with your class. The people here have not much zeal or energy
of mind. I had my ambitions for them long ago when I first
came to Dedmayne, but I abandoned them. If the people can
be persuaded to continue along the old rut, one must be
satisfied.'

Mary did not understand what he was saying but he had called
her 'my dear child', and she was grateful for his confidence. It
was almost the only time he did so speak. She looked back on it
with gratitude; he soon forgot it.

After some other failures she stopped initiating schemes of
utility in the village, and confined herself to the usual round.
Years afterwards the silent remnant of the economics class came
to see Mary. Ellen had left Dedmayne, gone to service, and

married. Sometimes she wrote, Mary thought with the intent of jogging her memory about Christmas presents.

'Oh, Miss Mary,' Ellen cried, 'it *is* nice to see you after all these years. Cook said you was pale, but I shouldn't have known you. I'm changed too, such a stout one as I am, and talk! "Why, you've found your tongue," they all say that at home. Oh, the dear old days! Do you remember the class? Dad used to have a rare laugh when I come back and told him what you said. I wouldn't set by you at tea, I was too frightened. Oh, that riddle, "What single word describes Miss Jocelyn?" and then I was too shy to tell the answer. "Perfection." I got it out of a book. "You silly," Mother says, "it's only Miss Jocelyn after all," but I thought you was quite a little goddess; there'll never be anything like it again, Miss Mary.'

So the economics class had not been quite resultless, but most of her schemes left no trace behind them.

When the parish phase passed, her energy found vent in writing. One day she showed her father in pride and trepidation an article she had finished on Education.

He read it and said, 'Yes, it is not a bad way of clearing the mind to write down your ideas, however crudely, though in this case I should have suggested waiting till you had a little more knowledge.'

She felt so dashed to the ground that she must resist him. She asked if he would show the article to his publisher. He never had been able to make allowance for youth, and he opened his eyes, which were often half-shut, and gave her a look before which she quailed. With the look came the words, 'I should be very sorry if any one of our name gave this kind of work to the public. No one should attempt publication until he is sure he has written the very best that is in him. In a few years' time you will thank me for what I say now.'

Mary tore her article up and threw it into the paper-basket.

'Yes,' said Canon Jocelyn, 'I think that is the best place for it.'

She went away and sobbed, and determined she would never write more, and for some years she never did. But during solitary walks she had much time for dreaming and thinking. Her silent, pent-up life made her inarticulate in speech, but she had much

13

seething within her waiting for an outlet. She wrote her thoughts down to get rid of them. But she was glad of her father's advice, and no one saw her writings.

When she was twenty-two, her aunt, who had always disliked Canon Jocelyn, could again make use of her rheumatism. She said Dedmayne was too damp for her, and retired to Tunbridge Wells. Then the sister, who had been for years in an asylum, was pronounced well enough to come home. She had become more quiet, but was childish and astray; she needed incessant care. Mary and a nurse divided the duties between them. Though incapable of steadiness in everything else, Ruth never changed in love for Mary. Mary returned her love, finding something to treasure in what others shunned.

No nurse stayed long; Ruth turned against them. They were with her at night, Mary a great part of the day; Mary left her as little as possible.

The doctor warned her that she must give herself change of thought and scene, and as the Rector's daughter she had other duties. She did well with the village people, less well with her own class. The village remembered her as a dear little girl full of spirits. They sympathized with her in her charge, understanding and admiring her devotion. Her own class, with their colder hearts, wondered at her, and considered it was morbid of the Jocelyns to have 'that poor thing at home'; it was making Mary so eccentric.

As time passed on her contemporaries married, or settled into spinsters with objects in life. The neighbourhood arranged its friendships. At the tea-parties she had neither the charm of novelty nor familiarity. She was rather a fish out of water with the married. She played games with their children better than they did, for she kept something of a child in her; but the Rectory never had to search for servants, so the topic of registries was closed. She could not hunt; she cared for no sport; she was useless at committees; she did not like gardening. This cut her off. She longed for friends, but friend-making needs practice and beginning early in life, and her best friend-making years slipped by unused. She had had a friend Dora in that Redland family that moved to Southsea, but their correspondence languished. Dora was no letter-writer; Mary had little to say. She could not accept Dora's many invitations to Southsea or ask her to the Rectory.

Her greatest friend at Dedmayne was Cook. Mary poured out freely to her, their perfect confidence only checked sometimes by the fact that Cook was a working woman of sixty-three, and Mary a lady with youth not so very far behind her. For if Mary could not make friends with her own class, she had an unusual power of intimacy with cottage people. She liked them best. She had more in common with them, and with them she was never shy. But she and Cook preserved most of the etiquette between mistress and servant; it did not occur to them to modify it.

Cook revered Mary's intellect, and thought no treat so great as Miss Mary's conversation. They did not choose the usual village topics, symptoms, and chit-chat of passing events. They roamed over poetry and the English classics in the study. They had mystical discussion, for Cook had one of the poetic peasant minds which Nature seems to have lost the habit of producing. Cook had come when Mary was six; Emma, the housemaid, had only been at the Rectory seventeen years. Both servants felt Canon Jocelyn a treasured child, to be guarded from the rough world. Cook looked on Mary as a child, too, in all practical matters, and constantly took things from her with, 'I can't bear to see you tiring your little hands,' so that when Cook and Emma were there, it was rather beyond Mary's capacity to boil the water for tea. Cook also did as much of the ordering and buying as she could. When Mary tried to resist, Cook would cry and say Mary did not trust her. If Mary had been more capable, Cook would not have revered her, only liked her.

Canon Jocelyn thought of Mary, not as a child, but as seventeen perhaps, 'heedless and slap-dash,' not to be trusted with his money affairs, over which he now fretted away hours in his study. The incompetent gardner 'couldn't abide young ladies interfering.' All this gave Mary more time for her duties in the village.

Dedmayne was small, and fewer and fewer babies were born there; but some there were, and the mothers would have thought it indeed 'strange,' 'funny', 'abrupt', and all their other terms of reproach, if Mary had not been the first outside the family to welcome the arrival. The old people sometimes died, but it took a long time – they were like tough gnarled trees – and Mary must be constantly with them to talk about their bequests. As the girl-babies grew up, they went away to service, and it was Mary who found the 'nice little places,' and sometimes escorted them thither. The day-school was not large, and was half-asleep, and Mary had to cheer it up with visits. These set aflame a passion for her in Miss Gage, the teacher, who lay in wait and pounced on her in the lanes. In a sense the whole village adored Mary, but quietly. Far from being grateful to Miss Gage, Mary could not bear it. She felt herself, though not worth adoring, worth more than that. But she would not neglect a parishioner, isolated by her intellectual attainments, and on tenterhooks about her status. Mary had walks with her on Sundays after Sunday School.

Of course she superintended the Sunday School, trained the Choir, had a boys' Bible Class and a Mothers' Meeting, and every fortnight or so tried to patch up those differences among the various layers of society which make the excitement of village life.

The year went round with its accustomed routine: Advent Sunday, Carols, the Christmas treat, Ash Wednesday, and a hope that people *will* come to Church this Lent (never realized); the Confirmation, with occasionally the Bishop to lunch; summer treats; garden- and tennis-parties, their own among the number; the Clerical Book Club Tea, with peaches on the lawn; the Harvest Festival, with the preacher to supper afterwards; and the Diocese and Government Inspectors. If they were gentlemen, and in addition classical gentlemen, Canon Jocelyn would enjoy himself, and make them enjoy themselves. If they were neither, Canon Jocelyn would get further and further into his shell. The more unobservant would say, 'The poor old man's ageing very much; he takes no notice of anything now,' but others, perceiving the sardonic gleam in his half-shut eye, writhed with nervousness. He could see the misery he was inflicting. He thought it a just punishment to the Universities and the Board of Education for sending Dedmayne such unsuitable representatives.

By October outside life was over, and as Mary wrote to Dora Redland, 'We go into our holes and live like dormice, nothing but ourselves and the village all the winter through, certain that for weeks and weeks on end the front-door bell will not ring.'

Mary liked the long Dedmayne winter evenings. In October, as regularly as the leaves fell, she began the winter habit of reading her favourite novels for an hour before dinner, finding in Trollope, Miss Yonge, Miss Austen, and Mrs Gaskell friends so dear and familiar that they peopled her loneliness.

Such was Mary's life. As the years passed on, the invalid's room became more and more her world. Sometimes she felt the neighbourhood, the village, even her father, becoming like shadows. On the whole she was happy. She did not question the destiny life brought her. People spoke pityingly of her, but she did not feel she required pity.

3

At two in the morning Canon Jocelyn sat reading Virgil in his study. He turned over the leaves quickly as his eye finished the page. The words were very familiar to him; it could not be said whether he took them in. The door opened; his daughter entered hurriedly.

'I think you had better come, Father.' She spoke in a low voice; the tension was evident.

He put down his book and followed her upstairs. His invalid daughter had had a stroke the night before; she was dying. She was not conscious, and lay motionless. He went up to the bed and pressed her hand gently. He asked a question or two of the nurse; he knelt down and read the prayer for those at the point of departure. Then he sat near the window; Mary was at the bedside. They waited in silence no one knew how long. The end, when it came, was peaceful. The nurse said, 'She's gone, sir.' He again looked at the form in the bed, and laid his hand on the brow. Then he went up to Mary and said, 'I think you had better come with me now, Mary.' She shook her head, and he left the room.

Her farewell was not so calm; she kissed the face again and again.

'You know it's best for her, Miss Mary,' said the nurse.

'Of course I know it is,' said Mary.

Her father heard her coming downstairs, and went to meet her. He took her hand and said, 'I believe there has just now been a joyful meeting of your mother and sister in bliss.'

He never mentioned the dead, or any of his convictions about them or about religion. But for the church services and family prayers he might have been a pagan, for all his daughter and household knew to the contrary. As he spoke of his wife he smiled. His smile was rare, and it encouraged Mary to do what she had never done before, fling her arms round him. She cried, 'Oh, what *shall* I do without her?' His smile disappeared, but he spoke kindly. 'Yes, yes I am sure you will miss her.' He did not return the embrace, but extricating himself gently, he said, 'I think I should advise you to go to bed; you can do no good by staying up,' and went back to the study.

She was standing, too wretched and bewildered to settle what she should do, when Cook came up to her and said, 'Miss Mary, darling, here's some tea, and Emma's got a lovely hot-water bottle in your bed.'

When Mary cried in Cook's arms, Cook did not reject her. 'Let me help you into bed Miss,' she said. They sat and talked till dawn. 'Ah,' said Cook to Emma, 'she *does* feel it.' But what Mary felt most was her father's want of feeling.

Beyond discussing the arrangements for the funeral, Canon Jocelyn never referred to his daughter again. He had, since her return to the Rectory, visited her twice a day for a few minutes, and talked quietly of the weather and the cat. On Sunday he read the psalms and lessons to her. Whether her affliction had been one of the calamities of his life, or her infirmity an irritation he was glad to be rid of, Mary did not know.

'My dear William,' wrote Aunt Lottie some days afterwards, 'I know dear Mary will be very much upset by poor Ruth's death, and I think that a change to Broadstairs will be just the thing for her. Unluckily I cannot get the lodgings that I am so fond of this year, for I am going rather earlier, as there is some papering we must have done, and most unfortunately Annie has to go home and nurse her mother, who was taken ill on Monday, otherwise she always goes with me. But I have heard of a nice quiet boarding-house where you can get good bedrooms, and really see *hardly anything* of the other people. I hope we shall get some pretty drives. I am telling Simpson at the livery stables I always employ, I shall want the fly every other day. I am sure drives will be good for Mary, and I am looking forward to some nice reading aloud. Annie will come back to take me to Victoria, but can Mary meet me there? I like to be there an hour before we start, so as to have plenty of time.'

Canon Jocelyn had himself wondered whether a change would not benefit Mary; this was the very thing. So Mary went.

She noticed many black figures, companions in bereavement, as she and Aunt Lottie walked slowly on the front; she could see from their heavy lids and weary eyes how many tears they had shed. She hoped they might be receiving more comfort than she. Aunt Lottie showed her sympathy actively by shutting up both the windows when they drove out in the fly. 'The sun is shining brightly, but I would rather, Mary, dear. You must not be catching a cold now.'

They saw more of the retired Anglo-Indians, officers' wives, widows, and bachelors of the boarding-house than Aunt Lottie had intended, for an old lady taught her a patience. 'Seven rows with three in each row,' she explained. 'You see how I am doing it. Leave out the Kings. It is such an easy patience; every one likes it. Now we choose any card we like. Oh, Miss Jocelyn, what are you doing taking out those Kings? No, it's the aces we must take out. Oh, we've turned up nine; I don't like nines. I shall put that back.' By a freemasonry of muddleheadedness, Aunt Lottie understood this explanation, and played her patience nightly in the drawing-room. Mary had time to listen to the talk round her: the Anglo-Indians, homesick for the jungle; the women, too idle to keep house, recounting their past triumphs of management.

There was an inevitable bore, a hanger-on to life, a middle-aged Mr Maltby with a stammer, who told anecdotes. 'I knew a feller travelling in the Highlands . . . He went off to fish – salmon it was – he doesn't do anything with trout . . . He took with him a feller from the village – gillies they call 'em . . . very decent chaps with quite a sense of humour of their own . . . My friend said to the gillie, "Well, Sandy," etc. So Sandy says, "Na, na, I'm no afraid of that," etc., etc.'

His anecdotes had no point, but through them all ran the English gentleman's kindly sentiment towards everybody as 'not half a bad chap.'

The boarding-house was tired of him, but Mary had not the presence of mind or the unkindness to snub him. He sought her out; his dismal face lighted up when he came near her. No man had ever sought her out before; she was too humble to be repelled by his dullness.

All the ladies liked her, for she waited on them when they had headaches. One, Mrs Grace, a colonel's pretty wife, said with prosperous warmth, doing almost more than justice to those less prosperous, 'Miss Jocelyn has beautiful eyes, only so sad, poor dear, and, what I particularly like, good eyelids, and there's a dear little line about the corners of her mouth. I'm sure she has a sense of humour. Of course she could never be pretty, but there is no reason why she should dress as if she came out of a jumble sale. It's a crime to be so unvain. I wish one could tell her.'

'It's extraordinary,' said another lady with married hardness, 'to see those crowds of girls getting older, and all unmarried. I'd quite forgotten about them; I've been out of England so much, and it comes upon one as a shock. Now a girl like Miss Jocelyn – I'm sure she's very nice and good, only people just pass her over. One can't be surprised nothing ever happens to her. All those girls are just as like one another as two peas.'

'I wish Mr Maltby would propose,' said a grass-widow. 'I believe she'd take him. She'd be so sweet to him; and didn't some one say he'd got quite a lot of money?'

'Oh *no*,' said Mrs Grace. 'She's much too nice. I'd much rather have nothing happen to me than poor Mr Maltby. Really she ought to have a Round Robin from all of us to thank her for taking him off our hands. He never will let her alone.'

'You know I think all you people are so wrong about Miss Jocelyn,' said a very handsome wife, who had been twice married. 'I believe the great passions and the lasting ones are for the plain women. They're the ones who can keep men, because they're loved for something inside them. They have only one affair in their

20

lives, but it's a big one. It's rather a snub for us who think ourselves good-looking, of course. Those eyes show Miss Jocelyn has something rather particular inside her. She may chance to meet a man who'll realize it, and then being very plain and badly dressed will simply make no difference at all. Only, of course, there are very few of those men about.'

In spite of this defence Mary was looked back on at the boarding-house as a kind girl, who would have been lucky if she could have found favour with Mr Maltby.

The time passed; the aunt and niece left Broadstairs. Mr Maltby said, 'This has been a very pleasant six weeks to me, Miss Jocelyn,' and sat for a long time after she was gone, looking out of window and thinking of her. Perhaps Mary would have liked if he had said more; she felt so desolate she might have taken him, but another lot was in store for her.

4

ALL the drive back from Cayley Mary had counted well-known trees, which told her she was coming nearer home. Her father stood at the study door as she entered the house.

'Oh, Mary, is that you? I think your train was rather late. How did you leave your aunt?'

She kissed him quietly, and said her aunt was better.

'How have you been, Father?'

'I have been just as usual. Why should I not?'

'Yes, of course, I know; there wasn't any reason. Oh, thank you, Emma. I've had tea, really, but it's very nice to have an extra cup.'

Canon Jocelyn watched her drinking it. She knew by his attitude that he thought it strange anybody should require tea twice in the afternoon.

'Has anything happened while I have been away?'

'I don't know what you call anything happening. Poor Sykes

has something to put up with in his new curate. He tells me he preached his first sermon last Sunday evening. In the course of it he spoke of the Medea of Virgil who slew her children. Sykes thinks of advising him to keep to safer themes another time. Apparently he is quite an authority on cricket scores. Sykes says the bishop warmly recommended the fellow. I'm not at all surprised to hear it.'

She laughed, but even when she was amused she could not be entirely at ease. It was want of ease made her remark, 'The dahlias are coming out already, I see. It's a very early year.'

He was not interested in flowers, and he cared still less for talking about them. This frame of mind cut off tracts of conversational openings. But he answered politely, 'The flowers must be still more advanced at Broadstairs.'

'Oh yes, it's much warmer there.'

It was his turn to start a topic.

'You say the train was late?'

'Yes, we were eleven minutes late.'

'I have no doubt they started from town at the correct time; they always lose at the junction.'

'Yes, it was just before we got into the station. I think we must have waited ten minutes outside.'

'The line wants widening there very much, but I remember Sir John Leyland telling me some years ago that they were demanding such heavy compensation for the land that the Company hesitated to embark on the expense.'

'I wonder who the land belonged to?'

'Oh, just small local tradesmen, I fancy.'

'I met Dr Mills at Cayley. He wanted to be remembered to you.'

'Ah, yes.'

He liked talking about trains. Does any man not like talking about trains? But at the mention of Dr Mills she could see his eyes wandering towards the door. There was a pause.

'I think there is time for me to do a little more work before dinner,' said he, and he went back to the study.

It was what she expected. She knew her father did not care for long conversations, or, indeed, short ones, particulary at unusual times, and between tea and dinner was unusual. Yet she felt wounded almost to tears.

That conversation was typical. They would pass the whole round of the year, spring, summer, autumn, and winter, without anything more intimate. In his sympathy for Mr Sykes her father had been unusually communicative. 'I should hate it if he snapped,' she thought, 'but it would make us seem more friendly.' It was only in his sermons, written in limpid and beautiful English and simple enough for the slow village congregation, that she heard the result of his learning and long meditation. Once, when she was much younger, she challenged some conclusion of his sermons. Looking back, she saw timidity had made her sound truculent. He said, 'I think one should only proclaim one's views on such difficult and serious subjects after systematic study. I have some books in the library which I could lend you.' Time and experience showed her she had asked for what would be difficult to many, and the hardest thing in life to him. For several years she had ceased to question him.

'If men are only to meet in this life,' she reflected, 'and pass most of it fretting one another because they cannot get nearer, it would all be intolerable.' She remembered her mother's smile when she was dead. She felt it a kind of guarantee that there might be a time when she would see her father face to face.

Then Cook came for a chat. 'Oh, he *has* missed you,' said she. 'There was the day the Archdeacon, and Mrs Waters, and the three young ladies came, and Emma had gone to her aunt, and he come to me, and he says, "I don't know what we shall do about tea." I says, "Don't you trouble yourself, sir. Everything shall be sent up just as Miss Mary should wish it to be." "Oh," he says, "if Miss Mary was here she would pour it out." So I says, "Let me put it before Mrs Waters, sir; you'll see that won't trouble her." Then two evenings ago he had an attack of his cramp. I heard him moving, for I was sleeping next door, as you give orders, Miss Mary, and I went in to him, and he says, "If Miss Mary was here she would know what to do." "Let me write to her in the morning," I says, "and we'll have her back on Wednesday." That soothed him wonderful, but after I rubbed him he settled down quite quiet, and he was well in the morning and wouldn't have you wrote to.'

Mary laughed and was comforted.

5

THE Rectory settled down easily into its new routine. The nurse left; Ruth's room became a spare room; Canon Jocelyn went on writing in the study. Every one else felt the death a relief, but Mary found the house empty and her life empty. Even Cook could not sympathize with her. She would not show her thought openly – that now Mary must marry. During Ruth's lifetime Mary had never contemplated it; it would be impossible to leave her. She had not repined at youth slipping away with its natural desires unfulfilled. Canon Jocelyn had not contemplated her marriage either. And now at eighty-two his mind could not expand to make room for such a new idea; his very few remaining years must go on in their usual way. He would have esteemed Mary more if she had been married; a range of consideration and pleasures would then have been her due. He would not have treated her as a little girl. As things were, she had had her change of air with her aunt; enough had been done.

Mary had come back at the beginning of August. The topic of the moment was the inauguration of a village nurse at Dedmayne. All had been settled by Miss Redland, the elder sister of Mary's friend Dora, an energetic 'Labour' spirit, recently returned to the neighbourhood. It was she who arranged the sale of work on the Rectory lawn, and the speeches from herself and Lady Meryton, the *grande dame* of the neighbourhood.

When Canon Jocelyn first came to Dedmayne he found Mrs Cann, who said charms over her patients. He had never disturbed himself to change her. He was inclined to regard illness (he was rarely ill) as an opportunity for resignation, and thought the modern concentration on health regrettable.

Old Susan, uncertificated, with no strings and no veil, had

24

taken Mrs Cann's place, and he thought she did very well. Susan had cared for Ruth, and Mary clung to her as part of her sad past, from which she refused to be free.

The inauguration ceremony occupied the minds of Dedmayne to the brim. There was always something to notice: whether it was Miss Redland's rough familiarity – she treated every one alike on principle – or Miss Gage's flutter of spirits – was she as a teacher sufficiently in the public eye? – or Susan's distress at Miss Redland's reference to 'no real qualification,' and delight at Lady Meryton's consolations. 'Miss Redland may be what they call an educated woman, but her ladyship's real gentry,' was the verdict of all. These would be topics for weeks when the great day was over. Even Canon Jocelyn was moved from his usual meditation to read Tennyson to Lady Meryton after tea. But Mary, to outward appearance the assiduous hostess, felt apart from the innocent afternoon, preyed upon ceaselessly by the sense of her loneliness. Her duties ended with an hour's talk with Lady Meryton, when Miss Redland and the village guests had gone. Afterwards she looked back on that hour as the turning-point in her life.

Lady Meryton was a cousin of Canon Jocelyn. In the daughter of a peer, married to a rich baronet, Canon Jocelyn scented the possibilities of patronage, and, in spite of advances from the Merytons, had very little to do with them. Mary remembered occasional afternoons in her childhood and teens at Meryton Court, when various tall sons and daughters of the house had terrified her because they were so old. By this time tall grandsons and grand-daughters were beginning to terrify her because they were so young. But she had fallen adoringly at Lady Meryton's feet, and was always ready to fall again.

Lady Meryton was over seventy, but she was still a beauty. Her head had never been turned. She was as used to being adored as having her breakfast. From childhood onward her relations, doctor, tradespeople, lawyers, children, husband, governesses, and secretaries, and now, above all, her unmarried daughter Claudia, shielded her from the roughness of the world. She had only to be charming. That duty she fulfilled to perfection, and she had a warm affectionate nature.

25

Claudia, apart from her mother, lived for hunting. She was like a Juggernaut car to everything that got in its way. 'If only my people would have a little sense, and sell the Court, and get something in Leicestershire. Everybody's letting their places go now. I don't say the hunting is bad here, but it isn't Leicestershire. But what my two excellent parents love is muddling about with tenants and old women and things, and the hunting goes to pot.'

Lady Meryton gossiped to Mary about the neighbourhood in the old-fashioned county way. 'Nurse Brown (the new importation) isn't a bad woman – we had her at Yeabsley, you know, a little apt to take offence and pet the richer cases, but I think in nurses one has to expect that, and I know several instances where she has been really kind. What a good little speech Ella Redland made, and how handsome she looked. My husband will call her "the Unnecessary Female," so I'm afraid she's only known to us as the U.F. She will be so terribly active, and her dreadful socialistic views – she really ought to know better. I always think those inspectors the Government send down should be excused, because they know nothing of country people, but Ella was at Clouston till she was quite grown-up, and Mrs Redland was such a nice comfortable thing, and I'm sure she got none of her views from Mr Redland; he was a most harmless little man.'

Mary wondered if she and her father were also described as 'nice,' 'comfortable,' and 'harmless' things. But Lady Meryton had adored her Jocelyn mother, and for her sake loved all Jocelyns. Only, among the host of sons, daughters, grandchildren, nephews and nieces, brothers and sisters, to whom she was fondly attached, and her husband, who was all in all to her, her life was over full without Mary.

Yet it was the superlatively prosperous Lady Meryton who understood and comforted Mary.

'Your life reminds me so much of my dearest sister's,' she said. 'She looked after my brother. He was rather like little Ruth, and when he died she looked after my father. She was the best of all of us; she was never married – that is so often the way, I think – and the whole weight of the family seemed to fall on her. My two older sisters were abroad with their husbands, and it was the time my children were coming. I cannot tell you how I envied her, really being able to serve those she loved. When I lost my little girl of scarlet fever, I was not allowed even to come near her because of the infection. I was nursing baby at the time. It's forty-five years ago now, and I've never forgotten it. A life like yours has wonderful compensations.'

Mary saw the tears in her eyes. 'I tell you, Mary dear, because I think you will understand, and some people don't; even my dearest Claudia, who is so good to me, doesn't. But, Mary, I wanted to say, don't let yourself get too much of a hermit.'

'I feel so different from people – so stupid.'

'Yes, that is what my sister Eleanor said. But it is just shyness, which you shouldn't yield to.'

'Sometimes I want to see people, and then when I do I shrink up.'

'That's right. You ought to want to see people, and though you say you shrink up, I assure you you manage to conceal it. You have a touch of your charming mother. It came out so today, when I saw you and Ella talking to the people, *such* a contrast. In little Ruth's lifetime, of course, you were tied. You gave your heart to her, and you will never forget her, but try not to pine. I know how you feel, Mary. Eleanor said it was like losing a baby, when my brother died. My niece, Kathy Hollings, is coming in September. You must meet her. She's a great tall thing now, and so lovely. We haven't seen as much of her as I should like, for her guardian, my brother-in-law, chose to have a stupid quarrel with my husband. She has no proper home, poor child, and her brother has married one of those dreadful smart people I cannot *bear*. I want to get her away from that influence. We're having a big house party for Kathy; she's up to all sorts of fun.'

Mary remembered Kathy, a crushing, beautiful child, an accomplished horsewoman at seven, having a *bande à part* with Claudia at twenty-four, because Mary made such a poor exhibition with an old cob of the Merytons. She had no wish to meet Kathy again.

Lady Meryton had kept her best bit of gossip for the last. 'Have you heard about Lanchester? Robert Herbert is coming to the Vicarage. It will be so nice to have one of the family at last. The Herberts still have the presentation, you know.'

27

The name Herbert took Mary back to her childhood. Mr Herbert's father had been her father's dearly-loved friend. She could remember Robert, a handsome, supercilious undergraduate. They had not seen him for many years. He would be a stranger, and her father did not like strangers. There would be duty calls; there might be a tea-party or two. Then her father would find something to criticize, and make excuses for not seeing anything more of his brother clergyman.

Other thoughts were occupying Lady Meryton – the same thoughts which had occupied Cook and the boarding-house. How nice if Mary married Robert. She was quickly adding up ages, and planning *tête-à-tête*.

'You must be sure and get him to Dedmayne, Mary; it is so good for the younger clergy to meet your father.'

When she went to bed that night Mary felt less solitary; she knew not why.

6

THE news of the appointment to Lanchester was confirmed in a letter to Canon Jocelyn. In old age letters, genuine letters, apart from bills and circulars, resume the thin trickle of childhood. Canon Jocelyn was the more *intrigué* that he could not think who his correspondent might be.

It was Mrs Herbert, the widow of his friend. He had always kept up with her; according to both their ideas they were frequently corresponding. But it was nine years since she had written – so time flies in old age – and he had forgotten her handwriting.

'He is very much looking forward to the pleasure of seeing you again,' she wrote. 'He well remembers your kindness to him in his undergraduate days.' The object of the letter was now completed, but there was more to come in Mrs Herbert's pointed hand.

The miserable weather we have been having lately has been a great disappointment. After that long cold spring, which put everything *late*, our poor almond blossom was actually flowering in April! I had hoped that the summer might have been a *compensation*, but the cruel winds we had in August made the temperature actually *lower* than in December. My sister and I have missed the drives to Beachy Head and Hurst Castle, which we always look forward to so much; but September is sometimes a lovely month, and we are hoping for a few bright *restful* days next week, when my niece will be staying with us. My sister-in-law begs to unite with me in very kindest remembrances to yourself and Mary, whom I remember seeing *how* many years ago! – Yours most truly,

EMMELINE HERBERT.

Such a letter was pleasant to Canon Jocelyn, recalling his early days. He would not have written it himself, but the ladies he had known and liked best, all, literary and intellectual, and unliterary and unintellectual, wrote in that manner, nor, however intimate they might have been, would they have omitted one fact about the seasons, or have cared to add much of a more personal nature.

Mary's recollections of the writer were of herself at an awkward ten, thirteen, and seventeen, and of Mrs Herbert, as what at that time she called 'fashionable and satirical.' Since then Mrs Herbert had been delicate, and living at Eastbourne with a sister-in-law; she had not come to Dedmayne again. She had invited Mary to pay long visits, but Mary had declined them; for some years the invitations had ceased.

The news roused an interest in her father which she had seldom seen. That early friendship had been, next to his marriage, the deepest feeling of Canon Jocelyn's life.

A few days after the letter Mr Herbert came to call. He was paying a preliminary visit at Lanchester before settling in. He was now neither handsome nor supercilious. Mary thought he had interesting eyes, and liked his long, rather wolf-like mouth. She could watch him as she sat at the tea-table, for he was listening intently to her father, unaware that she was staring at him.

Canon Jocelyn was talking about Mr Herbert's father, and his voice was faltering, almost breaking, when he said, 'There was no one like your father – no one.' The emotion from an old man of eighty-two was touching. Mary was glad that it was displayed before some one who would know how to treat it. She thought of a noisy clergyman or two of their acquaintance, and shuddered. Her eyes met Mr Herbert's; he had turned his head a little to give her father time to recover. He had been moved also, and she liked his expression.

Canon Jocelyn had, when he chose, unusual powers of pleasing in conversation. Mary was accustomed to visitors becoming engrossed in him. Politeness satisfied, or hardly satisfied, they left her alone. This she did not mind in the least.

Mr Herbert satisfied politeness entirely, with something left over. It was Canon Jocelyn who impressed him certainly; it was of him he thought continuously as he walked home, but he remembered Miss Jocelyn's face, when she looked at her father. She had a sweet smile.

He rose to go shortly after tea, but it had transpired that he was bringing out an edition of Donne, whose sermons were particular favourites with Canon Jocelyn. He was begged to come into the study and see a rare folio, and then other old editions were shewn, and Mary could hear the continual rise and fall of the two voices. The first gong rang while they were still busy looking and talking, and when Mr Herbert stood up in compunction, Canon Jocelyn invited him to dinner, saying, 'If you share your father's taste for port, there is a very fair wine I should like you to try.' And the precious vintage, which lingered in the cellar year after year, was brought up in his honour.

Either it or Mr Herbert's society unloosed Canon Jocelyn's tongue. Mary had hardly ever known him so genial. Mr Herbert was a Cambridge man, which was a refreshment in a dry land, for what University men there were in the neighbourhood were Oxford, or came from upstart places, which Canon Jocelyn would not call a university. Such unfortunates could not relish the full flavour of a Cambridge joke, and recently there had been little chance for Canon Jocelyn to remark, as it gave him pleasure to do, 'He had no depth; the foundations had not been securely laid – more what one might call the Oxford stamp. There have no doubt been certain eminent and really sound scholars among them, but I think it is fair to say the Oxford mind is superficial.'

After dinner he brought forth his Cambridge University Calendar, which was to him as the peerage to Sir Walter Eliot, and dissected the distinguished classics of sixty-five and sixty years ago, recollecting accurately the senior, second, and third classics of several generations, and their coaches as well.

'Miles was fair certainly, hardly a first-rate man, a good grammarian, but his verses were lamentable. Now Fullerton turned out as neat a set of Alcaics as I ever saw, but he had a finicky mind; there was a want of manliness about him. He went into the Church, and they made him a bishop. He was a ritualist – excessively pleased with his tippets, and so forth. Webb was an excellent scholar, but he fidgeted every one with his absurdities, and his appearance was unfortunate; his face was hideously marked. Poor fellow, he lost his reason. Armstrong was second-rate in every particular, a puny creature, and immoderately vain. He was always wondering what people thought of him. He pestered your father with questions, until at last even he lost patience, and said, "I can set your mind at rest on that point for ever. They do not think of you at all, because there is nothing to think of." He took to politics, and flattered the mob. I believe they made a baronet of him.'

Mary liked hearing of old Cambridge. She had heard of it from her childhood, listening half-dreamily, while her father discussed it with his contemporaries – contemporaries who, however else they might differ, relished good wine, were uninterested in smoking or athletics, rather despised the rest of Europe, honoured the Conservative party and even its vagaries, and treated her, whatever their opinion of her might be, with polished deference.

They had dropped away from her father by this time through age or death, and their favourite topics had all the sweetness of early associations. Mary had imbibed their horror of false quantities, though she had forgotten most of her Latin and Greek, and from constant repetition she knew when the point was coming in the classical jokes much better than some of the new curates, who slipped through the theological colleges with as little learning as they could.

Mary could remember some unwary ones embarking on Latin names and being annihilated in Canon Jocelyn's silver tones. Once a Bishop had come, Colonial, it is true, who told a classical story, prefacing it genially with 'You must "tick me off," as the boys

31

say' (it was no recommendation to Mr Jocelyn that the boys said it) 'if I make a ghastly howler.' He did, but Canon Jocelyn thought it unbecoming his own dignity to correct him in the presence of the clergy, whose flocks he was shortly to confirm. He was tracked down afterwards in the Book of Books, and it was discovered he had taken a Poll degree. From that day Canon Jocelyn gave up the Church as lost.

The conversation passed away from Cambridge to other things. Canon Jocelyn talked of his travels abroad with Mr Herbert's father, and of Alpine climbing. 'Your father helped to start the Alpine Club; I was a humble follower, but we had some climbs together before they tamed the mighty Alps and put them into harness.' Mary heard of parties at the English Legation attached to some of the smaller German courts. 'They were very merry, very merry, those old days; they seem part of another life.'

Mr Herbert said his father had told him of Canon Jocelyn and a certain beautiful Grand Duchess.

'Yes, the Princess Sophia did me the honour of accepting the roses I had the temerity to offer her. That was all the bright sunshine of morning, and now it is twilight, and one sees the grave beauty of the approaching night.'

Mary could not help a twinge of indignation. She wondered which had been the bright sunshine of her morning. Had not her life been rather the twilight of a river mist, or even of a London fog? And there had been years before Ruth came back, when she, too, might have been gay. Common sense, her mother's legacy, came to her aid. Her father must have been born suited to Grand Duchesses, and she, with all the pushing in the world, would never have suited Grand Dukes.

'It has been a very pleasant evening,' said Canon Jocelyn when Mr Herbert was gone. 'I have always said there is nothing like a first-rate Cambridge man. Sometimes one is afraid the type is dying, when one remembers certain specimens of Cambridge men among the Inspectors the Government is good enough to send us; but I see it is not.' Mary had rarely heard her father so enthusiastic.

The weeks passed, and Mr Herbert read himself in. Canon Jocelyn paid his call, and Mr Herbert returned it. The friendship so happily inaugurated prospered, and Canon Jocelyn began to say now and then, 'I wonder whether Herbert will be looking in on us this afternoon?'

Meanwhile Lady Meryton sent her promised invitation. 'Cannot you manage to stay a night or two with us next week? Kathy is here, and I shall have two of my boys with their wives and a nice heap of grandchildren. I am sure you can trust that dear old cook and the nice housemaid to look after Canon Jocelyn while you are away.'

Here was the chance Mary had complained she never got. She thought of the men servants, the vast rooms, the corridors in which she lost her way. She thought of Claudia; she thought above all, of Kathy, superlatively smart and beautiful. She refused, and felt herself a coward.

'Well, now, Mamma dear, do be satisfied,' said Claudia. 'She doesn't want to come; she likes her dungeon at Dedmayne, and you ought to be very grateful to her, for I don't believe she plays a single game, even ping-pong, and you would have had her on your hands the whole time, for I couldn't have helped you. I don't know what to say to a person who can't play a game.'

In the happy rush of grandchildren, Lady Meryton forgot Mary.

Life generally has some pervading interest, often a very small one, which engrosses the mind, until it is its turn to be superseded. Ella Redland, the Merytons, Nurse Brown, Mr Herbert, faded into the background. Their place in Mary's mind was taken by the anticipation of a visit from Dora. There was now no reason there should not be visitors at the Rectory. She was invited and she accepted.

7

WHEN Dora arrived at Cayley Station she saw, among the motors and governess-carts, a shabby phaeton with a long-maned, wily pony. He found more than one hill to walk up on the flat road to Dedmayne, but neither Dora nor Mary wanted to go faster.

'This road,' said Dora, 'I haven't seen it for sixteen years; it's not a bit changed. *You* are, Mary. I shouldn't have known you, and of course *I* am. I'm getting so stout. It was clever of you to recognize me.'

'Your face has hardly changed at all,' said Mary. 'I always thought you so lovely.' Dora had been an unusually pretty, fair, pale girl.

'Did you, Mary? How nice of you. Yes, I think I was rather pretty. But,' with enthusiasm, 'you remember Gertrude? She married, you know, and her eldest little girl is the loveliest child you ever saw.'

When tea came, Canon Jocelyn waited on the visitor with trembling fingers and shambling, yet stately, tread. It seemed as if he must upset the cup. Dora longed to help him – she loved helping, but she knew old people felt it when little offices were taken from them. He liked to perform the duty in silence, so that he might give his whole mind to it. When all wants were satisfied he had leisure for inquiries about the journey. That two hours from London – Dora had come from London, not from Southsea – was referred to as something exceptional.

'You will hardly care to take much of a walk after your journey, but perhaps when you have rested sufficiently you might like to have a little turn in the garden.'

'A little turn,' 'a stroll,' 'a saunter' on dry gravel walks – these were what Canon Jocelyn, with a flattering assumption of their preciousness and fragility, proposed to lady visitors. But the suggestion was a part of old-fashioned, hospitable politeness. He would have thought poorly of Mary if she said she were tired or wanted to go to bed early, therefore she never did either.

There is a special pleasure in walks round a country clerical garden. It is large enough for variety and small enough for cosiness. It adds to the pleasure if the garden lies next the church, and the trees from the churchyard cast their shadows on the path. But perhaps the charm can only be felt by those who have known both vicarages and the country from their childhood. Nature helps lazy, inexpert gardeners with particular kindness in September; now the asters, Michaelmas daisies, dahlias, phloxes, and that whole autumn tribe of bright yellow flowers were sprawling in abundance all over the Dedmayne beds.

Canon Jocelyn walked beside Dora. He picked her flowers, first one and then another. The stalks were short, the petals sometimes withered, the species inappropriate for a nosegay, but there was a peculiar charm in the way he handed them. This charm was lost on her. Is all charm only an illusion – the emperor's new clothes? But by its means, and a certain slow way of shutting his eyes, which created the other illusion that he was formidable, Canon Jocelyn exercised dominion. His learning, integrity, untiring industry, clear judgement did not count for nearly so much; the neighbourhood could not understand them.

He went in; the friends remained in the garden.

'Father doesn't often come round the garden with people and talk so much,' said Mary exultingly. 'I am sure he enjoyed it.'

'I am so glad,' said Dora tranquilly. 'It *is* nice he is well enough to enjoy life. I am afraid I don't quite understand all those stories. I *did* say I don't know any Latin, but he didn't quite realize.'

Canon Jocelyn had formerly been an austere critic of young women, demanding little of them in action, but everything in repose. He had been too fastidious; his children and other young people had never been at ease with him; he had not known them as they really were. He was particularly severe on any trace of affectation or vanity. 'She is not perfectly natural,' he would say, and the girl's doom was sealed.

Mary had fallen short of the ideal in several respects; so had Dora, as the young, unformed daughter of a dull fellow-clergyman with a poor degree from some obscure, small college – 'I can't recollect its name, there are so many at Oxford.' He had approved her good looks. 'She is a pleasing person,' he had said, 'but I wish she had a little more colour, and I fear from those spectacles her sight cannot be very good.'

Then came other strictures.

'Your friend is very busy with her Sunday Class, and seems admirable in every way, but could she be persuaded to – there is a little, lisping affectation in her way of speaking which is somewhat irritating.'

'I wonder if Dora Redland ever reads. I am not speaking of the volumes of light fiction which young ladies devour at all hours, but does she ever *read*?'

Now Canon Jocelyn was old; his still alarming exterior was a shell from which the life inside was gone. His sight was dimmed; he had grown humble; he was even tending towards gratitude to young people for their attention. This showed itself in his comment, 'It is very pleasant to have Miss Redland with us. She enlarges our circle, which you must not allow to grow too narrow. I did not remember how good-looking she was, and she certainly has much more ability than her sister Ella.'

This was not true, but Ella Redland had made an unfortunate impression on him. She had started the subject of *progress*. 'We mustn't let ourselves be groovy, Canon Jocelyn,' speaking to him as if he were deaf. 'We must have a scientific point of view.'

'Ah yes,' said Canon Jocelyn. He pronounced 'Ah' as if it were 'myer', with an indescribable intonation of aloofness.

'I mean, however much you object to it, we can't go back. We must be progressive. *Eppure si muove*.'

'Groovy,' 'scientific', 'progressive', he winced at the words.

'Indeed, but it is possible that by progress we may mean different things.'

This much he allowed himself to say. Fearing he might have been discourteous to the daughter of an old friend, he went on: 'At my age one loses the capacity and, I am afraid, the desire for change. You were quoting Italian just now. We have been reading in one of the magazines an interesting account of the progress,' with a gracious smile, 'to use the word, I hope, in an uncontroversial sense, of the new tunnel through the Alps.'

And, in spite of struggles, to the new tunnel Ella was kept till she left.

She had worn a becoming hat, and Canon Jocelyn was melted by beauty, giving it moral qualities which did not belong to it. But he said to Mary, 'It is remarkable how objectionable some well-intentioned ladies can make themselves.' This was why Dora had much more ability than her sister Ella.

'Come and see if there are any more autumn crocuses in the churchyard,' said Mary to Dora as they wandered happily in the garden. 'I always look every day.'

A robin flew up to greet them; a toad crawled forth and squatted on the path, turning his bright eyes to Mary while she talked to him. He shared the general predilection of the animal world for human conversation. Mary and Dora stopped to look through the gap in the hedge at the view beyond, quiet, domestic, English scenery – a pond, meadows, and elm trees. These are the solace of the lonely in the country.

Then they walked in the village, a rustic saunter of admiring gardens and tasting fruit. Dora shared in the cottage talk in the special, pleasant voice she kept for parish visits.

'*How* difficult the poor are,' said she on the walk home. 'Always grumbling. Poor things, I suppose they can't help it, but I feel in despair about the working-class sometimes.'

'Do you, Dora? They hate anything new. I rather sympathize with them. I like them better than our class; we understand one another.'

'Really, Mary, I should never feel that. I love trying to help them, but there's such a barrier.'

'I think there is always a barrier with every one,' said Mary. 'Even if some unusual emotion seems to break it down, it is there again the next time.'

This thought was beyond Dora; she rarely reflected on life; she *did*.

When they came in Mary showed Dora curiosities. Households such as the Rectory contained many curiosities – carved chessmen, ivory balls within balls, enamelled snuff-boxes. There were port-folios of sketches by aunts and great-aunts. Sweet landscapes of bright, showery days in October, the earth always brown after a drought, so that no crude green need be employed. Then there were the photograph albums. Several generations were represented: crinoline ladies, none of them pretty, and almost all beautiful; lovely girls of the seventies and eighties; the neat, tight-laced nineties, then a lady-like elegance; lastly, the theatrical period. The whiskered men were a curious combination of mildness and severity; the era of moustaches following, characterless and commonplace.

'What a number of ancestors you have,' said Dora. 'We have none, you know. My grandfather kept a small shop somewhere in Hoxton. Then it was moved to Ealing, and my uncle has it still. I always meant to tell you years ago, and I didn't. Not that I think it would have made a difference to you, Mary!'

'No, not with me.'

'But it would have with your father.'

'I think it might a little,' said Mary.

Canon Jocelyn thought trade so inextricably connected with fraud that any one engaged in it must not be expected to be treated on a level with gentlemen. He looked on rich tradesmen with more contempt, supposing that the poor tradesmen had remained more honest. He found few to agree with his harsh, unwordly view.

'I wish you would tell your father, Mary,' said Dora. 'Not that it matters now. Once I thought –'

'How do you mean?' said Mary.

'I'll tell you later.'

The evening was just a repetition of the visit Dora had paid the Rectory twenty years ago; for the Rectory life was like a chapter of history, twenty years did not count for much with it. Canon Jocelyn offered his arm to form the procession to the dining-room. There was grace before and after meals, proposed by Canon Jocelyn with 'Shall we ask a blessing?' Tea, cake, and bread and butter were brought into the dining-room at nine. Then Canon Jocelyn read Shakespeare and Milton aloud, those fireside bulwarks of the old-fashioned home evenings.

'Thank you *very* much', said Dora. 'We're always saying we'll have some Browning at home in the evenings. We go to the theatre so seldom we want to see something bright, so Shakespeare never seems to come my way.'

When Canon Jocelyn had gone out of the room she added, 'What a nice interest for him it is. We try to get Uncle Tom to read, but he gets tired of things so easily.'

She was not idle during the reading; she devised comforts for Canon Jocelyn.

'I was wondering if he would wear a cardigan if I knitted one for him. I gave a dear old man in my district one, and he's delighted with it.'

There were prayers at ten, with verses of the psalms read by the family and servants in turn. Then came bedtime. A hip-bath was prepared before the fire in the spare room. The four-post bedstead with crimson canopies and tassels, so high that it had to be climbed into by steps, the lamp and candle-light were all relics of the past.

Mary lingered behind a moment to break to Canon Jocelyn the news of the Redlands' shop.

'Oh yes,' said Canon Jocelyn, with a slight touch of repressing inquisitiveness, 'a draper's shop somewhere in the outskirts of London. Mr Redland used sometimes to consult me about his brother's affairs. The brother was not very capable, nor, for that matter, was Redland himself. He would have done wisely, I believe, to have consulted Kekewich' (Canon Jocelyn's man of business) 'as I advised him. It might have saved him from getting so seriously embarrassed. Redland became involved himself. Mr Sykes and I were able to be of some assistance, otherwise it would have been an unpleasant business.' This was the time when Canon Jocelyn had refused to lay out the tennis-court.

Canon Jocelyn was never conceited, but while deploring his too slight knowledge of Hebrew, he took pride in his business acuteness. He was pleased that he had so often been consulted.

8

AT night Mary took Dora into her room. She showed her Ruth's photograph. The face was feeble, sad, and vacant; it had sometimes been redeemed in life by a glance of affection or merriment. This did not appear in the photograph.

' *You* don't think, like Ella, she should never have come back, do you?' said Mary.

'Oh no,' said Dora, 'I should have loved to have done what I could for her. I should have liked to be a mental nurse; it's so sad for them. But it's better it's over, isn't it?'

'I know it is, but I felt all the happiness of my life went with her.'

'Really, Mary, I think you're wonderful,' said Dora, taking Mary's hand.

'No, there's nothing wonderful about me,' said Mary, disengaging herself. As dutiful parsons' daughters they were alike, but there were regions in Mary Dora could not enter.

'Mary dear, you've had a very hard life.'

'No, I don't think so – only loneliness. I do long for a sister.'

'Yes,' said Dora. 'There's nothing quite like a sister. Gertrude was my special, you know, and she married. One doesn't lose them exactly, but it can't be the same, though we're very good pals the rest of us. You must treat me as a sort of sister. Will you, Mary?'

'Darling Dora,' cried Mary, flinging her arms round her friend.

Quiet warmth, not heat, was what Dora liked. She was perhaps relieved when the arms were taken away.

'I thought once we really should be sisters,' said she. 'It's all so long ago. Did you know – you must have guessed – Will and I were in love?'

'I knew Will was; I didn't know about you.'

'I was stupidly shy. I dreaded it coming to a point.'

'You would have taken him, wouldn't you?' said Mary gently. 'Do you mind my asking?'

'Mind your asking,' said Dora; 'no, of course I don't. Oh yes, I should have taken him. But of course I was nothing like clever enough for all of you. And I think your father didn't like it. And Will seemed so nervous of him. I sometimes wonder if that was why he never did propose.'

'Everything went wrong about Will and Father,' said Mary. 'For one thing he was so bad at Latin. It was one of the great disappointments of Father's life that none of my brothers really cared for classics.'

'Really, Mary?'

'You don't know what he and his friends felt about Latin and Greek. They were dearer to them than almost anything else, except the Bible.'

'How funny, Mary; don't you think so?'

'I don't know.' Mary had often heard her father and Mr Sykes deplore the decline of learning – one of the principal reasons they had for shaking their heads. 'Learning must be carried on. It's a kind of apostolic succession.'

'Oh no, Mary,' said Dora, bewildered. 'And anyhow *you* like Latin. Don't I remember you one day reciting Latin poetry?'

'I was never really good; besides I was a girl. It was his sons he cared for. Will's Latin lessons with Father – I shall never forget them. Things got much worse when Will was older. He drank, you know; he was very unhappy. It was that, I think, and Father was so hard. He had to go to Canada.'

'You're shaking all over, Mary.'

'Am I? Yes, I think I am. I used to hate Father about Will, Dora; he was as cold as ice. Telling you has brought it all back. It seems to me parents didn't think it necessary to understand their children in those days. Besides, Will always showed his worst side to Father from fright. I know so well what that is.'

'Are you afraid of Canon Jocelyn, Mary?'

'Not exactly, but I never knew any one who could make one feel so small. Will has done very well in Canada. I suppose it's better he went. Only we used to be so close to one another, and I've lost him altogether now he's married.'

'She's a Canadian, isn't she?' asked Dora.

'Yes.'

'Any children?'

'He's just got his fourth.'

'How splendid. Any boys?'

'Two boys. Here's the photograph of them.'

Dora looked at it with no trace of envy.

'Aren't they sweet?' she cried. 'And *what* a nice face his wife has' (her kind, optimistic eye passing over the commonness). 'I know she *must* be nice,' with the feeling that nothing could be too good for him. 'Dear me, I hadn't thought of those old days for years. Dear Will.' Her smile had always been sweet; in middle age it had become more sweet. 'But I must not be sentimental. I have a very happy life, and Gertrude's infants are such darlings.'

The time for romance was past. She had certainly retricked her beams, but Mary thought there was a little connection between her old love affair and the speech she made pensively, when they

41

took a walk in the twilight one evening. 'How glad one is, Mary, that this life isn't all.'

When Dora went to her room after the long talk, the fire had burnt low, and not all the beauty of the silver sticks could compensate for the very small oases of light created by the two candles. The wind was up, and kept tapping a branch against the window. Tranquil and prosaic to a fault, she felt tonight as if the sorrows of the past, the solitude of the present haunted the room. She wondered if the mad girl had died in the high bed. She longed for her cosy villa home at Southsea, for companionable tram bells. She tossed for hours, with bitter thoughts against Canon Jocelyn.

The wind died down in the morning; the sun shone; she felt her calm self again.

In compunction at unkindness she suggested, 'Do you give your father a cup of Benger's at ten? Mother has it and quite enjoys it. At their age the night is rather long for them.'

To be coupled with Mrs Redland and 'at their age' was a revenge Canon Jocelyn would have felt.

He and Mary were both occupied at breakfast with the prospect of the Meryton's garden-party that afternoon. As Claudia put it, 'The animals come out of the ark, and we polish them off with an annual feed.' The strange history of last night seemed far away. At breakfast, too, a letter from Will arrived with news of his crops, church, and investments, such a letter as any church-warden might have written. There was no trace of Jocelyn erudition. With it came a photograph of Will and his family – a prosperous, not distinguished, not at all handsome father, a stout mother, with the commonness much increased, healthy children.

'Very nice,' said Canon Jocelyn, without special enthusiasm. 'That is my godchild little Frances, I think, on the right. She was the eldest, but I cannot remember the second; was it Lilian?'

'No; Lilian is the baby, you know, Father.'

'The baby. Yes. Well,' as though addressing a child, 'you must be sure and write a letter of thanks and send my kind love, and you had better look out some fairy-tales for them for Christmas later on; perhaps the *Arabian Nights*.'

'We gave them that last Christmas, you remember.'

42

'Did we? But no doubt you can find something for them.'

The son who had nearly broken his heart roused but tranquil and inaccurate interest now. The tempests of life can die down as though they had never been.

9

MARY's appearance for the Meryton party occupied Dora. Her own dressing was quiet, neat, tasteful, late in the fashion, but not behind it. She looked a model for clergymen's daughters.

Mary had never been a good manager of dress. Her allowance was ample for a schoolgirl's pocket-money, but not sufficient for a woman. From a mixture of pride and shyness she had never explained what was her due. She had to give endless small sums, relieving village wants. She had only an absolute minimum for herself. Crêpe de chine underclothes and such had no attraction for her. She was too proud to become the slave of money for luxuries, but she was in a cage; money would have let her out.

She had her best dress made by Miss Wantage in Cayley and her everyday by Miss Porter in Dedmayne. Miss Porter produced a dreadful parody of the fashion-plates. But she was an old friend, whose feelings must not be hurt. In hats Mary constantly feared she was buying something extreme and must alter it, making it flatter if high hats were worn, higher if flat hats were worn.

'Mary, dear,' said Dora pleasantly, 'let me do a little something to that hat, may I? I always trim mother's and the girls'. And those little ends of hair – shall I fasten them up with a slide? Mother was very particular when we were young. She used to say dressing carelessly was burying a talent. I always thought that so helpful.'

'Nobody ever noticed much when I was young.'

'Your aunt was so busy, wasn't she, with her reading and her beautiful needlework?'

Never had woman been lazier than Aunt Lottie, sitting on a

sofa even in early middle age, putting occasional stitches into cushion-covers. Mary left Dora to her kind impression.

The pony took Dora and Mary to Meryton Court.

They approached the wonderful, dignified old house, reposing placidly in the afternoon sun.

'Are you shy?' said Mary. 'I am to the pitch I am not quite sure what my name is.'

'Oh yes, I never go to these sort of houses,' said Dora easily. 'Of course they make me shy.'

The interior was not merely beautiful, though it was beautiful in the highest degree. The pictures, both frames and canvases, softened by the lovely bloom of age, seemed as natural to the house as the elm trees in the park. The oak panelling, like black shining water, the rich red crimson brocade on the chairs and sofas, the Indian and Chinese cabinets, the porcelain, even the profusion of today's hot-house flowers – all had a landscape's power of looking not new, but fresh, not faded, but immemorial.

Lady Meryton smiled her sweetest on Dora and Mary. When her time must be given to others, she herself took them to the rose garden. 'I believe Kathy is there and you must see her.'

There *was* Kathy, the Kathy Mary had dreaded. She fell captive to her beauty on the spot: the broad forehead, the large grey eyes, serious and true; the exquisitely shaped mouth with its sweet, very benignant curve; the straight tall figure like a beech tree. In former times, when beauty was more thought of, Kathy might have had wars waged for her.

With her was Claudia. In contrast to the guests, who had bought best summer dresses with an eye to the Meryton garden-party, Claudia wore a coat and skirt – perfectly fitting, but a coat and skirt. She always looked as if she were in a riding-habit. Lady Meryton wore a lovely grey silk.

'Claudia, dearest,' she had said, 'couldn't you put on something prettier? I think it pleases people.'

'No; there is one thing I draw the line at,' answered Claudia, 'and that is the party-frockers, all decked out with beads and chains like squaws. I'm afraid they must miss the bliss of seeing me got up to kill.'

Claudia was thin, weather-beaten, and born to the saddle. She

44

and Kathy had retired to the rose garden for a quiet discussion on harness.

'Claudia,' said Lady Meryton, 'here is Dora Redland. I remember you and her toddling about together so well. Miss Hollings, Miss Redland, and this is my niece Kathy and my cousin, Mary Jocelyn. You are not really relations, but I feel as if you were.'

Lady Meryton went off to other guests.

'Mamma seems to think we swore an eternal friendship in our cradles,' said Claudia to Dora. 'I suppose the nurses pushed our prams side by side now and then. My mother has such an imagination.'

'I remember coming to tea here sometimes. I think you had a white dog called Scamp,' said Dora.

'Did we? Oh, by the way, would you tell Ella – I think Mamma said she wasn't coming today – there's no need for her to trouble herself about Fred Parry's hens? The Hunt has given him the usual compensation. Of course the cases are gone into systematically, only he likes to get somebody fresh and pour out his woes. All the rest of us know him rather too well.'

Dora came from that section of the middle class which is so good and kind it *cannot* be rude (Mary came from the section above it which *can*), but there was a touch of dryness in her answer. 'Won't you see Ella yourself? She's coming back tomorrow.'

Meanwhile Mary, like a romantic lover, was speechless in awe before Kathy. Kathy did not speak either; the two stood and looked at one another.

'I don't quite know why Mamma brought you here,' said Claudia, turning to Mary. 'The rain's ruined the roses. Kathy and I supposed no one could possibly want to look at them but there are some rather good kinds, I believe. I ought to know them and don't; they've got the names on them.'

'Roses don't do very well with us at Southsea,' said Dora to Kathy. 'I expect we spoil them.'

Kathy turned her beautiful eyes on Dora in silent indifference, and made no answer.

'Did you enjoy Florence very much?' Mary asked Claudia. 'You were just going off when we last met.'

This harmless question was answered crushingly.

'I didn't go in the end. I can't bear churches – it's enough to be dragged to one every Sunday morning – or pictures of naked females, and that's all there is at Florence.'

The ordinary coinage of small talk did not circulate with Claudia. She hated London, she went to buy clothes sometimes. If compelled to stay the night, she relieved the tedium by a farce or revue, roared with laughter, and was bored. She hated ordinary parties; she hated everywhere abroad, except the resort of big game. The only books she read were Jorrocks, *Pickwick*, and *The Adventures of an Irish R.M.*, so that one or two further topics broached by Dora and Mary died at birth. Kathy had been silent, because she was thinking of something else. Now she spoke to Claudia across Mary, as if Mary were empty air.

'I don't see how you mean about Taffy,' and Claudia, in her husky county voice, resumed the discourse on martingales Lady Meryton had interrupted.

'That's a lovely crimson rose,' said Dora to Mary. They made conversation with one another about pinks and crimsons.

'They gave you tea, I hope,' said Claudia over her shoulder to Mary. 'There are some peaches in the tent. I always think the one point of a party is the peaches.'

This broad hint could not be ignored. Mary was generally without initiative at parties, staying just where her hostess put her. She took Dora back to the lawn.

'Why I was supposed to want to see Dora Redland!' said Claudia to Kathy. 'Mary Jocelyn has always been a pet. Dora is just a vicar's daughter, not even our vicar, and Mamma used to have a mad freak of Mrs Redland coming to stay for two or three days. I used to think she was Dawson's sister, only it was a bit rough on Dawson' (Lady Meryton's maid), 'and say a kind word before I saw my mistake. Dora is a regular Sunday-frocker – that isn't so bad as a party-frocker, I own – but don't you feel it in your bones she'd call her coat and skirt a *cos*tume, and do rather funny things at dinner?'

'Claudia,' said Lady Meryton that evening, 'how could you desert our guests.'

'Now, Mamma, Kath and I toiled like niggers stuffing the

beasts of the people with tea. Then we thought we might have some respite.'

'Dearest,' said Lady Meryton, speaking with even more than her usual gentleness, 'I do wish you were kinder.'

'Don't speak to me like that, Mamma,' said Claudia, blushing. 'I never knew any one who could make one feel so small as you do. I'm sorry; I will behave better.'

One day the Jocelyns and Dora went to examine the remains of an Augustinian priory, and had tea afterwards at the Vicarage.

'You may not have heard that much more has been discovered of the Priory since your father's time,' said Canon Jocelyn to Dora. 'The Augustinians were especially numerous in this part of the country. Of course we owe several of our finest churches to their zeal, but no one had any idea till lately on what an immense scale the Priory was planned.'

When the Roman Church was sufficiently remote, Canon Jocelyn regarded it with the same affection as his own. When it was near at hand, creating perverts, he hated it.

'I'm delighted to see you all,' said Mr Sykes, the rosy, white-haired vicar, who, with Mr Herbert, met the Jocelyn party at his church gate. 'And it's a particular pleasure to see Miss Redland again. I hope your mother and sisters are well. I wish you could persuade your mother to revisit these parts; we should give her a most hearty welcome.' His duty done by Dora's affairs he went on, 'I've got Herbert to help me, you see. He has the Augustinians at his fingers' ends, and I hope Miss Redland shares our harmless madness for the Augustinians, because I'm looking forward to a peculiar treat today, Jocelyn. There's a French priest I met at Rouen in June, an excellent fellow, who has been examining the archives of one of the Augustinian priories over there, and, if you'll believe me, it's a kind of Mother House of ours here, and they have documents relating to us, which shed any amount of new light on the topography. I have a letter from the priest I must show you after tea. He says we are to suck him dry for any information he's got.'

The mantle of learning covered all the priest's theological errors.

'There were some things we had got wrong about the refectory. And you remember the arch you and I disputed about. I parti-

47

cularly want to look at that again, for we have proof that you are right and I am wrong. I hoped in that one matter of the arch I had caught your father napping, Mary, but it was not to be.'

They walked round and round the church, ascended and descended stairs, retraced their steps, peered at inscriptions, went down on their hands and knees. They passed to the churchyard, where some mounds and grass-grown masonry enabled the three clergymen to construct a graphic picture of a past civilization. Yet with all of them this was merely a pastime; their serious interest lay elsewhere.

'By this time we have earned our tea,' said Mr Sykes. 'I've asked young Baston in. I hope you won't mind. I wanted him very much to see you; I wanted him to see a scholar.'

'Come, he sees yourself, and happily he can, in addition, see Herbert,' said Canon Jocelyn.

'Oh no, my classics are entirely gone where the rest of my memory is very shortly going. I am an old man of seventy, recollect, not an infant of eighty-two like yourself. I am beginning to feel the infirmities of age. As to Herbert, I am not sure. He hails from a strange place called Peterhouse, which Trinity men know nothing about.'

'Has Mr Baston made any more classical allusions in the pulpit?'

'I have tried to check his ardour. It all came from exuberance of mind, induced by the reading of a miserable translation of Virgil, and another still more miserable of excerpts from the Greek tragedians; some society he belongs to had recommended them. He confused the two. Everything is the same to him, "most interesting," as he says.'

'Perhaps it is in his favour that his exuberance gets the better of him. One must be thankful for the very smallest mercies in these days.'

'It's ungrateful to cavil, but there is *un peu trop de zèle*. Is that correct French, Mary? You know the Baptists opened a little chapel here some years ago, and as Widow Hankey used to say to me, "Their congregations is very pore, sir, very pore indeed; there's nothing for us to trouble about," and nobody did trouble I believe, certainly not the preacher that they sent on Sunday

48

evenings; but now Baston is harrying them into the fold. I caught him making a black sheep of a Baptist's little girl, and he's at some new Irish people that have come, when really their souls are in most respectable keeping. Father Murphy is a diligent little man, you know. In the eyes of the Creator these differences must appear so infinitely little, and to Baston they appear so infinitely great.'

''Myes,' said Canon Jocelyn. 'The Papists are wary in England, and make the differences *appear* small to allay suspicion. I don't think the Church of Rome really changes. You must be glad Baston is not a ritualist. It is the weak mind engrossed in coloured scarves which she gets into her clutches.'

'Oh, I don't think that's his danger. Anyhow, he's not at all a bad fellow. But he's too much *of* the village people; he mixes up in all their quarrels; there's a perpetual commerce of affronts between them. They realize it perfectly well. But what can one do? Sad to say, that's the prevailing type one gets now. Look at Yeabsley, Mansbridge, and Milverton. As the Church must have clergy, I suppose one must be very much obliged to them for taking Orders, but whenever I meet a grocer's assistant with an earnest countenance, my heart sinks in anticipation of hearing that he is reading the Greek Testament with the intention of being ordained.'

'One cannot see what is going to happen. I do not believe I told you, Sykes' (Canon Jocelyn told Mr Sykes every time he met him), 'that when the Bishop was ill the other day' (seven years ago) 'he sent a most objectionable individual to take the confirmation. He reminded me of a very inferior flash type of undergraduate at a small college. I looked him out in the Calendar, and you will not believe me when I tell you that he was a non-collegiate Pollman. But what can one expect? We have a Government bent on destroying the foundations on which, not so much the greatness, but the very existence of our State depends. And there is no foresight, no quiet thinking over whither all this so-called reform is leading us. There is simply a child's pleasure in breaking its toys.'

'I agree with you from the bottom of my heart,' said Mr Sykes. 'I see no gleam of light anywhere.' Then the two old friends felt happier, and went indoors.

Mild Mr Baston, when he had handed round the tea, threw away his chance of intercourse with scholars and talked to Dora. She welcomed him with a smile but, preferred feminine conversation. They began on choir boys, and soon Mr Baston was telling her comic anecdotes about howlers. Meanwhile the three clergymen continued the archaeological discussion. Even the excessively polite Mr Sykes and Mr Herbert had thoughts for nothing else. Mary sat by and listened; Dora tried in vain to draw her into the comic anecdotes.

Dora could hear scraps of conversation now and then. It, the learning, the jokes, the enthusiasm, the whole afternoon opened a new world to her, a dull world. And Mary really liked it. Had they been right when they used to call her that poor little odd thing?

'You're rather tired, I'm afraid, Mary,' said Dora that evening.

'Oh, no, not a bit, thank you,' said Mary. But she was surprised at herself. She had *not* been wholly absorbed in the Augustinians. She had been disappointed because Mr Herbert, who had often seemed to want to talk to her, had shown clearly that he preferred archaeology.

Next afternoon the Jocelyns gave a tea-party in Dora's honour. By twelve o'clock the household (excepting Canon Jocelyn and the gardener) began to prepare for it. Mary was already agitated and her agitation spread to the servants. The pie-crust was burnt at lunch, and they had no spoons. 'I am very sorry,' said Mary, 'but do you mind our managing without? They are *so* busy.'

Canon Jocelyn did his share of distraction. He said three times at lunch, 'I cannot remember what friends it is you are expecting. The Venns are away, I think you told me. Will Mr Sykes be coming?'

Mary, with forced calm, enumerated the company in slow, clear tones.

'The Archdeacon and Mrs and Miss Waters are coming, you say. Then they will want to put up their horse and carriage here. We must tell gardener. Is there a stall ready for use?'

'They have given up the pony, you know, Father. They will come on their bicycles.'

The conversation moved away from arrangements, but soon

Canon Jocelyn was back at 'The boy should be told to leave the gate open if people are coming this afternoon. Will you see that he is told?'

'He does know already; Cook told him.'

'But I wonder if he quite understands. I think,' with a sigh, 'it will be better for me to see about it myself.'

'I wonder, do the roses look better *here* or *here*?' said Mary about three o'clock. 'I *wonder*. Which do you think, Dora?'

'Very nice indeed in both places.'

There was nothing to choose between the two.

'I'll put them there, then,' said Mary, and five minutes after they were back in the first place.

This distraction was the legacy left Mary from the care of Ruth and anxiety for Will. She struggled against it, but she was like the reed before the wind.

The party consisted of two clerical spinsters, a curate or two, a stray girl, Mr Herbert, Mr Sykes, and an old squire. He was a relic of the cultivated aristocracy of the eighteenth century, lasting on in complete mental solitude – 'absolutely mad' his compeers called him. His delight was to cap quotations from Horace with Canon Jocelyn on the rare occasions when they met.

There were the Archdeacon and his wife and spoilt daughter with painted lips, impressed at her goodness in coming. Canon Jocelyn thought the bustling Archdeacon all a clergyman should not be. But the Archdeacon was a successful preacher; his Church of England's Men's Society and his Retreats were highly popular. The Archdeacon disliked Canon Jocelyn's superiority; as a member of many more committees, and still in the vigorous years of life, he felt the old man should have looked up to him. In spite of mutual enmity, occasionally each entertained the other.

Dr and Mrs King were also of the party. Canon Jocelyn was against their coming. 'No doubt Dr King is very attentive in the discharge of his duties,' said he. 'Most kind, but whether one wishes to encourage an intimacy – it would be hardly worth while to have them constantly visiting here.' One day Dr King, in delight at her father's good health, had remarked to Mary in Canon Jocelyn's hearing, 'The Canon is full of beans today.' This familiarity confirmed Canon Jocelyn's views on doctors –

people to be treated with the greatest courtesy, even friendliness, in their own sphere. Their sphere was never dinner at a house like the Rectory, and rarely tea.

On the arrival of his guests all Canon Jocelyn's agitation vanished. One would never have imagined his composure had been ruffled by the Archdeacon's party and the front gate. Mary remained flushed, but she made a charming hostess. It may be because shy people have suffered so much from being left out that they, above all others, make their guests feel at home.

Canon Jocelyn's courtesy froze the circle round him, but if not enjoyed at the time, his guests felt afterwards they had been in distinguished society.

The friendly words that the visitors exchanged with the servants who handed the cakes; the servants' old-fashioned desire that the visitors should enjoy their tea, and pleasure when it was manifest they did; the lovely china, the general shabbiness, the dignified silhouettes of the clergy in their long coats; the tacit acknowledgement that the old people, the squire, Canon Jocelyn, and Mr Sykes, were the most important members of the circle – all these things made up another scene from the past Dora remembered. The Archdeacon's powdered daughter with the screeching voice should not have been there; she spoilt the effect.

Dora was not handicapped by a desire to be preferred, or troubled by the smallest touch of shyness. Since Will had gone to Canada, she had put away the world and its pleasures as resolutely as a nun. She looked on parties benevolently, rather as an aunt might be glad to see her young nephews and nieces enjoying themselves. Mr Sykes liked parties much more youthfully.

The talk ran on herbaceous borders, hens, and parochial treats, the roads, the rain. There were shakes of the head over the bad manners of the young people, the deterioration of the servants, the sad state of England. And the old and young people smiled on one another and spent a pleasant afternoon in spite of all; the formidable young people pleased at the friendliness of the old, the formidable old people flattered and grateful at the notice of the young. The unformidable middle-aged people pleased, flattered, and grateful at the notice of either.

When Mary had poured out the second cups of tea she had time to look about her. She had introduced Mr Herbert to Dora and to the rouged daughter of the Archdeacon. He noticed their good looks with indifferent pleasure, particularly Miss Waters's pretty complexion; he thought it her own.

'I feel I ought to be helping Miss Jocelyn instead of being idle,' said he, and crossed over to Mary.

To sit half an hour by an elderly lady getting deaf, another half an hour by some awkward spectacled girl, a third half hour by the shyest curate, such was generally Mary's fate at the parties of the neighbourhood. When it was over she had accomplished a duty; for pleasure she preferred reading under the chestnut-tree. Today the one of all others she most wanted to talk to most wanted to talk to her, and there was no archaeology to spoil her happiness.

'I've brought over that new fellow's poetry,' said Mr Herbert. 'I thought one or two of his things would please your father.'

They talked of the poetry; it was a peg on which they hung thoughts of one another.

He mentioned Kathy.

'Have you seen the beautiful and charming Miss Hollings?'

'Yes,' said Mary, 'she is so beautiful I could not think of anything to say to her.'

'I understand she's going tomorrow, so I've missed my chance. But I'm sure I should have disliked her. These astoundingly charming people are generally sharks. Don't you agree?'

Mary laughed and felt a pleasant dart of satisfaction.

They continued happily discussing. It seemed like two minutes, but Dora said to Mary afterwards, 'What engrossing conversation you and that Mr Herbert were having. I *couldn't* make you hear. What a pleasant party, Mary; I had such a nice talk with Miss Jackson about sweetpeas.'

In the evening Canon Jocelyn was not in the least tired. Mary had a headache, but she played backgammon with him on the supposition that he would not be up to reading aloud.

'Mary,' said Dora later. 'Why did you play backgammon when you had a headache?'

'I shouldn't like him to miss his backgammon,' said Mary.

'I know, only old people do get selfish, and we oughtn't to allow it. It really isn't right to them, and in a way they're like children, aren't they; I think all men are; they never grow up really.'

It made Mary wince to have Dora's cruel, penetrating, motherly good sense turned on her father. But her words may have had an effect.

A conversation took place between Canon Jocelyn and Mary next morning.

'I suppose,' said Mary, 'it will be about time to write the invitations for the Book Club. It is our turn this month.'

But Canon Jocelyn, for no reason but inertia, did not want to write the invitations. He answered therefore, 'Ye-es, I daresay we shall not have the meeting here; they might go to Mansbridge.'

'But, Father, you know how they like coming here.'

'Perhaps, but it is not always very convenient.'

'But we always have it here.'

'From time to time we have had it here, certainly, but it is better that it should not be a precedent; every one should take their turn.'

'But, Father, we have had it regularly every year since the very beginning.'

'I don't care about that. I think it is a very good thing to make a change now and then, and besides I am rather specially busy with work just now.'

'But it would be only just one afternoon.'

'I know, but there are a good many other matters to be taken into consideration. The days are drawing in now, and the weather is becoming very uncertain.'

These excuses were delivered in such a stately manner that Mary could hardly believe she was correct when she answered:

'But we have always had it the third week in September.'

'My dear Mary,' with disagreeable blandness, 'would it be possible for you to moderate the tone of your voice a little?'

'I beg your pardon. I am very sorry, but *do* have the meeting here. You know Mr Sykes said he felt it was such an opportunity for the younger men to get to know you.'

'I do not think there is any need for us to discuss the question

54

further. Have you decided where you will take Miss Redland this afternoon?'

'Father, I do think you ought to have it. It's wrong not to make the effort. You oughtn't to get into a shell like that.'

'Indeed. Since when have you felt yourself called to take my actions under your charge?'

'Oh, Father, you know I –'

'Perhaps you would not mind leaving me now, as there is some work I want to get done.'

Mary came out from the study, keeping back her tears with difficulty.

After lunch Canon Jocelyn said to Mary, 'I think you were talking of going to the Mill this afternoon. If so, perhaps you could leave these invitations on your way.'

Canon Jocelyn did not seem out of countenance with his *volte-face*. He came with particular affability to tell them about the weather when the phaeton was brought round, and referred openly to the Book Club. 'It is not worth while your leaving an invitation at Yeabsley. Sykes tells me Hartnell is confined to the house with rheumatism, but he has given Sykes his list of suggestions for new books.'

Canon Jocelyn could own he was in the wrong with full-hearted grace, which made the critic feel that it was himself who was guilty.

10

THE two friends talked every night. Not for many years had the spare room walls heard such animation. Mary had received many confidences; it was part of her business in life. To impart, to confide herself was an unfamiliar delight.

Dora was very sympathetic within her narrow range. Outside it she was often astray, and did not follow Mary.

Mary told Dora of her writings.

'*How* interesting!' cried Dora. 'Gertrude's sister-in-law writes things when she's wanting money for her Babies' Home. They're

simply fascinating, those infants. Oh, you *must* get yours published, Mary.'

'I am not sure if Father –' began Mary.

'Yes,' said Dora. 'The dear old man. I know everything new
worries them a little. I always like to explain any new scheme of
Ella's quietly by myself to Mother. Ella talks too loud, and then
Mother gets puzzled, and she does *love* to know all we're doing.'
There seemed no resemblance to Canon Jocelyn here. 'We'll
ask Ella; I think she knows some one who writes.'

The sisters criticized one another at times. 'What Dora does is
all very well in a way, but it's rather frittering and dabbling – the
kind of play philanthropy people were so busy about in the
nineties,' said Ella; while Dora's return criticism was, 'Ella
bores us so about her work, I'm afraid it all seems rather faddy
to us.'

But Mary's writings united them. The Redlands had the doing
of good deeds in their blood. Mrs Redland's forebears had been
clergy for three generations.

'They are not exactly stories,' said Dora, 'but I am sure they
are very good, and I am not at all surprised really, though it seems
funny our little Mary writing books.'

'I *am* so glad,' said Ella warmly. 'I was afraid you were sinking
into one of those many women who do nothing. I know a very
clever girl who is in with a number of literary people. They *were*
so alive, that set I met in town, and I am sure she will get them
taken for you. And now, Mary, I wanted to ask you, will you get
Mr Herbert to have a meeting for me at Lanchester? I want to
work Lanchester up, and if you could tackle Mr Herbert I think
we could get the schools.'

'I!' said Mary. 'I'm sure I shouldn't persuade him to anything.'

'Oh yes, you could, Mary. He told somebody who was saying
how wonderful your father was, "Oh, and Miss Jocelyn, too",
so I felt you would be the person to get at him.'

Mary lay awake some happy hours that night, going over the
words, 'Oh, and Miss Jocelyn.' He looked on her as a friend. She
had hoped, now she was sure. It was a delightful thought. It
filled the space which had been so empty when she came back
from Broadstairs; it filled it fuller than she knew.

Dora's good-bye was full of affection. Mary was established in her heart as a sister and a duty, beloved in both capacities. She decided to rearrange her Southsea work that she might be ready to go to that dear, solitary Mary whenever she was wanted.

Mary gave her writings to Ella, and in due course received the following in a small, clear, pointed hand:

Dear Miss Jocelyn – Ella Redland sent me your MS. I thought the form so novel, and the rhythm of some of your phrases quite arresting. I like your pattern – it is very individual. I lent it to Dermott O'Donovan. I expect you know his verse. He's quite new and rather young.

He wrote to me about your writings: 'I have never known any one on such intimate terms with toads, and this, coupled with a passion for Mother Julian of Norwich, indicates a mind I want to know more of. It must be arranged that I see her.' Do come for the night to my flat next week. It would be jolly to have you. Dermott can't be caught before eleven P.M. – Yours sincerely,

BRYNHILDA KENRICK.

This letter astonished Mary. She had written almost as a silk-worm weaves a cocoon, with no thought of admiration. That it should come from a young man was exhilarating. She had the same idea of young men as a very young girl; they seemed above ordinary humanity. Middle-aged men she knew were like herself, subject to unpopularity and making mistakes. Not that she had ever been near falling in love with any young men. She had never desired to please any one as much as her father. He, by the way, would certainly not think more of her because she brought out a book. On the other hand, if a friend of his own age should read and like it, he *might* be disposed to talk more freely to her.

She remembered that Mr O'Donovan was a Roman Catholic. Canon Jocelyn disliked Roman Catholics and the Salvation Army on account of their wildness and extravagance. When Mary was thirteen she had said, 'I simply detest Henry IV of France because he did not persecute any one.'

'That is a foolish way of talking,' Canon Jocelyn answered, 'and I dislike your slang use of the word "simply".' She had only meant Henry IV was not in earnest, but there was a strangeness in the speech, which made Canon Jocelyn feel she might get into

57

the hands of the Roman Catholics. Twenty-five years had elapsed: Mary was still a Protestant, but Canon Jocelyn would never say more than 'Um' if Mary told him she had met Father Murphy in the road. In his heart he regretted that 'Papists' had been put on the same level as Protestants at the Universities. He combined these views with admiration for the great Roman Catholic men of letters. In literature other matters troubled him – slang phrases and inadequate dictionaries.

It would be a bitter pill if any one of his family were beholden to a Roman Catholic. Nor was Mary sure if she wanted her inner thought exposed to the bored scrutiny of the public. But she wanted very much to go to London and hear Mr O'Donovan's compliments from his own mouth.

She accepted the invitation. Then the news must be broken to her father.

It needed breaking, for she had never proposed to do such a thing before. She meant to tell him of her writings, but her heart failed her; she dreaded his sarcasm.

'You wish to stay with a friend of Miss Redland, with whom you are not acquainted. That surely is a strange idea, and to go a journey of nearly two hours for one night only would not be at all worth while. I really think, Mary, you had better give it up; it seems a very wild scheme.'

'Perhaps I could stay with Mrs Plumtree for another night, if you could spare me, Father. She has often said I could propose myself whenever I liked.'

'I must say,' replied Canon Jocelyn, 'I am a little surprised that you should care to be running about in various directions at this time, when we are rather occupied with the Harvest Festival.'

She let pass the injustice of 'various directions,' and answered:

'I should be back by Saturday, Father, and the Harvest Festival isn't till Tuesday. It would only be two nights at the most.'

'But there would be the decorations, which are always under your charge.'

'Yes, but there would be plenty of time for them. I never do them till the morning before, you know.'

'Well, you must of course judge for yourself in such a matter. I merely tell you what I think.'

58

Mary kept to her resolution, but the heart was taken out of it. Had she known her father's real reason, she would have given up the visit in an instant, but Canon Jocelyn did not always like giving his real reasons.

He called up a picture of Mary run over in a London crossing. He thought, too, of himself, seized with a heart attack; he had slight attacks at night occasionally. He liked Mary to come and sit with him on the pretext that he must drink something hot. He was hurt that Mary should not realize all this without explanation. He indulged himself in some petty and morose thoughts, but he checked himself, and recollected that the young are naturally selfish; allowance must be made for them. He wished her a comfortable journey; he even said, 'I daresay Miss Gage can be your deputy at the decorations if you should be detained in London.' He would not entirely give up his point about the Harvest Festival.

She had won her battle. Her battles with Canon Jocelyn were few and her victories fewer, but many times she regretted her victory, and most of all as she mounted the stairs to Miss Kenrick's flat in Kensington.

II

In the flat a new world was opened to Mary, both of the eye and mind. The rooms were furnished with every new convenience. Nothing, even the books, dated back farther than four or five years. 'Books are like sucked oranges when the vogue is over,' said Miss Kenrick. Besides new books there were many magazines, pamphlets, and organs of small societies. There were, too, various thin volumes with thick pages. They contained poems, essays, short stories that the set was constantly publishing and presenting to itself.

The walls were orange; the paint royal blue. There were foreign posters still more emphatic than those at Basle Station; illustrations from comic papers of South-eastern Europe; Cubist studies by some Scandinavian artist. There were large cushions on the floor, which looked as if they had been sat on too much; they were covered in Cubist chintzes. These might have been harsh and crude, but were tempered by the dust, which everywhere lay thick; the windows were dull with London grime.

Miss Kenrick was a good-looking, imperturbable girl of twenty-five. She greeted Mary, who was trembling in shyness, with the cool, practised courtesy of one accustomed to seeing new people every day. She kept up easy talk.

'Isn't Ella Redland spendidly typical?' she said. 'We call her Great-aunt Ellen. The year before last we all had a season of causes, and she can't quite realise the season's over, and keeps sending us pamphlets. I've caught Dermott for tonight and one or two other people will be turning up, so would you like to rest for half an hour?' She gave Mary a book of new poems to read.

While Mary turned the pages she was supposed to be enjoying, her mind ceaselessly repeated the phrase, 'one or two people.' It was an evening of ordinary routine to Miss Kentrick, only diversified by the new, uncertain element of Mary.

Brynhilda, Dermott, and the rest belonged to the same set. Its members were almost all between twenty and thirty. They came from Hammersmith, Hampstead, Chelsea, Bloomsbury, and St John's Wood. Most of them had shaken off their families, and united in light elastic unions with friends. There were some husbands with *not* wives, and wives with *not* husbands. If one or two still lived with parents, it was understood that no one would take any notice of *them*. Most sprang from good provincial or suburban chapel homes. They were in the bloom of youth and lustiness with a remarkable proportion of good looks; they possessed youth's special quality – vitality. Those who have it find it irresistible; so do those who lack it. The old, the middle-aged, the young themselves bow before it.

When the set did not meet at Brynhilda's flat – it was a tribute to Brynhilda that it should come to such a wrong part of London as Kensington – it met at Hammersmith, Hampstead, etc. The flat was a house of call for the set, not a home. It had no permanence, no roots of sentiment. When Brynhilda left it – she might at any moment – she would not think of it again. As she said, 'You should never let the past get in your way.'

But how pleasant the atmosphere was, how sensible. There was no snapping, fussiness, or anxiety. Mary remembered many throes at the Rectory: if the cat took a day off in the woods, if a member of the household was late, or a visitor turned up unexpectedly for the night. And when they were agitated they all became cross, Mary included.

Neither was the set dull. Canon Jocelyn's circle really enjoyed dullness: dull talks, walks, books, newspapers, sermons, visits, and parties. Mary, under the aegis of the old generation, had some of the attributes of her own, which, though it endured dullness, did not like it.

Now it was night, and the set came in. They hardly greeted one another, and Mary noticed that they made no distinction in their manner to the other sex. But were the sexes really so indifferent to one another? Did they not perhaps drawl, smoke languorously, loll and lounge among the cushions, lie in long heaps about the floor, appear too silly to finish their sentences, laugh and ejaculate 'Isn't it?' at random more than they might have done if there had not been another sex present?

Mary found herself seated by a Mr Worsley of forty-five, the oldest person present. Feeling this disgrace, he was the most rebellious of the rebels, the youngest of the young. He took care to pay no attention to Mary, who was his nearest contemporary. He and his wife had discarded one another some years before. After different experiences he had now set up house with a girl of eighteen, and was trying to think and be just what she was. She was already beginning to find him 'mossy.'

On the other side of Mary was the fireplace, where once had been the grate and now was the radiator, not in full working order. If it was the place of honour, it had its dangers too, for all the ends of cigarettes were hurled at it. One missed, and hit Mary; another fell into a kitchen jug. There were four of them, filled with coffee, which was cooling on the hearth. Brynhilda introduced her to one or two people. They treated her as if she had not been there. On the whole she was grateful, though it was missing the only chance she was likely to get of coming into touch with the intellectual, young generation.

Mary had noticed a thin girl, Priscilla Leach. She was stretched

61

at full length on a couch, half-opening and then shutting her narrow, brown eyes, which looked like some not brightly polished stones. She was talking about *adventures*.

'One ought to have as many as one can, and go on and on and on. You get such jolly things from them.'

'Does one leave all the old shells of the victims lying about?' said an undergraduate called Tommy. 'Isn't that rather untidy?'

'Oh, if little me gets the kernel anybody else can have the shells,' said Priscilla.

'Excuse my seeming rude,' said the undergraduate, 'but I rather doubt whether little me will get my kernel.'

'The point, I feel sure, is,' said Mr Worsley, crushing levity, 'that whether one loves or hates, or is faithful or unfaithful, life is always a comedy and always a pageant.'

This topic continued for some time. Brynhilda placidly handed round coffee and cakes; she had heard it too often to be much interested. None of the men helped her. It pleased the girls that the men were rude to them; it pleased the men almost more to be rude. Mary listened in bewilderment, hardly believing what she heard. The coffee was cold, and there was not enough to go round, but such discomfort the set bore with an attractive lightness of heart.

At last Dermott came in. Brynhilda introduced him to Mary, and he took Mr Worsley's place. He was very handsome, and greeted her with a bewitching smile; he could not smile quite impersonally. Light friendliness lay behind it, and careless desire to please. Mary would have meant much by such a smile. She could not help thinking he must be a little attracted to her. It excited her; she longed to impress him. Looking back afterwards, she saw she had been ripe with encouragement for something warmer than friendship.

No chance came for her to shine. The talk fell on London. Dermott decried it. 'What is there to say for this corner of London at any rate? You have the large vulgar stores here just matching the large vulgar flats, and the vulgar motors spueing forth obscene and abominable cries, and portentous women with fat bosoms surging against the stores, submerging the men, who are absolutely as detestable in their own beady-eyed Hebrew line.

Now just tell me, is this a spot any breathing being could respect?'

'But why should any old thing ever respect another old thing?' said Brynhilda. 'London's ugly, and wicked, and screaming, and silly, and crude, and smelly, and democratic, and jolly, and tremendous, and it's today, never last week.'

'Who says London is ugly?' said Salome, a lovely serious girl, who wrote bad poetry, 'with its taxis scarlet and emerald, and its buses like dressed-up revellers at a ball, and its great racing cars like darting silver beetles. And the posters are like nursery picture-books for the giants' children, and the sky-signs are spelling lessons for the stars.'

'Say that all over again,' said Tommy, 'that I may take it down in shorthand, and send it to the Publicity Department of Metroland. You'll see it all up at Walham Green Station in a neat frame.'

'There is an incongruity about London,' said Mr Worsley, 'which makes it so splendid. I mean, always London goes on her way indifferent, whatever happens. Now Paris tries consciously to be beautiful, doesn't she? That produces in her an atrocious anaemia, which sickens one like the odour of garbage. I always feel Paris is longing to be crimson as blood, but I see her maroon like my grandmother's pelisse.'

'Now, Miss Jocelyn,' said Dermott, turning to Mary, 'I know you're concurring in my sentiment. Don't you feel that village of yours can despise London?'

'I don't know,' said Mary. He paused attentively, and, after ransacking her brains for something, she went on. 'I think trees and fields are more companionable.'

'To be sure they are, rather too much so, particularly on a night in November, when the wind is sighing among them.'

'I don't mind saying I think any company's better than the most communicative tree,' said Brynhilda. 'And you do too, Dermott. When do you ever cross to Ireland unless one of us goes and holds you by the hand?'

Next the set turned to the anthology Mary had looked at in the afternoon.

'What did you think of it, Miss Jocelyn?' said Brynhilda.

Mary had not understood the poems; their style and matter

were unfamiliar. She disliked them for this – the reason why the set admired them. She said more than she intended. Perhaps solitary people fall into the shyness of talking too much, more than others.

'Well, Miss Jocelyn,' said Dermott at length, 'you have demolished me pretty thoroughly. That unhappy little rhyme which especially offends you is my poor offspring.'

'I did not know,' cried Mary. 'I had no idea. Why didn't you tell me?'

'We none of us knew. How were we to know that Jonas Mudge was you?' said Brynhilda.

'Yes, that was my little private jest. I wanted to see if you'd know an O'Donovan when you met it.'

'I should have thought it was particularly individual; any one might have recognized it as Dermott's work,' said Mr Worsley.

'But why Jonas Mudge? Why particularly Jonas and why particularly Mudge?' asked somebody.

'Surely that's obvious. My own name is so excruciatingly pretty that it isn't to be endured more than it must be. It was to be mine for plain everyday life, but in the land of romance I call myself Jonas Mudge and enfranchise my soul – and he really is a very charming fellow.'

'I should fancy he is an earnest agnostic of the Herbert Spencer school,' said Tommy.

Mary's cheeks burnt. She was reminded of herself at fifteen, when she had either turned dumb and been reproved, or talked too much and been further reproved. She made more of it than necessary. All turned to something else and forgot her. They stayed very late. Dermott was the last to go.

'Wait,' said Brynhilda, posing herself on the floor beside him and Mary. 'I want to ask you what about Miss Jocelyn's writings?'

'About Miss Jocelyn's writings?' said he. 'I don't know that I have anything of special importance to say on the subject.'

'What do you advise Miss Jocelyn to do?'

'Is there any reason why I should advise anything? I am quite impotent, and quite incompetent. Did I tell you, by the way, Father Lecky has just been showing me the most amazing hymns of a girl of fifteen in Galway. She has had visions of Our Lady that are of superlative wonder and beauty. But I say, I must depart. I see even old Worsley has gone to roost. That is a sign the night is far spent. Goodnight, Miss Jocelyn,' he hardly glanced at her. 'Goodnight, Brynhilda. Think that I'm off to Oxford at ten, and I haven't packed up.'

'I'm sorry,' said Brynhilda later. 'He was in a mood. He really did like your work; he could talk of nothing else one night. You ought to have liked his poem; that was the misfortune.'

'I'm *very* sorry I was so rude to him,' said Mary, flushing almost to tears. 'It was shyness. You have no idea how terrified I felt of you all.'

'Oh,' said Miss Kenrick. 'On the contrary, it was so jolly getting a fresh point of view. Let's have some more coffee before we go to bed; there's nothing like coffee for making one sleep. Tell me what you think of all the people.'

'I couldn't possibly say.'

'Oh, do. Say quite frankly. I want to know what strikes you.'

'I don't understand any of them. Who was the beautiful fair girl?'

'Oh, Salome Barnett. She's religious, and she writes. She wanted to take vows somewhere, and she wouldn't cross herself, and they sent her away in a week. She isn't quite normal. What did you think of Priscilla?'

Mary hesitated. 'I expect you'll be rather hostile,' said Brynhilda.

'I think she's abhorrent,' said Mary.

'What a jolly word! She's rather a wonderful person, but she *is* a little abhorrent. She has a sort of perverted mind which makes her interesting. She likes to hand picture postcards round – you know the sort suburban people look at in twos, and are awfully shocked. I wonder if she'll have an understanding with Tommy. I thought she looked rather like it tonight, but you can't really tell. Aunt Ellen was horror-struck at her views, but I never feel they're my affair. Who is it says "Moral indignation is the only sin"? That's rather profound.'

'Do you think nothing matters, then – that nothing is right and wrong?'

'I think things matter extraordinarily, but as to right and wrong that the Victorians were so portentous and glib about, I don't know. I mean laughter and lightness and good-humour carry you through most things. Life is meant for experience; that's the thing that counts.'

'I can't agree with you,' said Mary, shutting her lips like her father.

'No, you would feel like Dermott. He specializes in disapproving; that's the Roman Catholicism. I quite see his point of view, but isn't it intellectually lazy? I wish you could see Dermott again. Stay another night.'

But Mary had determined not to meet Dermott again.

Brynhilda's talk bewildered Mary, repelled and fascinated. Some was incomprehensible. Brynhilda was versed in the arts of intimacy; she had a charming suggestion of flattery in her 'Of course you would think that.' Mary confided more of her life and her ideas than she knew. Friendship seemed easy; at Dedmayne even acquaintanceship was often leaden-footed. Canon Jocelyn chilled the beginnings with criticism. The society of Mrs Plumtree, with whom she was to spend her second night, loomed dully before Mary in comparison. She broke her promise of arriving for an early tea, and went with Brynhilda to a matinée.

Brynhilda on her side was attracted by Mary.

'You must come again,' she said when they parted. 'And I want to see your Rectory. I shall bring Salome one day – or are you too far off for a Sunday tramp? – then we could all come, get to you for lunch, and put in a Eucharist or something; it would be jolly to see it. I don't know anything about church and clergymen. They always seemed to me not real – just cardboard. It was stupid.'

'She's rather wild and crushed, and a perfect lady. Such an odd type – but nice, don't you think so?' said Brynhilda to Dermott.

'First I thought her dull and then I thought her a kind of governess; she talked my head off. Sorry, but I can't go into any raptures.'

It was late in the afternoon when Mary made her way to Mrs Plumtree. Rain had been falling; the pavements were reflecting the electric lights in long streams. There is a particular charm in those damp London twilights, a freedom from the weight of routine, responsibility, and duty, which suited well with Mary's present thoughts. She felt the fascination of Brynhilda's life. For the first time in her life she was envious.

Mrs Plumtree's face was glued to the window. She lived in a villa at Shepherd's Bush. She was one of the many Canon Jocelyn had secretly helped with money and advice. He was an oracle to her. To entertain his daughter was her best return, her greatest treat. This had only been possible at the rarest intervals.

'Oh, Mary,' she said tearfully, 'I thought there must have been a dreadful accident, and Gladys had made you one of her seed-cakes – but never mind. She *was* so disappointed; however –'

It was with difficulty Mary persuaded Mrs. Plumtree to have the cake for supper. She heard it described many times before she ate it, and the lemon sole also.

Mrs. Plumtree was a faded specimen of the generation that is almost gone. Mary knew through and through all the views Mrs Plumtree held on the minute range of subjects which interested her – servants, medicines, aspidistras, knitting patterns, sermons, and the wide range of subjects which shocked her and roused disapproval – dogs, barrel-organs, all hymn tunes earlier than 1860, all branches of Christendom (except St James' Church), especially Unitarians, white and magenta flowers, people wearing black (unless they were in mourning), the present fashions in dress, whatever it was – one might almost say the present fashion in anything. Mary could have screamed. She was not far from echoing 'Moral indignation is the only sin.' They sat and sat.

'I am staying up an hour later, Mary dear; it is *such* a treat to have you here.'

Twenty-four hours ago Mary had been shocked and miserable at the flat. Did she cherish a mad notion that it was better to be shocked and miserable in heaven than dull in hell? If so, going home in the train she returned to herself. She knew she excelled in one branch of knowledge – old ladies. She thought of the matinée. She had deliberately given Mrs Plumtree three hours of avoidable torment. For what? Nothing. For the future she would stay at home, and no one should see her writings again. She despised herself for ever showing them. She was, as Ella Redland called it in C.O.S. days, now long forgotten, 'unhelpable.' It was better to know; it would stop her restlessness. She wept. Not without a pang could she recall that she was despised by Dermott and the other intellectual young people, shocking though they might be.

Cook told her that evening Canon Jocelyn had been to Lanchester the day before.

'Prince knows the turn quite well there now,' said Mary. 'We go so often.'

'Ah, my dear, you'll be going to the Vicarage once too often,' said Cook. 'And we shan't get you back again.'

Mary did not understand, but laughed. In village life she often had to laugh at jokes without a point. Thinking it over, she realized the point. She knew it was impossible, nevertheless she did not care now who despised her.

Canon Jocelyn had missed Mary when she was away. Now she had broken loose and shown she could leave him, he respected her more. They had an almost flowing conversation on architecture at dinner.

The next day was Sunday, the busy Sunday of the clergyman's household, her favourite day in the week. It began with the early service, held but once a month, for Canon Jocelyn looked askance at early celebrations as a fruit of the Oxford movement. The early service was a delight to Mary. She loved the walk thither in the dark winter mornings, seeing the gravestones stand out in the fog. She would have liked to have fasted before partaking. But this Canon Jocelyn would have considered affectation and self-willed childishness, so Mary, in a spirit of abstinence, finished the tea and bounteous bread-and-butter provided by Cook with affectionate zeal. Mary thought fasting would have given her yet more share in the silence of Nature and of the dead, and in the stillness of the Church with its wondrous smell of old wood, old leather, and old sweet confined air, which recalled the generations who had worshipped there, their bodies now peaceful dust. At that time what was impossible in ordinary life became easy – to feel in communion, not merely with her mother and sister and the dead who had been known to her, but with the excellent Dedmayne fathers and mothers and grandfathers and grandmothers, of whom the old people had so often spoken, gone from the earth over a hundred years ago. Her contact with Brynhilda's set made the morning walk more precious.

There was a low arch and some tracery left, a relic of the old church, and one of the odd allegorical figures that the medieval masons amused themselves with sticking about their sacred places. Cromwell's generals must have forgotten to smash him. He had been Mary's playfellow in childhood during her father's long morning sermons, and he was her friend still. After Kensington and the flat she greeted him and his seven hundred years with particular affection.

Canon Jocelyn had an old-fashioned feeling of Sunday as a day apart. It was a busy day for Mary, with morning Sunday school, evening service, and a walk with Miss Gage.

'Miss Jocelyn, dear,' said Miss Gage. Mary did not like being called 'dear' by Miss Gage, but never summoned up pluck to check it; occasionally Miss Gage called her 'treasure.' 'You're looking a lot better now after your trip to town, but you were ever so white and drawn before you went away.'

Mary had her father's dislike to observations on health, particularly when they were a mark of affection. She knew she had never looked drawn, but Miss Gage must imagine it was her two nights' absence which wrought the change. Of course it was Cook's words about Mr Herbert.

On Sunday evening Canon Jocelyn read aloud Cowper, Vaughan, or George Herbert. The sleepy cadence of his voice, though he always declared he was not sleepy, mixed with Mary's dreaming thoughts. Then she woke up to play till bedtime from Handel, Haydn, and Mozart. Her father only liked slow and soft passages. He was not musical, but he loved certain things, going back as usual seventy years, because his mother had played them. He hummed the melodies incorrectly but sweetly to himself in a voice still true, though age had taken most of its sound away.

Mary thought to herself that Mrs Plumtree's mind resembled her villa drawing-room with its blinds half-down; Brynhilda's and her set were like the crude brightness of the flat; Canon Jocelyn's she compared to his study, sumptuous in learning and spare in luxury.

12

Mr Herbert's acquaintance with Dedmayne Rectory prospered. He came there constantly while autumn was turning into mild green winter. He went about the garden with Canon Jocelyn and Mary, sometimes with Mary alone. He enjoyed the robins as much as Mary did, the arches made by the bare branches, the early afternoon sun shining on the cocks' scarlet combs, the odds and ends of berries and brown leaves, and other tender beauties of winter. He and his had come from the country. Lanchester had been theirs for many generations, though the family had not been able to live there. He loved it the more, because much of his life had passed in factory surroundings. He had an affection for his eastern county stronger than any artist's admiration. He shared, too, Mary's fondness for old books or old anything, as links which bound the present to a loved past.

Not merely did Mr Herbert visit Dedmayne, he persuaded Canon Jocelyn to visit Lanchester. He had some rare seventeenth-century folios he wanted to show, and, the pony being ill, he could not bring them to Dedmayne. This bait caught Canon Jocelyn. In general he disliked having meals out of his own house. When he preached or attended meetings in the neighbourhood, he had to be entertained by his brother clergy, but these receivings of hospitality he considered a burden almost too heavy to be borne. He consented to come for an old-fashioned 'happy day,' with lunch, a leisurely afternoon, and tea to follow.

It actually was a happy day. Canon Jocelyn and Mr Herbert roamed about the Rectory study, each picking out books, taking them to one another to show and discuss. They stood with one leg on a chair, balancing the larger volumes against the back; uncomfortable arrangements, but agreeable to them. Sometimes Mr Herbert tried to make Mary talk, but she was just as pleased to listen. It was an indulgence she could not often give herself; she missed it as a departed pleasure. At her present age it distressed people if she appeared to be left out, so she found some one even shyer than herself who must be talked to.

At one moment Mary feared for the peace of the afternoon. Canon Jocelyn had been reading some stanzas of 'The Lotus Eaters' with exquisite intonation. Then he said, 'I cannot tolerate these young coxcombs who won't read Tennyson – that is to say, the early Tennyson. Like many poets, he wrote too much in later life. They spend all their time over the new-fangled poets. It is lamentable.'

'I don't think I agree, sir,' said Mr Herbert. 'It's hard on a writer if his contemporaries won't back him up. A man shouldn't stand aside from his generation. I did when I was an under-graduate, and I now think I was rather a prig.'

'Unfortunately for you there were only ephemeral names in your time, no one like Tennyson.'

'Yes, you have the affection, not exactly of a contemporary, but you were much nearer him than we are. If the generation of Tennyson's youth had carried out your principles, they would not have looked at any one more recent than Wordsworth. The lamp of literature must be handed on.'

'Possibly,' said Canon Jocelyn, 'but there may be a false light. Now Tennyson was a true light, a poet worthy of the name.'

'Possibly' was a great concession on Canon Jocelyn's part. He did not like to be disagreed with.

The discussion drifted amicably into a comparison of centuries – what sort of literature each century appreciated. Canon Jocelyn spoke of them as favourite friends or enemies – the eighteenth century, for instance, was an enemy – seeming more intimate with them, as indeed he was, than with his own.

He had been head and shoulders above the neighbourhood not only in learning, but in grasp and judgement. In old age this superiority was slipping from him. He felt it; he showed his feeling in snubs. It would have grieved Mary if Mr Herbert had been made aware of this weakness. People now found it safer to agree with Canon Jocelyn. They wrapped him in cotton-wool. Mary blushed when they agreed; then she did it herself. It pained him particularly if she differed. Being her father and a man, he felt he must know better, whatever her age. He had, as it were, knelt at the feet of his wise, unintellectual wife; he had a poor opinion of

71

other women's minds. It may have been because his bodily faculties were so powerful that Canon Jocelyn could not resign himself to old age, and so had not attained to the sweetening wisdom, the spirit above small matters, which may be old age's compensation.

Canon Jocelyn and Mr Herbert's talk turned to the Greek Testament. They had discussed a passage in Galatians, when Canon Jocelyn said, 'I have often thought of those words of St Paul, "I know when to abound and when not to abound." His powers were abridged; he was restricted, and he was not only contented, but joyful. The dimming of faculties is bound to come with advancing years, and one allows oneself to grow soured and melancholy.'

'But have not winter and the close of day their special compensating beauties?' said Mr Herbert.

'Yes, for those who have had the strength to learn the last and hardest lesson of life – to be content to be a cumberer of the ground. If not, the winter of old age is ugly.'

Canon Jocelyn turned to his book, as if not desiring an answer. Mary began, 'Oh, father –' but felt he would rather she said nothing. They sat in silence, then Mr Herbert asked him about a grammatical point in another epistle. They discussed it, leaving Mary time to indulge herself in jealousy. She had had the hope that she was making her father's period of age not unhappy. She had cheerfully sacrificed something for the hope, apparently in vain. It was in Mr Herbert, the comparative stranger, he confided, not in her. Her unhappiness was at its height when Mr Herbert proposed they should go into the garden.

She tried to think of some fresh topic – Mr Herbert and she usually had many – when he began, 'Your father was speaking sadly of the uselessness of age. I shrank from intruding my views upon him, but I think the world cannot get on without the special qualities which belong to old age. I cannot tell you what a privilege I have found my intercourse with your father.'

'Yes, perhaps for you it is,' she said, 'because he can talk to you.' Before she could stop herself she broke out, 'But I am nothing to him, simply nothing.'

She could not say more; she was in tears. She remembered in

72

childhood paroxysms because some one had been praised when she had not, or because she thought she had been unjustly treated. She had hoped her tears were things of the past.

'Miss Jocelyn – don't – I –' began Mr Herbert in perturbation. 'Let us sit down, if this will be not too damp for you.'

They sat. She tried to compose herself, but, having once given way, it was not easy to be calm in a moment.

'I believe I can explain what – er – what you speak of in your father,' he said stammeringly. 'It is not want of love, if you will let me say what I, an outsider, can judge of better than you. I see your father's reliance and dependence on you at every turn. But in that matter of speaking it is just those dearest to us it is most hard to open out to, because they are dearest; I mean if, as I am, people are cursed with a reserved temperament. I love my mother and my mother loves me, but I could no more speak to her as I am doing to you now than fly over the moon.'

He kept his head turned away. She looked at him, feeling too agitated to notice where she was looking; she saw him shake it energetically to emphasize his earnestness.

She whispered, 'Thank you, thank you very much.'

Each felt drawn to the other. It struck him how beautifully her eyes shone when the tears were in them. She seemed easy to talk to. As a clergyman he had sometimes been called on to console women, but he had never considered himself an adept with them; he had not liked them, shrinking in repulsion from the too patent fact how much some liked him.

He wished to go on comforting Mary; he wished still more to talk about himself; he was not in the habit of doing so. He felt an unusual zest in depreciating himself. At that moment a seed was sown from which a plant of love was to spring.

'I think,' he said, 'reserve is partly one's own fault. I would not venture to judge your father, but I feel it was so in my own case. I believe I first got the idea at Rugby. But when I was a young man I imagined reserve was a symptom of strength and manliness, whereas, on the contrary, it is a weakness, which has cut me off from the best things in life. By the time I had realized that, I could not get free.'

Mary had now recovered herself, and speaking steadily, she

said, 'I don't know what came over me just now. Father is so far above me in mind, I can't be much of a companion for him. If I could have been, he would not have become so shut up in himself. Now you are come he will be less lonely. I haven't seen him so happy for years as he has been with you.'

She could say this sincerely; her fit of jealousy was past. She knew her nature was grasping, the quality she thought most repulsive.

'I should think your father is far above most of us,' said he. 'I wonder why it is this generation has stopped producing people of any pre-eminence.'

'I *do* like to hear you speak about Father. He rather bewilders the clergy round about when he will talk to them, which is not very often. He dislikes the ones who want to be very High Church; and he is not interested in guilds and clubs. I can't think what he would do if he were set down at a boys' club.'

'Yes, playing soccer with the lads is since his day.'

'Of course the people call all the clergy and the doctors "old" So-and-so when they talk among themselves, but Father is always the Canon; one of the women told me. She said, "He treats us all like queens." I never can imagine what he with his reserve says when he goes to the dying or mourners, but people often say, "I shall never forget what the Canon was to me." '

'I admired your father very much as an undergraduate, rather against my intentions, for my father had spoken so often of him, and it is in the nature of offspring always to dislike what their parents like; but I had to own my father had shown good taste.'

'Oh, but your father,' said Mary, not quite understanding the slight causticness of his humour; 'he came to stay with us three or four times. I remember him playing bear with us, as if he loved it as much as we did. When I was a little girl Father was writing his commentary, and if we had games he came out of the library and told us not to make a noise. When I was thirteen, and had a passion for Scott, your father talked about him to me as if I were an equal. I remember him saying, "Don't bother about the heroines they're all stage pokers. Go for the kings and queens; that's where Scott's first-rate. Royalty was his natural element." I

74

remember his exact words, because I was so gratified and so shocked about the heroines.'

'Yes, he loved children, and every one else, I think. I would give anything to be more like him. I wish you would make me.'

He did not say this in what might be called 'a particular manner'; perhaps he himself could not have said exactly what he meant by it. At that moment he had a curious exalted feeling that he could say anything to her.

She was so taken aback she could only stammer, 'I, oh, I could never do anything,' and the servant summoning Mr Herbert just then on parish business, the conversation was broken off. At tea it was Virgil the whole time until they left.

After this intimacy both had a cold fit, but they soon were as warm as before. Mr Herbert showed Mary some scholarly translation he had made from Greek lyrics. The happy conversations these translations evoked tempted Mary to show her writings too. But the Dermott episode had made her go into her shell. She would not try again, and she had a hypersensitive fancy that she did not want Mr Herbert to like her for her writings, but for her own everyday self.

She supposed her winter was passing as ordinary winters passed, but she was changing. She began to have longings she never had before. Her mind frequently recurred to the question which occupied Shakespeare's heroines, 'What is love?'

One winter day when Dora Redland had come to stay with Ella, she and Mary met for a walk. Mary suddenly started the subject. 'I wish you would tell me something about love. I should think no one ever reached my age and knew so little, except of love in books. Father has never mentioned love, and Aunt Lottie treated it as if it ought not to exist. There were you and Will, but I was so young for my age I never took it in.'

'What a funny thing to ask!' said Dora. 'I don't think I know much about it either. There was one of the curates at Southsea – I never imagined he cared at all for me; I had hardly ever spoken to him. I think some one else had refused him. That makes them susceptible, I believe, and also the time of year and wanting to marry.' There was a mild severity, perhaps cynicism, in this speech, which astonished Mary.

'But, Dora, don't you think there is a Love

"Which alters not with Time's brief hours and days,
But bears it out even to the edge of Doom"?'

'Take care, Mary dear, you stepped right into that puddle. Wait a minute. Let me wipe your coat. I am not quite sure that I understand what you were saying.'

'Don't you think there is a firm, lasting love?'

'Dear Father and Mother's was, I feel sure, but people are so different nowadays. Now, Gertrude – you remember how lovely she was? – she had numbers of offers, and she married a man who seemed devoted to her, but – I don't mind telling you, you will never see him – it hasn't lasted. Hardly any of my friends have married, but one, a dear little thing, her husband went away with some one else; it was dreadful. And people are so lax about it nowadays. It's bad enough when a man does it, but when it's a *woman* – I cannot think how there are such women. Not that I come across it, I'm thankful to say.'

Mary's mind saw Brynhilda's flat and Priscilla Leach blinking and talking of 'adventures.' It was strange to think Dora and she belonged to the same nation.

'So you see, Mary,' went on Dora, 'I don't seem to have come across very happy marriages, but I oughtn't really to talk about it. I was never attractive to men.'

This admission might have come reluctantly from many women. Dora spoke of it with the same indifferent cheerfulness as she did of her beauty.

'Oh, but you had Will,' said Mary. 'No one has ever been near falling in love with me. I think it must be that I am meant to do without it. I can. There may be a woman who can't, and she has what I might have had.'

'Perhaps that is it. It's a nice thought,' said Dora. 'I think the best women don't marry. Men are so strange about what sort of women they like.'

'To love and be loved,' said Mary musingly. 'Did you feel it like a key, Dora, to let you out of prison, and open a treasure-house to you?'

'Is that a pretty bit out of your writings?' said Dora with a kindness that would have checked the flow, but Mary was not listening. 'I have *longed* for it,' she went on.

She spoke with an intensity that startled Dora. She turned round; she looked at Dora. Neither Mary not Canon Jocelyn often troubled to open their eyes wide. Once Dora as a child had seen his open, when they were blazing with anger. Now Mary's eyes burnt too, with a fire which made Dora uncomfortable. She turned away, and wondered when they would get back again to the dear, quiet Mary she knew.

'I have sometimes thought – ' Mary said with feeling, 'the kisses –'

They were alone, and it was nearly dark. Dora was middle-aged, if not Mary, but she blushed. Then she remembered something, and smiled. She too had had her fire, a little domestic fire that warmed the small chamber of her heart. 'One day Will kissed me. He oughtn't to have done it, still –' She gave a little laugh, which made her look ten years younger. 'But it's all over and gone out of one's life, and the working time comes, and I am not sure that I want it back. What was that striking? I must be getting back; I had no idea it was so late. I promised Ella to address some envelopes before post-time.'

13

SOME weeks after this conversation Mary and Mr Herbert were again walking about the garden at Lanchester. This had become a familiar occupation. The clerical gardens of Dedmayne and Lanchester had not been so walked in for many a year.

The equinoctial wind rushed through the branches of the old elms and roared like the sea. It gave a colour to Mary's cheeks; her eyes dilated and brightened; the spirit which sometimes showed itself in her writings looked forth. Mr Herbert saw her eyes. If Mary had only been meek and sweet, he would have liked and respected her, nothing more. Now in a moment he knew she was the dearest object of his heart.

He suddenly broke the thread of the conversation and did not answer her question. She thought he must be getting tired of her. People sometimes seem to think this at the moment they are being fallen in love with. She proposed they should rejoin her father. He implored her to stay in the garden. His 'you must' was not to be resisted. She stayed.

'That is to say, if you are sure this wind isn't too much for you,' said Mr Herbert.

'No indeed. I love it better than anything in nature, except black clouds.'

'That's a harsh, not to say morbid taste, isn't it?'

'There is something beyond ourselves in the wind and clouds. I never feel heaven can be at all like July.'

' "Thy gardens and thy gallant walks continually are green," ' he quoted. 'That authority seems to think, on the contrary, that heaven will always be July.'

'I should miss autumn and winter trees, shouldn't you?'

'I should very much. At the same time, I want to be rid of the east winds in heaven. Perhaps there may be a special corner for you, however, with hurricanes, hail, lightning, thunder, and waterspouts. I hope there will often be a lull that I may come and visit you.' As he said these words he became shy. She did not notice it, and laughed. He recovered himself and went on. 'You and the psalms rather agree in your favourite natural phenomena. I expect you include snow and ice, lions and high mountains dragons and all deeps.'

'If dragons mean snakes, I hate them, and they give me a sort of nightmare feeling that all good is an illusion and evil the only reality.'

'Oh, I don't agree with you at all. I like the old python at the Zoo. He's a friend of mine, and I never bothered about good being an illusion. Why should it be an illusion more than evil?'

'You have stronger faith than I. I envy you.'

'No,' said Mr Herbert. 'I carry the burden of our generation. We have lost the abounding, buoyant faith my father had. I had it too when I was ordained. I thought it would last for ever, but that was not to be.'

'It was a great strength,' said Mary. 'Things must be so easy when one has it.'

'Looking back on my own life, perhaps too easy,' said Mr Herbert. 'I don't know. And abounding faith is very exasperating. "Unclouded by enthusiasm," as Gibbon says. You should have heard Miss Redland and the Archdeacon clouded by enthusiasm last Tuesday.'

He pursed up his lips quizzically.

'You don't mean that, Mr Herbert,' said she, smiling. She went on with a sigh. 'I wish I had some of their enthusiasm. They do something, they care for something. "So thou, because thou art lukewarm, I will spue thee out of my mouth." I often feel that should be said about me.'

'*You*, Miss Jocelyn. I cannot tell you,' he said, stammering with earnestness – 'I wish I could tell you how I admire all you do, all you –'

'No, no,' she said, cutting him short vehemently. 'I do nothing.'

'Actual doing is of little importance.'

'No, I know what one does cannot be taken into account, so much of it is mistaken, but if one is stagnant –'

'Then let's have enthusiasm with all its horrors,' said he.

They both laughed.

'But don't imagine,' he added seriously, 'that I don't know the danger of middle-aged doubting paralysis and want of faith. I dread it above all things. I have never told any one – I should only tell you – but at one time the dread was so great,' his voice shook, 'I felt I should give up my orders. But faith returns, and now in times of dryness I see one must be content to trudge along in the dark, and occasionally a chink of light comes through.'

He smiled.

'Yes, it does,' she said. Tears came into her eyes, and she felt tears were near his also.

They were silent; soon they were again opening their hearts to one another. They told thoughts, hopes, speculations they had never spoken of. More than once each cried joyfully, 'I knew you were going to say that.' Neither ever forgot that talk. Mary thought, above all, of those wonderful words, 'I have never told

79

any one. I should only tell you.' Only once in their lives were they ever to feel so near again.

Both had hitherto put the thought of marriage away. Mr Herbert's father had lost money. Until quite recently, when a considerable fortune had been left him by a cousin, he had had only enough to support his mother. He had not even allowed himself friendship with women; he would not risk falling in love. Now he might taste its joys.

His love was already kindling a spark in Mary. Before she knew it, she was caught as thoroughly as he. He was not a coxcomb, sure that he must be acceptable, but he had a feeling that they understood one another and were meant for one another. He was not in the desperate hurry of a youthful lover. He was vain or middle-aged enough to go and take a cure for rheumatism before he came to the point; he did not choose to propose as an invalid.

His mother suspected that he was in love with Mary. She had suspected it some time before there was anything to suspect. In September she and her sister-in-law had paid him their annual visit. He had escorted them to Dedmayne for lunch and tea. It had always been right that the sister-in-law, as younger, stronger, unmarried, less accomplished in Italian and music, above all, as a Herbert not a Lessingham, should remain in the background, and the rule was not relaxed at Dedmayne. The fact that Mrs Herbert had lost her husband after a blissful marriage of twenty-five years gave her, according to Victorian ideas, a claim to unremitting attention from Miss Herbert. She, with no twenty-five years of bliss, had to our eyes, if any one was to be petted, a stronger claim. The two ladies were very happy together. Isabel carried the wraps, and was contradicted whenever Mrs Herbert wanted to contradict.

That Dedmayne day was long. Mary, enduring it, could hardly be amused to see the agonies of formality Canon Jocelyn and Mrs Herbert, both sincerely attached, were inflicting upon one another. Honoured by the presence of lady guests, Canon Jocelyn could not enjoy himself with serious literary discussion. The conversation wandered round the chilliness of the evenings, the damage done by storms, the dreadful news of floods in China, back to the chilly evenings without finding a resting-place. Mrs Herbert was an especially formidable old lady, and Mary was shy. She showed it in fussiness about the shawls and footstools. Mr Herbert was shy also; he became stiff and dumb. A ramble round the garden was proposed. Mary, from nervousness, ran to fetch Mrs Herbert's pretty bonnet; she fell down and cut her shin. She felt she was keeping every one waiting, and she took out her garden hat for rainy weather by mistake. Mrs Herbert's acute old eye noticed the hat at once.

In the garden the two gentlemen escorted Mrs Herbert. Mary had a friendly talk with Isabel, who had no dignity or pretensions to intellect. At the early tea Mrs Herbert could not bring herself to eat the smallest morsel of bread-and-butter 'so soon after my luncheon.' Mary was grateful to the 'chilly evenings' for taking them away at four, while a bright sun was still high in the heavens.

Mrs Herbert, with the awkward reserve of the old ladies of her day, stumbled into a question about Mary to her son. She longed for his marriage. But she hoped for a daughter-in-law like her two nieces, elegant and rather High Church, one writing books about saints, the other illustrating them. She knew Mary was sweet and good, but, content to endure personal shabbiness, she wanted something beautiful and more of the world for him. Though Mary saw eye to eye with her on all important points, Mrs Herbert was tempted to be exigeante and condescending with her.

When Mr Herbert owned his desire, Mrs Herbert remarked – she was lacking in worldly wisdom – what *plain* children good-looking parents often had, in a naïve hope that this would be a deterrent.

'That is true, mother,' said he perversely, 'but I must cling to the hope that Miss Jocelyn may overlook that and take me as I am.'

As regarded Mary, he was armed against every attack. He felt, with a lover's vehemence, that he preferred plain people, that she was beautiful, and that he did not care a jot whether she was plain or beautiful.

Mr Herbert came to say goodbye before he went to Buxton. He was without experience in such affairs. He had decided it was due to Mary to say no words of love till he proposed. 'You do not know what this six months has been,' said he, 'getting to know your father and –' Here he stopped, but something in his manner and his eye told a tale even to Mary which confirmed Cook's prediction

With the possibility that he was in love with her came the certainty she was in love with him. She did not dwell much on marriage, certainly not in that practical part of marriage, going to Lanchester. Curiously enough the question of leaving her father did not much perplex her. A romantic sentiment that if Mr Herbert wanted her she must follow him wherever he went was about as far as she got in plans.

After long hesitation she wrote and asked Dora her opinion. She felt it a kind of betrayal of Mr Herbert, but if Dora had been a sister, she would have confided in her. The first part of the letter sailed easily along, a continuance of the topics and small jokes they had enjoyed together. 'You thought Miss Gage would be the next to fall out with Nurse, and so she is. Nurse said to her, "Now then, Girlie, I shall smack you if you don't take care!" "But some people like that," I said. "Oh yes, the *workin'* class," said Miss Gage, "but not some one like what I am!" Isn't it unfortunate? Nurse says she thinks a bright manner in nursing is half the battle.

'Don't say I never go to the Merytons, for I did go, and Claudia and I talked about owls. She likes them as much as I do. She said, "You're the one person I've met who knows how owls do their courting; we *must* go and owl together," I saw her last week at the Archdeacon's and she wouldn't look at me, she was so busy with Lady Violet Ware.'

Now came the difficult part of the letter – Mr Herbert. After many tearings up and beginnings again, Mary confided to Dora her reasons for hope. She told Mr Herbert's 'I wish you would make me,' and then scratched it out.

If Dora felt surprised, in the smallest degree unfavourably surprised, her answer did not show it.

Dearest Mary – I think from all you say it certainly *does* sound as if Mr Herbert means something serious. I am *very* glad. I think he is such a nice man, and you will have all your taste for books in common. It is most fortunate that Lanchester is so near; it will hardly be leaving your father. It makes all the difference in a parish to have a good clergyman's wife; it is as important as what the clergyman himself is, sometimes, I think, almost *more* important. We have all been *very* busy with a baby show! Fancy me with two darling twins, one on each arm; such nice fat things. The mother is a dear little woman. The weighing was most exciting, and the mothers were all as keen as mustard. I must stop now. We all send kindest remembrances to your father. Mother says I am *particularly* to remember hers. – Your loving

DORA REDLAND.

P.S. – I shall not say again that the best women don't marry!

This letter encouraged Mary's hopes. Was she wise?

Canon Jocelyn was away for the night preaching when the letter came. Mary had the whole day alone to rejoice in. She called at a distant farm. She was past walking; she danced through the fields. There were some children there, idealized by her. She loved children passionately, she had sometimes thought it was better not to be with them too much; they roused a longing which turned her against ordinary life. She did not shrink from them today.

When she got back she lit a lamp and went into the disused nursery. The Rectory was too large for them now; they shut some of the rooms up. She opened the dolls' house and took out her favourite dolls. Thought moves so fast, she had pictures crowding before her of her babies, and boys and girls, and their different likenesses to him. She peopled the empty room. 'Miss Mary,' said Cook crossly, after knocking at the door unnoticed, 'didn't you hear the dinner-bell? Emma went to look for you down the road, we got so anxious, and then I saw the light under the door.'

It was half-past seven, and she had imagined it was five o'clock.

She was restless during dinner, wandering about under the plea to herself that she was looking for a book to read. After dinner she dashed off three sheets of exuberance to Dora. Of ecstatic personal happiness she had hitherto had none; it went to her head.

She came to her ordinary senses next morning. She could not remember last night's letter clearly, but there was a sentence, 'When he opens his eyes wide they transport me.' She went to the post-office and asked for the letter back. In vain it was explained it was against the regulations.

'I *must* have it,' said she. When Miss Jocelyn spoke in that tone it was difficult to resist her. She knew the village would not rest till they had probed the mystery; today that was a trifle. She was too late; the letter reached Dora. It was incomprehensible to her that Mary could have written it. The second following it immediately did not entirely obliterate the impression.

'Will you burn that letter? I have not had a mood like that since I was sixteen. I have a very unbalanced side, I am thankful to Father for checking it. I have been reading Bacon's *Essays* this morning. I think he and his contemporaries took a very hard view of human nature,' etc. The rest of the letter was all Bacon.

Mr Herbert wrote almost as soon as he reached Buxton, a friend's letter, with no word of anything else, but it satisfied Mary perfectly. She answered it at once; then there was an interval. When she got the awaited letter she was disappointed. It was enclosed in a bulky, promising envelope. But it was short, almost entirely about the photographs of surrounding scenery accompanying it, and, yes – it was dull. This time she did not answer it at once. Then there was a still longer interval.

One morning when they were at breakfast the third letter came. It filled only half a sheet. She read the opening sentence. 'We have known one another only a few months, yet I feel you are an old and dear friend.' She glanced at another sentence lower down in a kind of fever. 'You will laugh at me when I tell you the first moment I set eyes on you –' She could not read further for a moment. Rapture, certainty, uncertainty, a little fear, and particularly that it was too much and she could not bear it all struggled within her. She read some other letters – Aunt Lottie's meanderings. She could come, couldn't come, 'but it is all as you and your father think best.' She went back to Mr Herbert, and she saw a half-sentence, 'Kathy, as they all call her,' and then somewhere else 'she' and 'her.' She looked more closely, and read some lines without their meaning anything. The idea that her brain was going made her turn cold. She drank some coffee; she could do that at any rate, and understand what she was doing. She took the letter again; she found she could understand it now, and read it all through.

My Dear Miss Jocelyn – We have known one another only a few months, but I feel you are an old and dear friend, to whom I must confide my wonderful happiness. I am engaged to be married to Miss Kathleen Hollings – Kathy, as they all call her. You remember we both met her at the Merytons. I only got to know her six weeks ago, and you will laugh at me when I tell you that the first moment I set eyes on her I had decided what I wanted (it was 'her,' not 'you'; Mary had mistaken the pronouns), and have been simply pumping up my courage to tell her ever since. The necessary pitch was attained yesterday. I am returning to Lanchester on Wednesday, and shall hope to call on you and your father as soon as I get back. – Yours most sincerely,

R. HERBERT.

'Father,' said Mary, 'here is a very interesting letter you must see.'

He read it twice, being slower than she was in taking in a new fact. He handed it back, and said, 'I am sorry he is marrying a girl of twenty-two. It is a mistake; the distance is too great.'

'Do you think so?' said Mary. 'It sounds blissful.'

She hoped her voice sounded interested to the exact pitch of cordial friendship. After breakfast, besides Cook, there were several village people coming to see her for help, advice, chit-chat, and, with some children whose mother was ill, games and fun. These duties were a support. It was the leisure of afternoon she dreaded. She determined to tell Cook in the middle of the orders. The news came in well, following naturally on Cook's announcement of a niece's engagement.

Cook answered suitably. 'Well there, that's what he was after all the time.' Mary hoped to slip away from the subject, but Cook did not keep the suitability up; she suddenly burst into tears. 'Oh, my own Miss Mary,' she sobbed. 'I thought it was going to be you; we all did, every one of us.'

Mary threw her arms round her. 'Cook, darling, you mustn't,' said she. She bit her lips and tried to keep calm; she felt her own tears coming. She longed to get Cook's sympathy. It was a relief to hear it had not all been a foolish spinster's fancy. Yet she writhed at the intrusion on her confidence.

'It's an entire mistake,' she said. 'If there were nothing else you know, I couldn't leave home.' She considered truth all-important, but when it came to the point, the pride of a lady was her first consideration. She found comfort in hugging Cook's skinny shoulder, but she recovered herself quickly, and hurried on to the mothers' tea.

Her business over, she went to her own room, and when she re-read the letter her tears flowed fast. Hardly had they begun, before Emma was after her, ostensibly to ask her a question, really to sympathize. Mary dismissed her fractiously, and wished for the first and last time in her life she lived in London, where sympathy was not so omnipresent.

'Poor thing, she does take on, Cook,' cried Emma, flying to the kitchen.

Nature failed Mary at this pinch. The days just then were dashing and magnificent, large white clouds, brilliant ultramarine sky, all colours standing out vividly from sunshine and recent rain. Everything looked arrogantly happy.

Cook told inquirers that Mary had refused Mr Herbert and that he had become engaged out of pique, but the village preferred the truth.

Was it another case of 'the fraud of man was ever so'? Mary did not think so. She in her inexperience had imagined what had never been.

Alas for her, Mr Herbert had found the beautiful Miss Hollings staying at his hotel with her aunt and uncle. One beaming smile, and the mischief was done. He was frantic with devotion. The feeling for Mary seemed only to have prepared his heart. Now he could allow his natural desire to expand, he was extremely susceptible. When he thought of Mary he did not feel he was deserting her. What he had imagined for a short time to be love was on both sides nothing more than friendship. Thus Cupid deluded him. A man who knew more of women might have perceived that Mary was in love with him. He remembered he had thought there might be hope for him; he was sure he had been mistaken. He wrote without any *arrière pensée*. There was no notion of waiting now. He was in a desperate hurry, only terrified by his own audacity. If he had not been distinguished-looking and reserved, his passion might almost have been silly.

The neighbourhood had, of course, already given Mary in marriage to Mr Herbert, but in joyous excitement at an engagement it at once threw Mary over and applauded Kathy. Still, all could not forget that Mary was left in the lurch. Some showed their sympathy by special squeezes when they shook hands. Mary was glad to find she could assume unconsciousness, and start the topic of the engagement herself.

The recollection of her bubbling-over letter made her shrink from Dora. She wrote the fact with no comments. The rest of the letter was filled with ordinary news.

'Is there anything wrong, dear?' said Mrs Redland as Dora read the letter at breakfast. 'You look so flushed.'

'No,' said Dora. 'Oh no, Mother dear, only Mary Jocelyn seems rather poorly. I was wondering if I could get to Dedmayne for a night or two.'

'Does she, poor child? Yes, she was always an anaemic little thing. Ask her to come here for a little change if she would like it.'

'To think that Mr Herbert should have become engaged to that disagreeable Miss Hollings,' wrote Dora. 'I do not even think she is so very good-looking as you do. Her mouth is too large. I am afraid it is not likely to be a success. Dearest Mary, if Miss Hollings is the kind of girl he cares for, you need not regret him.'

Mary declined Dora's proposal to visit Dedmayne.

'Thank you very much for thinking of it,' she wrote, 'but the day after tomorrow is the confirmation, which always gives extra work, and as Cook has had a rheumatic turn, I want her to be doing as little as possible until she is better. She has been making fig and ginger jam from such a nice recipe Mrs Davis gave her. Cook has never tried it before. Emma is taking the letters to Bakham, so I will not say more, as I want you to get this at once.'

There was no word of Kathy or Mr Herbert.

But Mary's pride broke down; a moan followed. 'I was not ungrateful to you, no one ever had a better friend, but for the present I would rather be alone. I tried not to love him, but it overwhelmed me like a flood. I am *sure* he is right about Miss Hollings, and that she is everything he thinks her.' She would not face the possibility of Mr Herbert's being unhappy in his love.

Dora tried her best to understand Mary's feeling for Mr Herbert. In vain. She thought of her old days. Her love for Will, her strongest emotion, had been but a faint shadow of Mary's.

Life passed as usual at Dedmayne. Canon Jocelyn was writing his sermon for the Cathedral, so that he was rather particularly immersed in his own thoughts. One evening at dinner Mary sat without saying a word. Tonight she felt that if she spoke she would rail. 'And he would not care if I railed or if I were dead.'

After dinner she did not go as usual into the drawing-room. She rushed to the nursery. A large yellow moon was shining in. She could see the furniture quite well: the children's little chairs, nurse's low chair, the dolls'-house, and her dear rocking-horse – all looking like ghosts. It seemed a room of the dead. She remembered her last visit there, full of baseless hopes that the room might be itself again. Now it and all it contained were in their graves for ever. 'And Mother is dead,' she thought, 'and Ruth, and old nurse, and the children that used to play here are more dead than the real dead – the boys are quite lost to me, and Father, the father who used to carry me on his shoulder, is deadest of all, for he never, *never* shows what he used to be.' She cried out: 'I am thirty-six, and I may go on fifty years. I take after father's family; they all drag on to ninety.'

'If there were children,' she thought, 'they would make everything happy, including the grown-up people. But a house without children has nothing, and is nothing, and the grown-up people in it are dead, even if they have to wait fifty years to be buried.'

She sat on till she heard the bell ring for prayers.

But her father was not as indifferent as she thought.

After prayers, when he was bidding goodnight, he laid his hand on her shoulder and said, 'I think we are letting ourselves get too silent. I have been missing your laugh at dinner. Shall we ask Dora to come and cheer us up? No one knows better than I do that I am a dull companion for a young thing like you. She who made it bright for us all is gone.'

She kissed him, hoping that the tears which rushed to her eyes would not fall on his cheek. She could tell him nothing. She had been having toothache, she said. 'That has made me stupid. But I will ask Dora. Thank you for suggesting it.' She felt he would think her cold and ungrateful, but for once he understood her. He had observed the growing attachment of his daughter and Mr Herbert. In old age's procrastinating way – for old age often thinks there is immeasurable time for important things though hurry for trifles – he had contemplated a possible engagement at some distant date. He grieved for her, but doing as he would be done by, he let fall no word of sympathy. He had some fear of a scene. He remembered her as a schoolgirl, effusive and given to repentant outbursts. After the disastrous fashion of his generation, he would not trouble himself to see that time had passed and she had grown out of that stage years ago.

She walked to the door. Then she felt she must not miss the chance. She turned back and said, 'I don't mind loneliness, I shouldn't mind anything if I thought you cared.'

If he had repelled her she would not have been heart-broken, but she could not have helped despising him. At last he let his real feeling out. He said, stammering with the unusual effort, 'I do care – I care very much.'

She wanted no more. She said, 'Do you, Father? Thank you,' and went upstairs.

To think that her laughs were noticed. They were sometimes hard work; they had to be loud for her father to hear, and not too loud lest they should appear 'unrestrained.' She smiled that she, oppressively middle-aged as she felt herself, was a laughing young thing. He very rarely mentioned Mrs Jocelyn. Mary would have liked to hear and talk of her. He, after a bygone habit of mind, thought the dead too sacred to mention.

At that moment, in tenderness for her father, Mary could feel content that Mr. Herbert had not loved her. This feeling was intensified by a letter she had just then from Lucille, her American sister-in-law, the wife of her eldest brother Hugh. He had lately married in middle life. He had been in the United States for twenty years, and had seldom revisited Dedmayne. 'I want you to read some of Hugh's letters,' Lucille wrote, 'just to show you a little how dear and lovely he is to me.'

Mary thought that Lucille must have sent one letter by mistake when she read the following passage:

'My own best and dearest, if you knew how I am throwing myself at your feet in gratitude at your love. I have never imagined any one could love me, and *you* – I have had an utterly loveless life; partly my own fault, I know. Since my mother's death – her loss was unspeakable for all of us – we never had any tenderness at home. My aunt was a worthy woman, I suppose, and my father did his best to inculcate in us his own high principles. For this I am grateful, and I respect him, nothing more. You have literally opened paradise to me.'

It was an incredible letter from the cool, fastidious Hugh, never much excited about anything or anybody.

Mary's sympathy should have been for Hugh. She did not think of him. She flung the letter down; she cried out, 'Oh, Father, my darling father.'

She would have felt more sorry still if she had seen into Canon Jocelyn's mind.

An old clerical friend came to see Canon Jocelyn one afternoon. 'So you say all your sons are out of England, Jocelyn,' said he. 'That often has to be, but I should be very thankful that I have my two close by. They have livings a few miles off, and are constantly over. We talk over everything and help one another. When one is old it's a great thing to have sons to turn to. We lost our little daughter, but we often say how good God has been to give us such sons.'

And the mild, affectionate old man went on prattling till the visit was over.

Canon Jocelyn did not listen with much show of interest, Mary supposed because he disliked any mention of God in common talk. But it was not that. He was cut to the heart with envy. 'We talk over everything and help one another.'

'I am nothing to my sons,' he thought, 'and never have been.' He could not understand why he had failed. He had not had a natural tenderness and delight in children and boys and girls. Without it, it is difficult to become intimate all at once with grown-up sons and daughters. Yet at the birth of his eldest son he had expected much. He could remember an evening walk alone, when he had been transported from his somewhat cold self with hopes of what that son might be to him. None had been realized. His mind turned to his daughter, and he was comforted. Mary was not what a son would have been to him; in certain respects she may have been more. He would like to have shown his grateful tenderness. Shyness stopped him. If it had been Mr Herbert, he might have found words. He did not know what to say. If he had known, would he have said it? Sometimes that generation seemed to use language chiefly to hide its thoughts. He could only go to the cellar. Mary heard him fumbling and stumbling. Soon he was back again, with a bottle in his hands. She knew he disliked questions, and said nothing. It was the Madeira he kept for clergy of the right sort.

'Let me induce you, Mary,' he said at dinner, 'to try a glass of this Madeira. It's an excellent wine, and' (in the warmth of his feeling he said 'and,' not 'but') 'it is particularly well suited to ladies.'

Mary had told him she did not care for wine. He could not reconcile himself to such a gap in her taste; he felt if he ignored it it would turn to liking. It did. Seeing it pleased him, Mary drank two glasses. He thought taste in old Madeira unnecessary for many people – Mrs King, for instance.

At their backgammon he still further showed his good-will. 'Never mind about throwing, my dear,' said he. 'Suppose *you* begin tonight.'

In spite of his learning and sarcastic tongue, there was a vein of childlikeness, simplicity, almost clumsiness in Canon Jocelyn. Mary missed all he meant to convey, but the excellent wine enlivened both him and her, and she was pleased.

14

LADY MERYTON had been full of solicitude at Mr Herbert's engagement for Mary's sake. As the fairy godmother of the neighbourhood, it was her due to know all the gossip.

'It's a thousand pities; he would have suited Mary so exactly,' said she to Claudia.

'It's a thousand pities for Kathy,' said Claudia. 'And it's an absolute disaster to lose her in the hunting-field, for I presume she won't go on hunting three times a week.'

Miss Hollings herself had no misgivings.

She announced her engagement to her brother's wife, Lesbia, in the following letter:

My Dear Lesbia – Well, I'm booked, and it's a parson. Don't faint. He's got a job near Aunt Edith's. He says he saw me there last year, but he didn't, for I should have spotted him in an instant. He's awfully ugly, and he doesn't know one end of a horse from the other; and he can't shoot for nuts. He's a Blue, all right, rowing. He's appallingly brainy, but *I don't mind a bit*. I like hearing him talk. You will think me an awful ass to have taken him, but I'm not. I can't explain, you know I never can, anyhow you'd never understand; but he's different from our men. You know they're rather rotters in a way. Jim-jam says she quite understands, and thinks I'm jolly lucky, and *so I am*. You see I'm staying at Jim-jam's. KATHY.

He's miles above me. I didn't know there were any men like him.

'My dear old thing,' ran Lesbia's answer,

of course I'm overjoyed if you are. Various poor unfortunates will be left lamenting, but that doesn't matter. I didn't faint, but I couldn't help *screaming* with laughter! ! Don't be cross. I don't think much of our men, but I think I prefer them to a parson. I suppose we shall all have to be awfully virtuous and sit twiddling our thumbs, and speak when we're spoken to and not before. Quite seriously, my dear, I wonder if you are wise. I know you've been awfully restless lately and wanting to settle. It was so unlucky about the Caswell boy, but you're still quite young. I really shouldn't jump at just anything in a hurry. I feel as a good sister-in-law I ought to give you some matronly advice, but from your ecstatic letter I know it will be a pure waste of time! – Your devoted LESBIA.

Kathy turned red with annoyance as she tore the letter up. Nothing short of falling desperately in love would have made her unlock her heart to Lesbia. She never would unlock it again. Most of the congratulations she showed to Mr Herbert.

'Of course they think you're simply throwing yourself away,' said he. 'As you are.'

The answer satisfied even his lover's nervous vanity.

Mr Herbert paid his promised call on the Rectory as soon as he came back. Of course he brought a photograph of Kathy. It could not do her entire justice, but her picture without her snubs was irresistible He was ecstatically proud, ecstatically pleased. His eyes danced, so did his mind. This gave him an irritating restlessness, unlike himself.

'I want you to know Kathy so much,' he said. He pressed Mary's hand. To have the hand pressed in an overflow of enthusiasm for some one else is specially uncomplimentary. 'You must be friends. I think of you as in some sort sisters, elder and younger, for she is such a child.' His face glowed with delight.

When she could study the photograph quietly, Mary did some worshipping of her own; she would like to be not a sister, but a sort of middle-aged cousin. She and her father sent an edition of Jeremy Taylor to Mr Herbert. She made a sketch of the prettiest spot in Lanchester as a private present to Kathy. After a short engagement Mr Herbert was married and brought home his bride.

Mary was one of the first to call.

She put on Dora's hat, by this time hoary in her service, thought it too startling, and pulled it to pieces.

Mr Herbert was out. Kathy was in the garden talking to three smart people. These were her sister-in-law, Lesbia Hollings, who showed her teeth too much; a friend, Miss Bassett, plain, but very smart; and Captain Wyndham, an elegant officer.

The girls were wearing their oldest clothes, 'simply in rags.' The rags had a wonderful air, and would have cut Mary's hat, even when it came fresh from Dora's hands. Not that any of the girls gave outside appearance more than its due. Within their circle each respected some weather-beaten old lady, stumping about her garden in ploughman's boots with a hat put on anyhow, the companion of so many years that it seemed as much part of her as her chin. The faultlessly smart Lesbia had, in addition, an aunt who wore a dilapidated gold wig and crude muslins the reverse of fresh. It would never have struck Lesbia, though she laughed at her, to think her less entirely one of themselves, raised far above the charmingly dressed office girls, or the stockbrokers' wives with Paris frocks. She put them in a bunch together, unless the stockbrokers' wives had unusually rich husbands. Once one was in the circle nothing much mattered, certainly not clothes. As for Mary, she could not yet be placed. The time has gone by when the clergy, as a matter of course were accepted and pressed to the hard but faithful bosom of the county. Until Lesbia and Miss Bassett had seen Canon Jocelyn they could not tell whether he might not be 'a nice little man,' or even 'quite a nice little man.' If so, the utmost praise Mary must expect would be 'really rather a dear thing.'

But she was not a dear thing yet, only a tiresome caller whom nobody wanted. This was perhaps made clearer (not much) than Kathy intended in her cool 'Oh, how d'you do?' She did not introduce Mary to the others. She asked her if she had gone to the otter hunt on Wednesday. Mary said she had not.

'It was topping,' said Mrs Herbert in her ringing voice. She continued discussing details of the chase with Jim-jam, Miss Bassett, and Cocky, Captain Wyndham.

'Are you keen on otter hunting?' asked Lesbia.

'I think it's detestably cruel' – this was her true opinion, but she did not dare to express it.

'I don't hunt,' she answered. Unable to think of anything else to say, she added, 'Do you?'

'I should rather think so,' said Lesbia, showing her teeth still more. The conversation dropped as far as Mary was concerned, for Lesbia turned to Captain Wyndham and said, 'Do you remember that run near Lynne?'

Mary did not get a chance again for some minutes, when a puppy, just past the pretty fat stage, came straddling towards them.

'Oh, here's Bimbo,' cried Mrs Herbert, 'Come along, my infant. He's only been here four days, and he's homesick, he says. He likes you,' turning to Mary. She was grateful to Bimbo. He was a nice puppy, but she sycophantically petted him more than she wanted, as a means of finding favour. They seemed to have settled to a fairly steady conversation about the train service apropos of his arrival at Cayley, when he made a pounce on Mrs Herbert's bag, which had fallen to the ground, and began gravely tearing it up.

'Drop that, you scamp. That's your mummy's. He's a thorough sportsman. You should have seen the way he went for a mouse; didn't we, old man? though we didn't succeed in catching him.'

Rescuing the purse cut the thread. Whenever there seemed a chance of its being resumed, even in a direction in which Mary would have found it hard to follow, such as the special points the Kennel Club required in otter hounds at their shows, Bimbo did something, which either demanded correction or admiration, and all was again confusion.

'What's wrong with his paw?' inquired Jim-jam, who had hitherto said nothing. 'Come here, my friend, let's have a look at it. Kathy, look; quiet, old chap, I'm not going to hurt you; that claw's growing in. You ought to have it cut. Get me some scissors and I'll do it.'

The operation was performed with address and gentleness by Jim-jam, Cocky and Kathy assisting with professional interest.

Some desultory talk between Lesbia and Mary about the surrounding country, which Lesbia seemed determined to consider ugly – in spite of smiles Mary thought she liked to contradict – bridged the gulf till the operation was over. Then there was another active duty; Mrs Herbert, Captain Wyndham, and Miss Bassett all liked active duties better than conversation.

'Cocky, Taffy pulls so. He all but ran away with me yesterday.'

'You ought to get his mouth softer. What kind of a bit do you give him?'

'That's it. I don't think the one he's got now's much good, though Perch says it is. Perch is rather a fool.'

'Let's have a look at it, and we might see what one can do.'

'Righto. Come along, Jim-jam. You'll come, won't you?' indifferently to Mary.

They were quite happy surrounding Taffy, with whom they were at once on the same excellent terms as with Bimbo. It was considered ample entertainment for a stranger to stand and look on.

Then they came back and roamed a little in the garden. Kathy struck up, 'Keep off the grass like a good little boy.'

This was an inane and rather indecent song. During the chorus she gave a push against Cocky, and he gave a push back. They did not sing more than a verse and a half, but their resounding voices – Mary bitterly reflected restraint did not appear to be one of Mrs Herbert's qualities – must have reached not only the kitchen, but the cottages next door. Bimbo thought it a delightful song, and scampered and yapped like a mad thing. Her half-hour of call being now complete, Mary could say goodbye, and present the little sketch which she had brought with her.

'Oh, must you really? That for me? How awfully sweet of you! I must undo it on the spot. Look, Lesbia, I call that most awfully clever.'

Just then Mr Herbert came out to them. Kathy hastened towards him and pulled him forward, keeping her hand on his arm longer than was necessary.

'Crab,' she cried. 'This is Miss Bassett, *alias* Jim-jam; this is Miss – I'm so sorry, I didn't hear what Dennis said your name was.'

'Miss Jocelyn, and I don't want an introduction,' said Mr Herbert, smiling at Mary.

'Now you are *not* to spoil my A1 introduction,' interrupted Kathy. 'This is Captain Wyndham, *alias* Cocky, and this is the Right Reverend Robert William Herbert, Archbishop of Lanchester, called Crab on account of shortness in the temper.'

During this speech Mr Herbert beamed upon his wife in such delight that Mary described it afterwards to herself as maudlin. He and Kathy showed plainly that they were in that stage of love when nobody else counted.

'You two are cousins,' said Mr Herbert, looking at Mary and Kathy. 'Haven't you discovered it?'

'Oh, are you Mary Jocelyn?' said Kathy. 'I've often heard the Merytons speak of you. They declared I met you there last September. Didn't you stay years and years ago at the Court? They had an awful white slug of a thing, Joe, do you remember? and you couldn't ride it for nuts.'

Mary's 'awfully clever' sketch, prettily tinted and wavering, not clever at all, was shown to Mr Herbert. The great interest seemed to be that in that scene they had had some very special interview. Mary cut his delight short and his thanks and messages to her father, and said goodbye.

'So that was the Jocelyn person Aunt Edith's always worrying about,' said Mrs Herbert, leaning against her husband. 'I thought she was a kind of church worker; she looked it.'

In his infatuation he did not resent her way of speaking.

Mary tried to be fair, but her jealousy was beyond all bounds. Possibly Mrs Herbert had been shy. Possibly she might be something more than beautiful, rough, rude, brainless, vulgar. This was Mr Herbert's serious permanent choice. She had been an amusement, a very small incident. 'But I *am* superior,' she thought.

Mrs Herbert was a little shy, and too happy to notice anything. She came also from a set that must not be bothered to care if any one outside it is happy or not.

Mary determined that she would, as a revenge, ask the Herberts to lunch, and be as polite to Mrs Herbert as she possibly could. Her father often tried to wriggle out of people to lunch. This time she forced him to yield, and to consent to the invitation of Sir Charles and Lady Meryton as well. Sir Charles was a dull, jovial, old country gentleman, whose jokes crushed Canon Jocelyn by their heaviness.

'Mary Jocelyn asks us to lunch next Tuesday, Charles,' said Lady Meryton. 'You'll come, won't you, dearest?'

'When I'm asked like that I always know I have to go,' said Sir Charles. 'But happily I really can't Tuesday. There's a special sub-committee of the County Council, and they say the Labour people are going to make themselves unpleasant, so I must be there. And I can't say I'm sorry. Old Jocelyn's such a schoolmaster I alway feel I ought to recite my Latin verbs to him. I know he has the best brains of any one about, but that doesn't make me love him more.'

'But, Charles, you like Mary.'

'I don't remember much about Mary, but if you say I like her, I'm sure I do.'

'No, Papa dear,' said Claudia, 'that doesn't in the least follow. Mamma likes everybody, and she has a devouring and particular passion for bores, of which Mary Jocelyn is one. Poor darling Mamma going to lunch at such a forsaken spot as Dedmayne. You shouldn't be such a saint, Mamma. It's very silly of you, for when you die you'll go to quite a different place from Papa and me, and you won't like that, for you can't possibly get on without us.'

When the day came Mary ransacked the house for bits of old silver, of which there were so many that they lay year after year forgotten in the pantry cupboards. She wore more of the old family rings than she approved. She was certain Cook knew what it meant from her lavishness in the menu.

Lunch passed off well. Lady Meryton, Canon Jocelyn, and Mr Herbert talked a good deal; Kathy looked beautiful; Mary saw that every one had what they wanted. She did not say much to Mr Herbert. To try to make his wife jealous by displaying their old friendship was not her idea; but she and Lady Meryton helped Kathy when she was floundering in the mire of Canon Jocelyn's civility. She was preserved from blurting out anything which would have outraged him, so that Canon Jocelyn said afterwards, 'I think Herbert has chosen an unusually charming young lady.' Mr Herbert himself was in that state of bewildered bliss that he was utterly unaware of any danger. During every possible interval he and Kathy were gazing at one another. Occasionally Kathy appealed to him. 'I'm sure *I* don't know. I daresay Crab does, because he knows everything.' Whereon Crab would break off everything instantly to come to Kathy's aid.

All Mary's preparations were thrown away on the bride. Old silver and old rings were as common as blackberries to Kathy; she would never have seen the difference between them and anything else. Art in all departments, small and great, meant nothing to her. But just now her mind was almost entirely occupied with Mr Herbert; the small residuum was reserved for enjoyment of the good things at lunch. The Jocelyns made no impression on her either way.

Lady Meryton stayed a little while after the Herberts had gone. She, with invariable kindness, complimented Mary on the lunch. 'And that lovely old muffineer. I shall certainly come and steal it some time or other. Isn't it a joy to see people so absolutely happy as those two? I wish she was just a few years older and he a few years younger, but sometimes those unequal marriages are the happiest of all. Little Kathy has been so lonely, I cannot tell you the comfort it is to have her in the keeping of a good man who loves her as Mr Herbert does, and whom she loves with her whole heart.'

When the excitement was past, Mary reflected that she had fallen into what a Russian calls the slave habit, trying to impress people by outside appearance.

Mary met the Herberts from time to time at the small entertainments with which the bride was welcomed by the neighbourhood. She did not have much talk with either of them, but Kathy gave her friendly smiles, and a smile from Kathy was so pleasant that Mary could not help reconsidering the severity of her criticisms.

15

MR HERBERT'S infatuation for his wife lasted a year. There was a reaction after the infatuation. He found much exasperating which had hitherto appeared attractive. Kathy went on being in love with him. Under her flighty exterior she was steady, constant, and affectionate.

She had lost her parents early. She and her brother – there were only the pair of them – had been brought up by relatives who had two or three houses, and left the children in the country to servants and governesses. Kathy did not get on well with governesses; they had little influence over her. She liked the nurses, grooms, and ladies'-maids, people born on the estate, their families connected with hers for several generations; she had much more in common with them than with the governess layer of society. From them she learnt to be rather rough and coarse, for she knew them well without the gracious, official manner.

He had fallen in love with her beauty in the old-fashioned way. He supposed her face was the mirror of her mind. She was undeveloped, in many ways an ordinary country and county girl, fond of sport, amusements, and men to flirt with; she also liked, in a less degree, clothes and bridge.

His appearance had not attracted her, that is to say, she did not think him handsome. His face was finely moulded, and he had expressive and beautiful eyes. The type was too ascetic for her. She admired a more ruddy, athletic sort; but she loved his smile, and would give an answering smile to herself when she thought of it.

To Mary she appeared an all-conquering beauty, but she had not had a very fortunate life. There had been long visits with relations, often with the uncongenial guardian aunt and uncle, with whom she was at Buxton when she met Mr Herbert. Her relations were more interested in themselves or some one else than in her. Her brother's house was supposed to be her home, just as she and his wife Lesbia were supposed to be allies, but Lesbia was jealous of her beauty. Various advantageous offers had been made her. The attraction of being no longer in the way had been considerable, but not sufficient to make her accept any. She had seen some unsuccessful marriages, her brother's among the number. It was before the war; there had been no idea of settled occupation for her. She was well-off; necessity did not urge exertion. She had associated with people richer than herself, who had lived in a rush of amusements; but she did not pine after their luxuries when she was without them. She was not one of those who demand everything that life can offer. She was perfectly happy leading a jog-trot existence in the country with two dogs, a horse, and her husband.

Her happiness did not last. Mr Herbert became moody, irritable and silent. Sometimes he poured out a flood of sarcasm. She neither understood the sarcasm, nor what had brought it about. Her own wit and sarcasm were just a schoolgirl's. She had no defence against him.

Her slang was a constant annoyance. One day he burst out, 'I cannot conceive where you have picked up that excruciating jargon. I don't imagine even a boy in the Lower Third of a Modern Side maltreats English quite as you do. If slang enriched the language there might be something to be said for it, but as it happens it invariably impoverishes it. Yet it always seems considered a humorous embellishment, which view you evidently share. Could you explain why?'

She got very red and answered, 'I think you're jolly rude.'

'I beg your pardon,' he said. 'I was detestably rude.'

'You were,' she replied, and walked out of the room. She could walk with the dignity of an angel, though she usually rolled about with her hands in her pockets. He was ashamed. His irritation partly came from the reaction of nervous excitement and the strangeness of living with some one after years of congenial solitude. Ever since he had been ordained he had had no one to consider but himself, only short visits from and to his mother, or two or three nights with men friends.

He had had many doubts, many fears, before he married, but merely the delightful doubts and fears of love – that he might not be worthy, that such a heavenly being could not care for him, that some younger, more attractive man would be preferred. She was not a stately goddess after all, but a child, defenceless against the hardness of life, to whom he was rough and impatient. The burden of his unkindness weighed him down. A looker-on might have made more allowance, seeing that he also was a child in experience, quite as incapable as Kathy. And that this love should all end in his irritation against her, when she had so much more right to be irritated against him! He felt the degradation for her more than she did for herself, and lay awake in remorse when she was calmly sleeping.

She had refused him when he first proposed, intoxicating him with adoration for her by her words, 'It wouldn't do. I'm not at all brainy, and you're top-hole. I can't think what on earth you want it for.' When she had accepted, she said, 'Righto, I'll take the risk if *you* will, but it's a big risk for you.' The last thing he had ever felt himself was top-hole. Before her wonderful face he had specially realized his unworthiness – greater unworthiness than he had felt with Mary.

Mr Herbert's mother came on a visit at the end of September. The visit was to be longer than usual that she might get to know the bride. Miss Herbert was left behind. They had met hitherto at interviews in which both sides were determined to be pleased. Mrs Herbert had been ill at the time of the wedding, and for the greater part of the year following.

She was not a difficult guest to entertain, having many resources.

101

Beside her good works, which could not be carried on away from home, there was refined playing (getting slow now) of classical music, intricate embroidery, and a study of books other than fiction: Ancient Babylon, the Catacombs, and English Cathedrals for Sunday; for week days, *The Flora of the Andes*, a study of Italian verse, and French memoirs of the eighteenth century, not with the spicy bits left in and the dull historical parts left out, but solid memoirs in several volumes.

Most old ladies do not like paying visits. Mrs Herbert tried not to long for home, but she missed her good works, her own chair, own habits, her sister-in-law to sit on. She had found years ago that Mr Herbert would not be sat on.

Kathy was as busy as Mrs Herbert, but on different lines. After hunting, she liked gardening, the care of poultry and all animals, dress-making, and every game. She was just as annoyed with Mrs Herbert's *parti pris* not to take bridge seriously as Mrs Herbert was with her refusal to be persuaded into refined tastes.

They were playing bridge one evening, not auction bridge – Mrs Herbert had not got so far – plain bridge. Mrs Herbert did not play very well, and was always surprised when the thirteenth trump took a trick at the last.

Now she chose clubs for trumps, having an equally good hand in hearts. When Kathy protested she answered that clubs had not been trumps all the evening; she liked to have a change.

'But, confound it all,' said Kathy, restraining her language with difficulty, 'think what the score was, and you chose clubs. But that's what happens if you don't play for money; the game goes to pot.'

'I don't care what the score is. I like a game to be a game.'

'If you don't play for the score, what's the good of playing at all?'

'I think it's a *pity* to play a game in that sort of way.'

'A pity' was a favourite expression with Mrs Herbert. 'A pity' to go out in the rain; 'a pity' to have a celebration at 7 A.M. instead of 8. It is to be translated 'unfortunate,' 'disagreeable,' 'wrong,' 'infamous.'

'Well,' said Kathy, 'I don't know what you suppose yourself to be playing. Perhaps it's spillikins. All I can say, it is not bridge.'

Mr Herbert had been called from the room by a parishioner. The timid curate from Cayley, who was making a fourth, afraid of Kathy's beauty and very much afraid of Mrs Herbert's snubs, did not know how to bring peace to the disputants.

'I think bridge is a simply capital game,' said he. This satisfied neither; each chewed the cud of real annoyance till Mr Herbert's return.

That argument about bridge meant more than met the ear. There in a nutshell lay an important difference between the nineteenth and twentieth centuries – what is passing away and what is taking its place. If Kathy had probed her, Mrs Herbert would only have repeated it was a pity. The ladies of her generation were incapable of discussion. They were as inarticulate as the uneducated, though often almost erudite. And why should they discuss, since everything they thought was right? Besides, they, never liked to expose their inner thoughts. Here Mrs Herbert's inner thought was *noblesse oblige*. It was wrong to use hours of leisure – she never questioned her right to them – on anything so frivolous as bridge. To play it scientifically would be the misuse of a talent. To that proud idea the upper middle-class owed its thousands of cultivated homes, now all crumbling away.

Mrs Herbert did not exactly mourn the loss of her son through marriage. He had given her dutiful, but not ardent affection; his passion had been for his work and for books. She had longed for him to find in marriage what she knew sadly she had not been able to supply. But that he should have chosen such a girl as Kathy! How she regretted Mary. She was not far from actively disliking Kathy; therefore she was scrupulously polite. She had to approve and love before she snubbed.

She and her husband did not come from Kathy's stock. Their forebears had been statesmen and bishops, distinguished in learning and courtliness. The contempt which the rustic, un-cultivated county had for such as the Herberts they heartily returned. Neither side realized that both alike were doomed, their one hope a combination against the 'new rich.'

Mrs Herbert used all her powers of self-command to endure silently. She only expostulated after strangled coughs at Kathy's cigarette in the drawing-room, though not merely had no one, male or female, ever smoked in her drawing-room, she did not know such a thing was a possibility.

'My cig. Oh, cheerio. Sorry.' Each word choked Mrs Herbert more than a cigarette.

There was a still wider gulf between them. Kathy was not mercenary, but she viewed with indulgence the hanging-on to rich people for what could be got out of them. Many of her friends were hard up. Money they must have for maintaining the old park and mansion – that came first with them – then for personal matters, hunters, motors, clothes, amusements. These things the vulgar could help to provide. Kathy herself never gave such people intimacy; she thought it reward enough to minister to the wants of a Hollings. But she described her friends' clever plans for captivating the vulgar; she discussed what degree of wealth cancelled what degree of lowness of origin or occupation. This indelicacy was an open sore to Mrs Herbert. Needless to say, for no material possession or pleasure would she have condescended to be indebted to any one beneath her. She would have welcomed favours only from her sovereign or her elders. There was the tale of a Jew, light-heartedly related by Kathy. 'Bernstein was a little pawnbroker beast, and he talks very hot stuff, but, after all, Valerie doesn't have a bad time, though we all said he might have cleaned his nails for the wedding. See, you know Valerie Bassett, don't you? Jim-jam told me you knew them when they were kids.'

'Valerie Bassett, that lovely girl, she *married* the man you are speaking of?'

'Yes, poor kid; what could she do? She hadn't a penny, and he gives her topping pearls.'

This terrific tolerance, especially the sentence about pearls, made Mrs Herbert cry in her bedroom. Mrs Herbert would not for the world her son should realize what was amiss. She was not one who would relieve herself by pouring out the unfortunate story as soon as she got home. But Mr Herbert, his senses of the mind just now all on edge, could detect from her unnatural brightness when she spoke of Kathy most of what she felt.

Kathy had never had to do with old people before, except village crones, pleased at any notice. Deference, clear, soft, slow speaking, chit-chat about the coming out of buds, delighted acquiescence that the wind was in the north when it was in the south – such duties were unknown to her, and she would not have had any turn for them. The more athletic duties, picking up shawls, bringing footstools, a helping hand down steps (not too ready – Mrs Herbert did not like much helping, though she liked some) – these Kathy would have gladly fulfilled if the idea had occurred to her. She was not given to wondering whether people liked her; she had none of a bride's nervousness at the first visit of a mother-in-law. She was neither jealous nor afraid of her. She thought of her as an old thing sitting in the drawing-room, of which she need take very little notice.

He was on tenterhooks with apprehension about her behaviour, and often on thorns with the certainty. His own scrupulous courtesy and respect to his mother escaped Kathy's observation. They made her rudeness stand out the more. It was unintentional. She treated everybody who was not of her own generation and set with a brusque and almost imperceptibly condescending bonhomie. She had no shades and distinctions. She did not think, she was certain, that most of the world was far below her, because she was a Hollings. She was so certain that no one in Lanchester or elsewhere questioned it either. People, particularly working-class people, often prefer those who consider them inferior, and she was soon on very friendly terms with her neighbours in the village – men, women, children, and animals, being especially appreciated by dogs and little boys. She might have been criticized by the old women at Dedmayne, for she rushed through symptoms faster than Mary; but it is not every village that has a Mary, and her smiles made up. They adored her beauty, after that her smart clothes. Even her own faithful Dedmayne would have thought more of Mary – they could not have loved her more – if she had dressed better. Kathy was not a confidant; she was too gay for the post. Nor could she induce the feeling Mary did, that it was hardly possible to be polite enough to her, because she was so tenderly polite herself. But whereas Mary might be put upon, Kathy could not. She did not disturb herself, with certain exceptions, to be interested in any one who was indifferent to hunting. This excluded most elderly and all old ladies. It was a remarkable tribute to Mr Herbert that she could have got over his terrible lack to the extent of falling in love with him.

Although the Herberts had recently had little connection with Lanchester, he and his were treated with the honour due to the family. The village and household showed their sentiment by calling Mr Herbert 'he' and Mrs Herbert 'she.' 'He' and 'she' standing by themselves meant them and no one else. In like manner to Kathy and Mr Herbert 'they' standing by itself meant the household and village. The tie that bound them was still so far feudal that each had a special importance for the other, they felt differently, if not more warmly, to one another than to the rest of the world. The doctor, known to Kathy by his surname *tout court*, 'I shall send for King,' was of no account in her mind. She put him somewhere among the chemists and bank managers of Cayley. Her manner did not convey this too unpleasantly. He liked to talk of 'that charming girl, Mrs Herbert.'

The news that Mrs Herbert would sing at the parish concert brought hearers from the most scattered farms; rain and cold could not keep any one away. They returned to their homes well pleased when it was over, without much recollection of anything and no criticism, just a pleasant haze of fire, lights, fancy-dress, and sounds.

There was one stern exception. Mr Herbert visited the Dissenters of his flock in illness, for there was no resident pastor. He paid special attention to Mrs Prior, because she was so tiresome. She was a deacon's widow, left well off, and a former beauty. These qualifications she felt called for unremitting notice, which Kathy had not given her.

A call on her was due a few days after the concert. Mr Herbert had not himself been present – he had been kept indoors by a chill – nor had Mrs Prior, but she knew more than if she had. After she had listened to Bible reading – when she made comments as if it were her special book, read by her permission – and had described her pains and medicines, she started a new topic. 'Maybe she's a dear young lady – she ain't been nigh me, so that I can't say – but she don't sing songs what I think at all nice. Heavin' up her legs, too, and her petticoats with pink bows and all. "Mother," Amos says, "be glad you weren't there. There's

106

a-many talkin" about it, and I says, "I shall certainly mention it to him himself, for he didn't ought to let her misbehave herself." '

'Ah, yes,' said Mr Herbert, looking out of window, 'there are some nice wallflower plants you have out there. They don't seem hurt by the cold as we are; gillyflowers, don't they call them in some parts of the country?'

'That I can't take on me to say, Mr Herbert, but what I says to Amos was –'

'I should think yours must be the best in Lanchester.' He was not looking at them, nor were they fine wallflowers. Mrs Prior, as a bed-ridden old woman, possessed great advantages over a healthy clergyman and gentleman, but she was daunted. They talked of things for a few minutes. He endeavoured to throw the same good-will as usual into his farewells. This encouraged her to try again.

'You don't mind what I said to you, sir? I thought it only just you should know it.'

'Yes, tell Amos I am sorry to have missed him. I thought I might have caught him coming so late. I hope your rheumatism will be better with the milder weather.'

He was out in the road now, his pride and self-respect wounded in their tenderest place. That his wife should be the subject of patronage, blame, and coarse scandal, gloated over by low, ignorant – his opinion of the village at the moment too much resembled Caius Marcius' of the Roman mob. He did them wrong. Mrs Prior had told her tale to one or two hearers; she got a snub back perhaps more severe than she deserved.

'I don't think you have any call to speak like that of our young lady. If the gentry will have smuts, that isn't your business. She's very young. I daresay she likes a little life. My mother used to say, "I'd rather cut my tongue out than speak a word against the family." She always spoke very just, my mother, but, being chapel, you can't be expected to know.'

If the snub was unmerited, so, perhaps, was the defence.

He must tell her. How was he to tell her? He brooded over it. He had no aptitude for correction and no confidence; no consciousness of superiority. Unless stirred up by irritability, he hated telling unpalatable truths.

He waited too long, till he was not angry, but miserable. At last he spoke.

'What was the song you sang at the concert the other night?'

'The song I sang? See, what was it?' Kathy's brain was untrained; her memory retained very little. 'Oh, I remember. "Every time a little bit more." We heard it in town, and Cocky made me get it, and we were always singing it. You know how it goes.'

She sang him a verse.

'That's more than enough,' he said bitterly.

'Don't you like it? I sang it to you when we were engaged, and you didn't mind then. You liked it.'

'That I am sure I did not.'

He had, but all was a haze of bliss in his memory.

'But *why* don't you like it?'

'If you don't see yourself, what's the good of explaining?'

'Oh, they like rather hot stuff.'

'There you are mistaken; it was people in the village who complained of it.'

'Did they? Well, I call it very narrow-minded. I sang it at Merton Cross, and every one simply lapped it up.'

The idiocy of her use of the word narrow-minded fretted him. He answered, 'Long may they remain narrow-minded.'

'And long may I remain broad.'

He went out of the room and set himself unavailingly to soothe his mind by writing in the study. What did soothe him was the thought of Mary. He had banished it hitherto; today he gave it welcome.

When Kathy's lustrous eyes had first rested on him he had imagined anything like vulgarity must flee at her glance. She had shown herself to be noisy and vulgar, but nothing more. She was incapable of suggestiveness, not because she was ignorant, but because such things made no difference to her. Her smile was the wrong smile, full of friendliness for all it fell on. It seemed strange that she should occupy herself with what was alien to her; but she followed other people. In hunting she was bold and rash; in things of the mind she was too indolent to have a choice.

Later in the day Kathy said to Mr Herbert, 'We seem to have had quite a lot of scraps lately, don't we?'

He had never seen her cry or near crying, but her voice sounded changed as she added, 'It seems a bit of a mistake our marrying at all.'

It was strongly his feeling at the moment. That she should be nearly crying did not soften, but made his heart hard against her. He answered with a laugh, which wounds so much more than abuse. 'Crabbed age and youth cannot live together, so Shakespeare said, who knew everything, particularly, as in this case, age is no doubt very unreasonably crabbed. Age forthwith apologises.'

Such a jocose vein was not natural to him.

'Everything I do seems wrong,' said Kathy. 'Tell me what to do and I'll be different if I can.'

'I am not a judge over you. What I admire is not what you admire apparently, and I certainly don't propose to change my views to your way of thinking; but that does not mean necessarily that I am the arbiter of what is admirable.'

'You see I don't know what you meant about the song. Everybody's singing it, and you said you liked it.'

Her persistent, innocent wonder that he should dislike the song made him feel the breach between them.

'I don't believe discussion ever has done any good to anybody. I should be obliged if you would not sing it again, however beautiful you may think it. Is that six? I ought to be at the Parish Council at this moment.'

As he sat at the Parish Council, peacemaking, wise, and benevolent, he loathed himself.

On his return a paralysis of reserve and shame kept him from speaking to her, but she threw herself in his arms, saying, 'You know you are everything to me, though I don't seem much to you. I will do anything you want, only let us be as we were first of all.'

This enabled him to speak. 'It is simply that I am the most detestable, contemptible, damned' – she did not know how intensely his feelings were roused when he swore; damned was a common word with her – 'scoundrel that was ever blessed with a woman's love. I ought never to have married you. I would give anything to be different from what I am, but it's too late to change. I was always moody, and living alone I indulged in moods, and now they are my masters.'

They got on better after this for several weeks, but they relapsed. Lesbia came on a visit. Her husband had got an appointment in Nigeria. The privations of the life and the disagreeable climate did not invite the comfort-loving Lesbia to join him. She disliked staying alone in her flat also. She was extravagant; living on her friends suited her better.

She had a curious effect on Kathy, setting her into a screaming flutter of restlessness. They constantly rushed up to town to buy clothes, and show themselves at restaurants. Kathy became insistent on buying the most expensive clothes. Lesbia was a natural mischief-maker; she brought out a side in his wife Mr Herbert had not seen. They seemed to have formed a league to have stupid, schoolboy hoaxes against him. Kathy showed a spiteful relish at his discomfiture. He felt heavy and elderly. He realized he was a wet blanket from a nervous striving to please. Far from being Kathy's prime source of happiness, it seemed she had turned against him. He was jealous and too proud to own it.

One Sunday Cocky came over. His cousins lived at Mansbridge Hall. He was constantly making his way to Lanchester, that the task of entertaining himself might be placed in Kathy's hands. Without initiative in that or anything else, he was appreciative of her efforts. Whatever the faults of Kathy and her friends, they were not blasé. The shrieks of mirth which startled the vicarage came from genuine enjoyment.

Now the entertainment was morning service and a half-dead, belated fly crawling over Mr Herbert's surplice. Kathy, Lesbia, and Captain Wyndham followed its wanderings like little boys of ten. They wrote comments to one another in the vicarage prayer-books, large eighteenth-century volumes presented by a Herbert predecessor, with ample margins to scribble on. Would the fly reach Mr Herbert's neck before the end of the lesson? Kathy ticked off the verses as Mr Herbert read them. 'Ten to one he will.' 'He won't.' 'Great Scot, the poor chap's come a cropper in Crab's hood. He's deaded! No, he's resurrected! ! Cheers. Come on, man, put your back into it. Stick it. He's gone down Crab's back! ! He's tickling Crab like mad. Look at Crab's wriggles. I shall have a fit!! Careful, Crab, you'll kill the poor dumb animal.'

They passed the prayer-books to one another. Each sally was greeted with suppressed whispers and giggles. The choir-boys were enchanted; the blacksmith's eyes (leading bass) started out of his head. Mr Herbert could hear the whispering; he could even hear the words, which were supposed not to reach him. He never had had the animal spirits to be mad with joy at a fly. As a superior, scornful small boy he would have despised the commotion.

After service, when it was possible to secure Kathy alone, he said as pleasantly as he could, 'I don't think that business this morning was quite fair on the choir-boys. Jim (the blacksmith) and I, when I first came, had to knock some of them down for their merrymakings in church; you know I told you Arnott had let the place get a bear-garden. We can't very well knock Cocky down, though I shouldn't be sorry to do so. Won't the boys feel sauce for the goose is sauce for the gander? Don't you think so youself?'

'Oh, but I never could sit up and be prunes and prisms,' said Kathy in a sentence after Lesbia's own heart. 'I wasn't made that way.'

He bit his lip in irritation and said no more.

One Sunday on their honeymoon they had gone to the early communion at a remote church in the fells. When they came out Kathy had taken his arm, and said, looking up at him with a graver expression than usual on her face, 'I shall *never* forget this morning.' Inarticulate about everything, she was specially inarticulate on such matters, but at that moment how near they had been, how perfectly they had understood one another, or was it only seemed to understand? Both thought of that morning now.

Kathy told Lesbia what Mr Herbert had said. She may have begun in a spirit of moderation; Lesbia turned it at once into derision.

'Oh, the *pet*,' she screeched. 'He's such a priceless prig, exactly like that old German thing we had when I was small. "I vill not hab ze yong latees scream zo lout."'

Kathy hated herself, but she did not defend Crab. She had sometimes tried; her defence had merely given Lesbia oppor-

111

tunities for further attack. On other topics she was in the habit of giving Lesbia as good as she got. But Crab was too sensitive a place; she could not be self-possessed.

'I shall go to church this afternoon,' said Lesbia, 'and I shall be a perfect lady, and so will you, Cocky; a perfect lady, mind, not a perfect gentleman.'

'Righto,' said Cocky.

'No,' said Kathy. 'We're going to look for rats in the Glebe barn.'

But this enticement could not keep Lesbia and Cocky from church.

'Well, I shan't go,' said Kathy.

She did go. All her compunction could not dash her enthusiasm at Lesbia and Cocky being perfect ladies. They pointed out the places to one another with unction. Cocky turned faint and Lesbia fanned him with her prayer-book. They had not intended to be so amusing, but success intoxicated them. The front pews watched their antics with horror; a rustle of excitement pervaded the church.

Mr Herbert stalked home by himself. He said not one word, good or bad, to Cocky during tea. He addressed Lesbia only as far as his courtesy as a host required it. He could deal with Cocky; he had dealt with several Cockies when he was head of his house at Rugby. He understood him – poor harmless thing – what there was to understand; he was not in the least afraid of him. But Lesbia; he felt as wax before her. What was there to appeal to?

Lesbia and Cocky were not so thick-skinned as Mr Herbert imagined; both were ashamed. Cocky left as soon as he could, with a feeling of discomfort that he had not quite played the game in 'guying the parson's show, poor chap.'

Mr Herbert took a walk after tea to fortify himself against Lesbia. He did not for an instant imagine that because Kathy played what she called 'monkey-tricks' in church she was incapable of serious feeling. But it was another indication that he and she were poles apart; Kathy should not have married a clergyman. Was his married life henceforth to be a series of remonstrances, recrimination, and bad temper, interspersed with repentant scenes, reconciliations, promises of amendment, and horrible tears? He had come to the conclusion that repentant scenes left them further apart in the end, though there might be a spurious immediate *rapprochement*. The prospect for the future filled him with dismay, almost with despair.

As he came back he saw Kathy. It was dark, but the starlight showed him her tall, stately figure. She was hurrying, and did not see him. She passed by him; he heard a suppressed sob. He had an impulse to spring forward and kiss her. The unworthy thought restrained him, 'What's the use?'

She was on her way to the church. She remembered his showing her the vicarage prayer-books on their first Sunday in Lanchester, pointing out, with the reverent delight of a scholar, the old rosy crimson leather bindings, the Herbert coat of arms finely engraved. It was the time when, for a brief spell, each felt that whatever the other liked they liked too, or would speedily come to like. Kathy rubbed the scribbling out and felt happier, but she could not rub out the fact that she had joined with Lesbia in making a fool of him.

Lesbia had been anxious to avoid a *tête-à-tête* with Mr Herbert. She was not as brazen as he thought; she was afraid of him. He caught her, however, and began.

'Lesbia, it seems to me Kathy changes very much when you are here.'

'Does she?' cried Lesbia. 'Poor dear, I'm so glad. I thought her awfully piano when I first came; well, really, we all noticed it.'

'What I meant was –'

'Kathy always was the life and soul of everything,' broke in Lesbia, 'and of course in a life like this you can't wonder she gets moped. It's such a *terrific* change for her. Of course I know her so well; we've always been such pals ever since she was an infant.'

Kathy had often told him how miserable she had been with Lesbia. She said one day, 'Now I know for the first time in my life what it is to be absolutely and perfectly happy.' He would not speak of this to Lesbia. Besides, Lesbia was right; lately Kathy had not been happy. He felt he had managed the conversation badly. He now burst straight into what he wanted to say.

'As the wife of Kathy's brother, our house is always open to

113

you when you like to make use of it,' he said, with some of Canon Jocelyn's stateliness, 'but I do ask one thing of you.'

He stopped for a moment, wondering how disagreeable Lesbia would make herself.

'I'm sure, anything to oblige, Crab,' said Lesbia.

'Will you never go to Lanchester Church again?'

She was grasping of the grasping. Still, she could not but recall that, becoming involved in some scraps up in town, she had thrown herself on Kathy's kindness to be whitewashed at the vicarage. She had arrived with large debts; Kathy had spent all that year's income on her trousseau, and Mr Herbert had paid them.

She blushed, and said, 'I know it was awfully tiresome of us but it's all right. Kathy talks so loud, but we'll all be like the little girl with the curl down the middle of her forehead next Sunday.'

'Still, I would ask you to keep to that rule,' he said, frowning at the sentence about Kathy.

'Oh, but, Crab,' she said, idiotically hoping to please him, 'I must come. I think your sermons are so topping.'

'I fancy that will not be a serious deprivation,' said he.

This conversation helped to tire Lesbia of Lanchester. She set her heart on the Riviera. She found a doctor who ordered it, and, as she said to Kathy, her own sisters, 'Bee and Muriel, never put themselves out for a soul, and are simply absorbed in babies. I wish you would come for a week or so. I'm sure Crab could spare you; I was going to say *more* than spare you, only that's catty; but I feel we are a little overwhelming for him, and yet you can't drop out of everything.'

Kathy refused, but after more arguments she consented. Mr Herbert felt aggrieved, but he put no objection in the way. Besides, was it not the wisest thing to do? To break, come back and start afresh, might give their married happiness a new chance.

'Do you see much of the Herberts, Mary?' said Ella Redland. 'I called, but I think she's an utter bore, just games and hunting. She'll give Mr Herbert such a wrong impression of women, and I don't consider him at all sound on the subject anyhow.'

'I don't see very much of them,' said Mary. 'We don't see much of anybody, you know. Father took to her.'

'I am rather wondering how it will turn out. Some people say they don't get on very well.'

'Who say so?'

'Oh, the village people. One of them told my landlady they had a regular row one night, and I do think it's a mistake a clergyman's wife hunting. I don't know what Father would have thought. He never liked Mr Dyson hunting.'

After all her London experiences and association with big movements there peeped out the old natural love of village gossip and tendency to feel shocked.

'I am certain you are wrong,' said Mary. 'You must have forgotten what village people are if you trust to what they say. What struck me, on the contrary, was how ecstatically happy they are. Lady Meryton – she's Mrs Herbert's aunt, you know – is delighted about it.'

'Oh, well, I only just wondered. We had such a splendid meeting on Wednesday, Mary. We had a Labour man down from town, only unluckily the local association is so jealous, and one of the committee –'

The talk turned away from the Herberts.

Mary did not know that she wanted the marriage to be a success, but she could not discuss Mr Herbert's affairs with Ella Redland.

The gossip was confirmed next day. Lady Meryton came to call. They had touched on various subjects with spirit when Lady Meryton said, 'Mary, I am so worried' (she had seemed, as ever, the entirely prosperous queen). 'I have come to consult you. It's about Kathy.'

'Mrs Herbert?' said Mary.

'I was always a little anxious. This quiet life in the country is such a complete change from what she's been accustomed to. But she seemed so absolutely happy first of all, and now that horrid sister-in-law of hers has got hold of her again. They had quarrelled, and I had hoped it was a permanent break. She's not good for Kathy and she associates with dreadful rich people who have made their money one doesn't like to ask how, and pay to have their names in vulgar papers. They go on in a way I can't bear. I know Kathy doesn't like it really, but she's very obstinate, and here's Lesbia wanting her to go abroad with her. Lesbia *ought* to join her husband in Nigeria, of course, *some* women can, and she's at a loose end, and Kathy is good-natured about every one. I wonder if *you* could do anything.'

'*Me*. I am sure I should be no good.'

'You and your father have known Mr Herbert so long. I did speak to Kathy, but naturally she thinks me antediluvian, and she doesn't like me. Her uncle always set her against us. Claudia says I managed it badly, and that it's no good interfering.'

'But I hardly know Mrs Herbert, and I am sure she doesn't like *me*, whatever she feels about you.'

'Yes, she does. She thinks you a little like my sister, the one I told you of. Kathy was very fond of her as a child.'

'But I can't think what I should say.'

'Of course you couldn't say anything at once; but do try to get to know her, or could you possibly get at Mr Herbert? Sometimes I wish he'd married Maida Bassett; she's so fond of church.' (This was a new light on Jim-jam.) 'I don't think he knows how to treat a young wife. He expects too much of her, and she's such a child. I heard him speak so harshly to her one day, and I know Kathy felt it. She doesn't look happy now. That great difference in age is such a mistake. Either the man tries to come down to the girl's level and is absurd, or he's too much of the schoolmaster. I wish you would try, Mary. I know how everybody flies to you for help, and Dr King told me how wonderful you were about his sister-in-law.' Compliments were second nature to Lady Meryton. 'I really am in despair. You see there is *nobody*. She hasn't any real friends in the neighbourhood except us, and she doesn't like his mother. I don't wonder. Old Mrs Herbert is rather strait-laced and tiresome, and one can't expect too much of a girl in these days. There's much more in Kathy than meets the eye. She's so warm-hearted and so absolutely true. And now, Mary dear, when are you coming to us? Next week I am going to the Hirst Blacketts, and it's almost impossible to get away once one's there, the grandchildren are so fascinating. The Hunt Jubilee will keep us busy the week after, but after that you *must* come. I shall drag you by force if everything else fails.'

116

Mary wrote a note asking Kathy to come to tea. She was walking with the note to Lanchester when she met two riders, Kathy and Lesbia. Mounted on tall horses and in faultless habits, they looked particularly formidable. They both gave cool nods, and were trotting on without stopping, when Mary called to Mrs Herbert, 'Will you come to tea on Thursday? I was just bringing a note.'

'Thursday, what am I doing Thursday? Oh, I was going to Cayley.'

'Would Friday suit, or Saturday?' said Mary.

'I don't know. I'm rather full up. Which day is it we go to town, Lesbia?'

'I must have you up both Friday and Saturday,' said Lesbia. 'We shan't nearly get things done if you don't.'

'Oh, well, that looks rather hopeless,' said Kathy. 'Sorry, Miss Jocelyn. I'm afraid I'm not a good hand at tea-fights. Stand still, Taffy! There are no hounds in that field, you ass. Good-bye. The beast won't stand. Lesbia, you know this bit isn't really better; he's pulling my arms out of their sockets.'

They rode on. Mary could not observe a liking for her or a warm heart.

'Fancy invitations to tea-parties from the daughters of the clergy,' said Lesbia. 'How truly tragic. I pity you.'

'Remember I'm a wife of the clergy,' said Kathy. 'I've definitely joined the middle-classes.'

'I know you have, poor dear.'

'You needn't always be pouring in consolation; thanks awfully.'

'Needn't I? Well, of course you know best. I thought last night –'

'Yes, I *do* know best. Miss Jocelyn's quite decent. Crab likes her.'

'Oh, *Crab*. Do you know, Kathy,' said Lesbia pensively, 'she's just the sort of type Crab should have married really.'

'Don't wriggle, you devil,' said Kathy, giving a vicious cut at Taffy, who jumped.

'Did I smack old Taff then?' she said apologetically. But no animal minded rough treatment from Kathy; they understood her good-will to them perfectly.

'Let's have a canter. I agree with Taffy; it's a shame to waste the grass.' She soon stopped Lesbia's tongue.

After Kathy's obvious snub it had been difficult to take further steps, and just then Cook fell ill. Mary was much occupied nursing her, so that for two or three weeks she heard nothing of Lanchester.

The Herberts had what Kathy called 'one of our usual' on the night before she started. In the course of it she exclaimed, 'I think marriage is an utter wash-out.' He said, 'Do you mean that?' and she answered, 'Of course I do, and if I had fifty thousand tongues I should say it fifty thousand times.'

He did not know she had it in her to speak so violently. She expressed something of what he felt himself; he was none the less indignant with her.

In the morning there was no time, or neither would make time, for a reconciliation. There was the usual disagreeable scramble. Mr Herbert felt any attempt would be useless; he would write later.

'I want two minutes with Crab before the train goes,' said Kathy to Lesbia. 'So mind you clear out.'

The drive to the station had been merely hilarious. When they arrived Lesbia walked off to get a paper. 'Let me do that,' said Mr Herbert. 'I haven't a night journey in front of me.'

'My dear man,' said Lesbia, 'do realize that I have a few grains of tact about me. I must leave you two devoted people to your farewells.'

This speech successfully froze up any tender words from either.

'Say good-bye to the village for me. My best love to the whole crowd, my bestest to Mrs Prior, and ask her to think of "Every time a little bit more" whenever she says her prayers. Do go and hurry Lesbia. She always misses trains when she can, and where's Mansfield and my dressing-case? She's much more precious than Lesbia.'

He was not sure afterwards; he fancied she had wanted to give him a caress at the last moment. He had rejected it.

The train started; he turned to leave the station. He looked back; he saw Kathy watching him. She was saying to herself, 'He never *once* said he was sorry I was going.' She did not know how the words showed on her face. He was dismayed. He took a step forward; he cried 'Kathy.' Some one looked round at him. She was already out of sight.

'Well, here we are on the razzle-dazzle,' she shouted uproariously to Lesbia.

'Yes, I know. Now, where on earth has Mansfield put my flask? She's so outrageously careless; you know that flask Crab filled last night. I'm absolutely dished if I don't have it for the crossing. You really ought to speak to that girl.'

'Turn her down yourself if you're so outraged. She's only two carriages down. I've not the slightest doubt it's in your bag. We always have these stunts, and they're always all for nothing.'

She took *The Tatler* and held it glued to her face.

'But, Kath –'

'Oh, let a fellow read in peace.'

So the razzle-dazzle began.

Mr Herbert determined to write the letter of reconciliation at once. But it was difficult to find the words. It was not written. Post cards came from Kathy – several picture post cards; they were cool and hurried. He did not feel his own letter satisfactory. At the end of three weeks Kathy wrote that they were having much too good a time to think of coming back yet. He was angry and relieved. The return to solitude was sometimes pleasantly familiar, he even imagined sufficing. But his thoughts wandered constantly not to Kathy, but to Mary. Lately he had not seen her, but he knew that he had decided not once, but many times, that in missing her he had missed the happiness of his life. When he realized it, he made up his mind to go to no place where he might meet her; he must not call on her father. It was on those calls that they had had talks with one another which the only sensible thing now was to forget. Soon after his wife's decision to prolong her absence he met Mary again.

16

THE opening weeks of the razzle-dazzle were more successful than had seemed possible from the journey out. Kathy and Lesbia found several of their old set already arrived, and every day there were new smart rich accretions. Kathy enjoyed the sports and gaieties with which the days were crammed. She was popular, particularly now that noise is so much appreciated; her good looks and clothes helped too. She liked the flattery and petting. They were not the breath of life to her, but she had been without them for some time; now she basked in them. She had many admirers; she was not so inhuman as to get no pleasure from admiration. She put her husband out of her mind as much as she could. There seemed several husbands and wives on the Riviera getting on comfortably, even uproariously, whose partners had lost all feeling for them. If so, why should not she? She did. She wrote sincerely when she said she was enjoying herself too much to come back. But after the first month her interest flagged. She longed for Crab, however beastly he might be. She wanted also – it would have been impossible to make Lesbia understand, though some other gay Riviera sparks were wanting the same thing – to be back at her regular duties – feeding the fowls, ordering the dinner, teaching the village boys woodwork. But it was clear from his letters Mr Herbert was not longing for her. She was too proud to go home when she was not wanted. In a clumsy attempt to stir up his jealousy and make herself desired she wrote the following:

'It's topping now; the hotels are packed. Nobody has any brains, which is a bit of a relief. Some of the women are awfully good-looking, and there are one or two really smart men. It's rather a blessing to see a person who goes to a decent tailor again. Here are some snaps of Captain Stokes and me. We've done a lot of golf and tennis together. He's riding in the Steeplechase this week. He's first-class; so he is at golf and tennis. He's just my sort. Of course we see a lot of one another.'

She had meant to dilate on Captain Stokes's admiration – he was the principal aspirant at the moment – but when it came to the point her pen refused to say anything more. She was perfectly aware of her beauty, but she had never set much value on admiration, and scorned any one who paraded it.

The snapshots had trodden roughshod on Kathy's beauty. She came out with a huge, triangular, *Daily Mirror* smile, but Captain Stokes's perfections of figure, face, and attire were preserved almost intact. He looked worthless, but what did that matter?

Mr Herbert had been disturbed in his supercilious childhood by compliments on his beauty. He had decided that he grew up extremely ugly, and had never thought further on the matter. He found himself wishing for his good looks back to compete with Captain Stokes. He was ashamed, but that sentence about the tailor rankled. Of course he would have been the same to Kathy if he had dressed in tatters. What sentiment she had for Captain Stokes depended on his faultless appearance. Mr Herbert imagined he had ceased to love Kathy, but his feelings were all raw about her, everything wounded him.

A letter from Lesbia by the same post did not mend matters. It was written in a spirit of aimless petty malice.

'I really feel I have undertaken a rather heavy job in chaperoning your gay and giddy wife. My hands are quite full with her affairs, not to mention my own, and we are quite *the* sensation this season. Seriously, I rather wish she would not go the pace quite so much. The present one and only is not exactly your sort. I've spoken once or twice, but without much effect. Still, no doubt, it will turn out all right in the end, and there's safety in numbers.'

Mr Herbert knew Lesbia's faculty for making capital out of what was harmless. He had no real distrust of Kathy. It would have been impossible for him to spy on her or accuse her causelessly, but he made up his mind that it would be well for him to go out to Monte Carlo. At present it was impossible, for he had had an accident and injured his knee, which meant weeks of inaction. He would pay no attention to Lesbia's letter, but he read Kathy's again and again. What should he answer? How had he dared to take upon himself the happiness of a young girl brought up like Kathy? Her natural affinities were with the Captain Stokes of this world. He could provide her with nothing she wanted. He was a wet blanket in what, no doubt, were legitimate pleasures if one had a mind that way. An unclerical desire to beat Captain Stokes in a steeplechase flashed through him. Why, *why* had he married her? He felt a shiver of shy distaste at the prospect of meeting her in Monte Carlo.

On the same morning that Mr Herbert received Kathy's and Lesbia's letters Canon Jocelyn suggested that Mary should go to Lanchester.

'I wanted to ask Herbert what his reading of that passage in Tertullian is. I wonder if you could copy it down for me. I rather thought he would have been calling here. It seems a long time since we saw him.'

'Of course he hasn't so much time now there's a Mrs Herbert,' said Mary.

She felt compunction that she had done so little to keep her promise to Lady Meryton; she was glad of a definite reason for going to Lanchester.

The parlourmaid said Mrs Herbert was away, but Mr Herbert was in the study. She entered. He did not look pleased to see her. She missed the warmth which used to welcome her.

He said, 'My wife is away; the servant should have told you.' He spoke almost rudely.

She uttered a few commonplaces, which he answered briefly. She told her errand at once. The absurdity of such good friends having nothing but a hurried business interview simply because he was married made her delay a little, and endeavour to renew their old cordiality. She made a small joke; he let it drop. There was not a trace of his former playfulness. He did not seem to be listening to her; it was useless to stay.

She had risen and put out her hand in farewell when he said suddenly, 'Miss Jocelyn, sometimes one makes great mistakes in life. She made one, and I have made one.'

He had not meant to utter a word of his trouble, but the sudden longing came. He told himself Mary in her wisdom might help him and Kathy.

She trembled; she could hardly answer him. She said, 'Do not what are mistakes at first often turn out right in the end?'

'Do they?' he answered bitterly.

She looked at him. Some people can be unhappily married and injure their knee and have severe sciatica into the bargain, and remain stout and hearty. Mr Herbert looked white and starved. Indeed without Kathy's care his meals had been turning more and more into a bit of bread and cheese in the study. 'I'll ring for it when I want it'; and his eyes, which were naturally sad, looked almost tragic in their distress.

Mary wanted to support him, but that glance at him broke her down. She cried out, 'Oh, I *cannot* bear it if you're unhappy,' and burst into tears.

He put his hand on her shoulder, and said, 'Don't, Mary, don't cry.' Their eyes met. Before they knew what was happening he kissed her.

A thrill of indescribable happiness passed through her. He held her in his arms, repeating, 'Mary, Mary, Mary.'

She wanted to say something; for a few seconds she simply could not speak. She did not know what she wanted to say. She began, 'Oh –' She got no further. She had no idea what rapture she put into the one word. She came to herself; she walked to the door, and said, 'I must go.'

He turned away from her and made no answer.

She went out of the house. Neither he nor she noticed, in spite of a violent wind, the rain was pouring down. She ran as hard as she could. She was never a graceful runner, now agitation made her clumsier. Mr Herbert, watching her from the study window with his eye gleaming, thought her the most exquisite spectacle.

As she ran home the scene was already in a haze. She could hardly remember what had taken place. She could only feel that poets, far from exaggerating, had never done justice to love. He, being what he was, cared for her. She was exalted into an ecstasy, but as an excellent clergyman's daughter, with duty paramount, her ecstasy took the form of good resolutions. The thought of him should make her do her ordinary work better.

'It shall,' she said to herself again and again.

In the evening a letter for her came from Mr Herbert with the passage of Tertullian for her father. She had forgotten the object of her visit.

Friday, Feb. 4th. – I cannot tell you how I reproach myself for this afternoon. I had avoided meeting you. You *must* know. [This he wrote and scratched out. Such a fall from his customary perfection of neatness marked the intensity of his agitation.] I had no intention, but at the moment I was overmastered. Your father in his note asks to see me. You will judge whether I had better come. There is only one thing to be done: the thought of you must make me face life with a better heart. With that remembrance I should be less fretful and complaining, and not so contemptibly inconsiderate for her. – Your

G.R.H.

This letter, the one love-letter of her life, could not be read often enough. There was one word she paused over each time with an exquisite thrill, 'Your' G. R. H. He had intended that the letter should end with the plain signature, but that word 'your' crept in. There was a mad delight that for that one moment in his life he could feel he belonged to her, not all his resolution made him scratch it out. She wrote an answer. 'Never, never regret what you did. It is the whole world to me. – Your own MARY.' She burnt it. It must be all or nothing; she could not trust herself. What she sent was, 'DEAR MR HERBERT – I hope you will come now and then and see my father. Thursday is the day that will suit us best. – Yours sincerely, M. N. JOCELYN.' On Thursdays she visited at the Cayley Infirmary.

She had determined never to see him if she could help it; never write to him or speak to him. In that case, might she not indulge herself by meeting him in thought? She brooded over the letter she did not send him. She composed many poems about him. Night after night she thought of him, imagining, with the terror of love, every sort of disaster and of death for him. She dreamt of him also, waking up in an uncontrollable torrent of tears because he was dead in some foreign country.

At first her meditations were a kind of gazing on his portrait. After a while she built castles. She described them to herself as concerning someone else, but she knew from her excited joy she was thinking of pleasure she was ashamed to own. She would picture Kathy's death. After a while she went further and pictured her going away with another man, Mr Herbert's freedom, and their marriage. If she had been told a month ago she would have desired the death, still more the sin of another woman, she would not have believed it. Such desires would have been impossible to her mother. The spirit of the times was making itself felt in her. She wished she had spoken to him when he kissed her. She had accepted all and risked nothing. She recoiled from herself, but she continued her day-dreams. She had often acted suddenly on wrong impulses. She had never deliberately pursued a course contrary to her sense of right, but some bonds seemed to have snapped within her. She longed for help; she felt incapable of standing up against herself.

Lady Meryton's words often occurred to her. 'Little Kathy has been so lonely. I cannot tell you the comfort it is to have her in the keeping of a good man, who loves her as Mr Herbert does, and whom she herself loves with her whole heart.' Mary assured herself many times that now they did not love one another, but she never satisfied herself. Sometimes when she lay awake in excitement, she could see Kathy's face looking mournfully at her.

She knew what Lady Meryton's feelings would be. Lady Meryton in general regarded the lapses of men rather as a matter of course, sometimes with amusement. She was even lenient towards the indiscretions of good-looking young matrons, though it was a satisfaction to her that the morals, though not the jokes, of her immediate circle were irreproachable. The questionable jokes she placidly endured – she could not participate in them – with, 'You young things really are outrageous.' They would have frozen old Mrs Herbert with repulsion. But, in spite of all this latitude, Mary knew no mercy would be felt for a middle-aged married clergyman who had been disloyal to his wife; less than none for a middle-aged spinster.

Dora was abroad just then. Gertrude's husband got an appointment at Hong Kong. Dora went to help with the children on the voyage; she had little time for letters. Mary was glad; she shrank from the thought of Dora. She knew she would have had sympathy from Brynhilda. She could imagine with what pleasant, easy principles of guidance Brynhilda would have supported her inclination. She shrank from that too.

One evening she wrote to Brynhilda telling her all. She put the case in its most favourable light, moistening the paper with tears of self-pity. When she had finished, she tore the letter up. She did wisely. If she had made Brynhilda the recipient of her vacillation, passion, repentance, and complaints, Brynhilda, though interested first of all, would soon have sickened of her; strong feeling repelled her.

About this time Mary had a joyful letter from Brynhilda announcing her engagement, shortly afterwards another announcing her marriage to a journalist. They were to live in Paris. It was unlikely that she and Mary would see much more of one another. Mary received the news with indifference. She felt now nothing was of account which did not concern Mr Herbert.

Sometimes she longed for confession, but the two local professional confessors did not invite confidence. Father Murphy greeted her with bad puns in an uproarious brogue; he was just a comfortable peasant. Father Lynne, the vicar of Long Clouston, confessed five penitents, so she heard from indignant Low Church parishioners. She thought he was more interested in baiting his bishop than in performing spiritual duties, however, irregular.

'Mary,' said Ella Redland one day when she was at the cottage, 'you've made a wretched tea, and I noticed when we were talking about that meeting you seemed distrait. I wonder if you're quite well.'

'Oh yes, perfectly well,' said Mary quickly.

'I don't think you are. The strain of your life undermines you more than you realize, the being always with an old person.'

'It's only that I have a headache today,' said Mary.

'You want a change. Let's go off together somewhere. I'm rather busy, but I think I could put off my small meeting, and I'll get Miss Bowes to run my two committees next week. It's a bad time of year, but somewhere in Devonshire would be sunny, and it's really rest from strain you want.'

Mary did want it – a rest from the strain of love, but not for the world would she leave Dedmayne, where, though she never began the subject, she constantly heard Mr Herbert mentioned, and there was the dangerous hope of seeing him.

'It's very nice of you to think of it, Ella, but next week Lent begins, and I am always busy then.'

'Oh, *Lent*,' said Ella with some impatience.

But Mary was grateful for the Redland kindness, which was less fitful than the Meryton kindness. Lady Meryton had no notion that it was so, but out of sight was out of mind with her. The invitation promised last September had never got beyond a wish.

At this time Canon Jocelyn broke a small blood-vessel in his eye, and both eyes had to be bandaged for a few days. She read aloud to him to relieve the tedium. She asked him what he would like to hear, and received the uncharacteristic answer, 'Anything you care for will interest me.' Some masterful people become meek if they have once consented to be invalids. His and her tastes in light literature were not similar, but she remembered hearing her aunt say that Canon Jocelyn used to read 'Mr Gilfil's Love Story' aloud to her and her mother. So Mary took *Scenes of Clerical Life*. When she had finished 'Amos Barton' Mr Jocelyn said, 'That is a beautiful tale, told very touchingly; but the older I grow the more I feel that pleasure in George Eliot cannot but be spoilt by the remembrance of her association with Lewes. I know that there are excuses made for her, but one cannot blink the fact that to indulge in love for a married man is always illicit, and the eminence of the guilty parties makes the sin more, not less, serious.'

Mr Jocelyn, exaggeratedly reserved in general, spoke sometimes with unaccountable openness. He was always more approachable and communicative if there was anything the matter with him.

She said, 'Yes, of course it is,' hardly knowing how she managed to articulate. He went on to describe his meeting George Eliot at a party in Cambridge. 'It was after Lewes's death, of course.' Once he had started, he continued his reminiscences, dissecting the celebrated people of his youth with clear-sighted mercilessness, so that his daughter almost cried out, 'Who, then, shall be saved?' She made answer within herself, 'Certainly I should not.' She had had a long course of taking part in conversations which did not interest her; she could keep up an appearance of attention while her mind was all the while repeating, 'He ought to know what I am.'

When he gave her his good night cheek to receive her kiss, and remarked, 'It has been a pleasant retrospect of old times,' she could bear no longer sitting with him under a guise of innocence, and stammered, 'I just wanted to ask you something – I meant about love. Do you think if a husband or wife loved some one, and perhaps also that some one might have loved too, and they never saw one another but once, could there be an excuse –'

'I do not understand what you mean.'

She recollected, more than twenty-five years before, when she and Will had gone trespassing against their father's strict orders. They had robbed an orchard; she had thought it wrong all the time, but had yielded to please Will. He had lied about it, and in the interview with her father in the study after the lie she had been too petrified to speak connectedly, and he had thought she lied too. She was able to recall clearly the utter blank in her mind. She had never entirely recovered her confidence. Whether she would really have confessed Mr Herbert's kiss to her father must be uncertain; at this moment she *could* not.

He waited, and then repeated, 'I don't understand what it is you wished to ask me.'

'I don't think it is worth – at least – I think I would rather – Good night, Father –' and she left him abruptly.

Her timid brusqueness, almost uncouthness, so different from the limpid, peaceful joyousness of his wife, always jarred on him. He might have understood her, perhaps he ought to have understood her, for the wild, uncontrolled side of her character came from his family. She was the modern and less extreme counterpart of certain good but odd aunts and great-aunts of his, who in the intervals of passions and hysterics had played delightfully with him when he was a child. Canon Jocelyn had become used to Mary's deficiencies and resigned to them. He thought little of this further instance. She lay awake many hours. One thing she vowed. She *would* have a clear conscience before her father. From henceforth she would not allow *one* thought of Mr Herbert to intrude. The next day she did think of him, on the sly first of all, as it were, to deceive her conscience, afterwards openly in defiance of it.

When she tried to check herself with the recollection of her father's words, she felt she hated him. In her struggles she could only say with St Paul, 'Oh, wretched man that I am, who shall deliver me from the body of this death?'

It was at this season of the year that she always had private talks with the girls who were to be confirmed. As she looked into each stolid, innocent face and spoke against yielding to temptations, she felt an outcast. The blacksheep candidate, who ran after boys, had promised she would not run after them any more. *She* was keeping her word. And though the wonder was, looking at her unattractive appearance, that the boys had ever allowed themselves to be caught, her reformation was none the less to be commended. On the whole, Mary's misery during those weeks was greater than her bliss.

There was a Spanish poem she had read and rè-read in the days when she had learnt Spanish. Spanish was a part of the honey of knowledge Canon Jocelyn had sipped by the way, together with Italian, considering it a dishonour to Dante and Cervantes to read them in anything but the original. What he had learnt once, he had learnt for his whole life. What Mary learnt she generally forgot, but the poem had chimed in with early romantic sentimentality. She had never imagined its feelings would be her own, felt at first hand.

She wrote a translation hot from her brain:

> For thee I am outcast from God,
> I have forfeited Heaven for thee,
> And, lo, I am doomed to remain
> Alone – all alone, woe is me!
> And lo, I am doomed to remain
> Without God, without Heaven, without thee.
> For thee I am outcast from God,
> I have forfeited Heaven for thee.

She put Mr Herbert's name at the top, and 'In remembrance of February 15th,' and the date. The writing of his name thrilled her as if he had been standing by her side.

In that bursting agitation she felt she must be going mad, and if her father, Mr Sykes, the Redlands, and all the neighbours with whom she was the gentle Rector's daughter had seen into her mind, they would certainly have thought her already mad. Mr Herbert, too, might have felt a little startled, yet it was for that very quality in her he loved her; he alone would have understood.

17

WEEKS passed. It was now the end of February. The days were unusually mild and balmy; the fields were basking in the sweet air, getting ready for spring. Mary was miserable. One day she had indulged herself in rage against Kathy. 'If she really loved him I could bear it, but she doesn't. She can't make him happy and I can –' An insane impulse seized her. She threw on her hat and coat and started off for Lanchester, walking so fast that people turned to stare at her. She did not know what she meant to do when she got there; her real, sober self would have recoiled from any idea of joining Mr Herbert.

She had passed the first knot of cottages belonging to Lanchester when she suddenly saw Mr Herbert in front of her. He did not see her. He had an unusual expression in repose, as if absorbed in sublime meditation. Mary thought now the look of sublimity was intensified. It was her eye of love that magnified it. His thoughts at that moment were of her, and bitter with longing. Her heart felt as if it stopped beating. She turned into a field and walked rapidly away from Lanchester, never looking back.

She went into the churchyard to her mother's grave. She was terrified at what she had done; her unbalanced side was hateful to the rest of her. She longed to die. She made four resolutions. She would destroy everything that reminded her of Mr Herbert. She would occupy herself more actively and allow no time for thought. If this failed she would go away on a visit. If the visit failed, she would kill herself.

She went indoors, took all her poems and his letter, and put them into the drawing-room fire. Her Lenten penance was a small fire; they would not burn. Then she heard footsteps and voices; it was her father and a guest. She worked herself into an agony that he might ask what she was doing. She snatched them out, and hid them as the door opened. The guest was a curate; he had come to consult her father about religious difficulties. Mary had seen the dejected expression in his eyes at tea. The weight was now removed. Canon Jocelyn had listened and advised with kindness, almost tenderness. To the stranger curate he could be fatherly. Much as the curate wanted fatherliness, his daughter wanted it more. The guest stayed to supper. When he was gone Miss Brewer came. Then Emma began one of her chats, which dawdled on interminably, because Mary had not the sense to stop her. Mary was so tired when it was over that there was no time to finish the task of destruction.

In the morning her resolutions were less rigorous; common sense prevailed. She decided it was unnecessary to destroy everything. She picked out Mr Herbert's letter and the translation from the Spanish, repaired and smoothed them, placed them in an envelope, sealed it, and wrapped it in paper. She put it at the bottom of a box in her room, where she kept her letters and papers. The Rectory abounded in great black boxes studded with nails. Some years hence, she reflected, when she was calmer, she would read them again, not till then.

Cook was in a temper that morning because, for the fifth day running Mary had forgotten her weekly cheque. 'But there, I don't know what's come over you; you don't seem like our Miss Mary at all, and Mrs Gibbs said she *did* think you would have been round to see baby, but things were so different now.'

'See baby, but I didn't know it had come already; no one told me.'

'Excuse me, miss, but I did myself. Last week I told you.'

'Did you really? I believe you did, and I completely forgot. I'll go at once.'

'You can't go in all this pouring rain; it would be quite ridiculous, and there's no call, I should say, to see Mrs Gibbs's baby at all. There's some say we'd better not ask how it was come by.'

'But I can't bear the people to think I don't care.'

'No one thinks that, but you always take up whatever one says.'

But Mary knew that out of the abundance of her heart Cook's mouth spoke, however she might tone it down afterwards. She *was* different. Only the week before she had forgotten the Bible Class, which in the fifteen years of its existence she had never forgotten. She remembered her resolution returning from Lanchester, but, on the contrary, she had deteriorated in the performance of every duty.

After the visit to the baby, she set herself to write a new catalogue for the village library. She was aghast to find she had lately allowed her mind to wander so persistently that she made numberless mistakes; twice she had to tear it up and begin again. She read three chapters of Gibbon's *Decline and Fall*, but that was a weak defence against thought. While her eyes had disposed of several pages she was settling the towns in Italy they would visit during the wedding-tour. She put on her mackintosh and went off to see Susan. She knew Susan must think this odd; she never called on her at halfpast eleven in the morning. In her comfortable society she strove to find forgetfulness. Susan saw something was the matter, and said in her soft country voice, 'Are you well, my dear? This dear white hand is so thin.'

'It's getting on for spring, you know,' said Mary, 'and I always think that's trying; but I believe I do rather want a tonic.'

In the afternoon – it was Saturday – she asked Miss Gage for a walk. To have an extra walk lifted Miss Gage into ecstasy. She did not cease speaking from the moment of starting till the door closed upon her on their return. As thus: 'No, Mr Clarkson' (the church-warden) 'and I don't speak. I would not make it too marked for anything, but we really *don't* speak. You remember the social – no, not last Christmas, the Christmas before. I was singing "The Holy City." I was asked specially, because it is always such a favourite. It was my second song – I had "Lavender" for my first – and fancy, Mr Clarkson, when he was writing the programme, put "Song, Miss Gage," not the title, when people would have made a special effort if they had known it was to be "The Holy City". It was a peculiar thing to do, wasn't it, Miss Jocelyn? But then, what hurt me still more was that when the time came for it he should get the Canon to say it was too late for it. We know what the Canon is, such a perfect gentleman in all his ways, so it wouldn't be like him to say such a thing. It was Mr Clarkson pushing himself forward. I didn't say a word – I'm sure you know I wouldn't – but the way he came up to me. "We all think the Canon's rather tired, so we'd better cut the proceedings a bit short and miss out your song." I just said, "I'm afraid there'll be a good deal of disappointment, Mr Clarkson, but every one must do as they think right." You were poorly, you know, Miss Jocelyn; you had one of your dreadful colds, but I said at the time, "If Miss Jocelyn was here it wouldn't have happened, because she is so broad-minded," and I always meant to tell you, for I knew you would see my point of view.'

Miss Gage was little qualified to be a diverter of thoughts. Mary's mind could not but wander, but she was always ready when she was wanted with, 'Yes, but I don't think he *really* meant it.'

Between tea and dinner were the special hours she had devoted to reverie. It had become like a drug; her ennui at everything else was almost unendurable.

> Refrain tonight
> And that shall lend a kind of easiness
> To the next abstinence.

She hoped this might be the case with her. She was ashamed to find that what calmed her most just now was not prayer, but patience. She played patience till her hands were too tired to hold the cards, and her eyes too tired to see them.

She asked one of the farmer's daughters to bicycle with her and come back to tea. Her activity in sending invitations and paying calls would cause widespread comment. She abandoned Gibbon and read Trollope. She did not exactly wish it had been possible to exchange her father for Trollope, but she felt if he had been more like him he might have had more mercy, more understanding.

There was a moment in the twenty-four hours which carried her through; it was when she mentioned Mr Herbert in her prayers. She found she counted the minutes to half-past ten, and devised excuses for going to bed early. Thereupon Reason and Duty bade her give up praying for him; she did.

Some talkative and at the same time interesting visitor to stay would have best helped her. Who was she to have? Aunt Lottie was talkative but she missed the other qualification. Bustling Cousin Maria rubbed all the household up the wrong way. Canon Jocelyn did not like visitors, except Dora. He would draw his daughter aside after the first two days with, 'Do you know how much longer your aunt will be staying with us?' They had some infirm, poverty-stricken, elderly pensioners who came now and then. Mary seized the opportunity to despatch two of them one after another – Mrs Plumtree, the widow at Shepherd's Bush, and one still humbler, Miss Davey.

By all the laws of logic, a deaf, crippled, ugly spinster, racked with rheumatism, should have been dejected, but life being para-doxical, Miss Davey was, instead, almost too cheerful. Seated close to the window, facing their uneventful lane, she derived endless amusement and subjects for chat from what she saw.

'Who can *that* be coming down the road? Why, it's the pretty little girl with the dark curls we saw yesterday when the Canon took me out a little walk – your dear father. Oh no, it's not; now she comes nearer I see it's *not* the little girl with the dark curls. My sight isn't quite as good as it was. No, she has red hair and spectacles. Dear me, *what* a plain little thing. Did you say she would be calling for the milk, dear? Or is this the little one you say helps Cook? Oh no, not that one, only ten; no, she would be rather young. Yes, *what* the girls are coming to. You say you don't find a difficulty. Mrs Barkham – my new lodgings; I told you about her, poor thing, she suffers so from neuralgia – she says the girls now – fancy her last girl wearing a pendant when she was waiting. Just a very plain brooch, no one would say a word against, costing half-a-crown or two shillings. I've given one myself to a servant many a time. Oh, that dear little robin – Mary, you *must* look – or is it a thrush? There, it's gone. You've missed it. Perhaps we could see it out of the other window. Thank you, dear; if I could have your arm. Oh, I didn't see the footstool. No, thank you, I didn't hurt myself *in the least*; only that was my rheumatic elbow.'

It tired Mary out transferring Miss Davey to different coigns of vantage, and steer as one might, Miss Davey in her energy for exploring always fell against something.

Mrs Plumtree was higher in the social scale, and pretended to wider interests. She talked to Canon Jocelyn at dinner about politics. She did not care for them, but felt it her duty as a guest to talk about what would interest her host. She bored him terribly. Her poverty forbade him to snub her. If the Archdeacon had said what she said he would have fared badly.

Mrs Plumtree did not like games; she said plainly they were a waste of time. Miss Davey liked them if dear Mary liked them; but she could not tell the difference between clubs and spades, so that anything beyond beggar-my-neighbour was a strain. Mary would not resort to it till she felt something must snap inside her if Miss Davey did not stop talking. There were times alone in her bedroom when she could hardly tear herself from her moment's respite to face the six hours of chat which lay between her and bed. She would go downstairs, and the effort was easier; the hours passed quicker than she imagined. At any rate, beggar-my-neighbour broke the six hours, so did their music, each more stumbling than the other. Mary preferred the virgin soil of no culture to the half-tilled field of Mrs Plumtree; but Mrs Plumtree's anti-ritualist society gave her more occupations in the morning.

Both thanked her with tearful voices when they left. She might feel she had made two harmless people happy for a month. She recognized that the ceaseless conversation was their means – almost their only means – of returning hospitality. It was, too, the bulwark they put up to hide their loneliness from the world. Such loneliness would probably be her lot. Would she be like them?

> Ready to give thanks and live
> On the least that Heaven may give?

She hoped so, and shuddered at the hope.

The days passed somehow, though she thought certain afternoons, when she was in bed with mild influenza, never would come to an end. One was a Thursday; on that very Thursday Mr

Herbert called. She had been fractiously insisting she must get up; she was so tired of being ill. She heard his voice; her heart leapt; she went back to bed. Emma came to say, 'I've just taken in tea, and the Canon hopes you will be coming down.' She said, 'Tell him I am very sorry I am not so well.' Canon Jocelyn was fussed at managing a teapot, and sent a second message; she refused.

She was up, but still feeble, when her father was asked by the Archdeacon to make a Lenten address at Yeabsley on whatever subject he chose. In spite of his contempt for the Archdeacon, he was gratified.

On the morning of the meeting he lost the address. Hours of agitation followed. He could not speak extempore. Writing, though he wrote as well as ever, had grown laborious to him. As he became more distracted, the weakness and querulousness of age were apparent. The prospect, which sometimes terrified Mary, that his mind would go, seemed perceptibly nearer. Something began thumping inside her; she became burning hot. The terror passed. She was able to soothe him and pursue the search, though she felt as if her own faculties would be the next to fail. The servants shared in the incapacity and despair. At last the paper was found; they could set off. They were lunching with the Archdeacon. The harshness of his tones were magnified to Canon Jocelyn by his deafness. Mary strove, not always successfully, to keep him from piercing the thick skin of his host with the needle of his sarcasm, or from sinking into himself, crouching up and hardly answering, as if his keen faculties were asleep. She knew she was irritating him by aggressive cheerfulness. When she was younger he had called it boisterous. She was not, and never had been boisterous, but it was unnatural.

Canon Jocelyn had looked forward to the gathering. While affecting contempt for the present generation, he could not altogether reconcile himself to being unwanted by it. He had, as was habitual to him, taken the utmost pains with his address. The Parish Hall was sparsley scattered with elderly ladies – the bulwarks of all meetings, orthodox or unorthodox. Mary felt tears spring to her eyes. She was disappointed for herself, and she read the mortification in his heart as if it were her own. She remembered how he had spoken of himself to Mr Herbert as a cumberer of the ground.

Mrs James, a clergyman's widow, came up afterwards and shouted sympathy. 'How d'you do, Canon Jocelyn. How d'you do, my dear. What a wretched attendance. When I heard there was to be so few I felt I must come, though my lumbago is bothering me dreadfully, and I can't hear a word your dear father says, and we had such numbers last time. It's most disappointing.'

She saw her father flush the feeble flush of age as he bowed his acknowledgements. Nor were the Archdeacon's apologies happier. 'That was a magnificent thing, Canon, packed with learning. You ought to make your father publish it, but I'm afraid the subject put our people off. They're not quite learned enough for Tertullian, and I say we spoil 'em a little with lantern and cinema shows. We had a big missionary rally last week, and the lads said it was as good as the Elite picture-house at Cayley.'

Canon Jocelyn wreaked his irritation, and punished her cheerfulness, by contradicting most of Mary's timid statements during the drive home. They were old remarks, which she had often made because he liked them. He was very weary when he got back, but he would not, of course, give up or shorten evensong. She knew he would be vexed if she sat down during the service, but the influenza and the strain of these last weeks had made her often feel as if her legs must give way under her. She envied the wonderful frame, which even in its decline could so easily tire her out.

She went up to her room after service with every nerve on edge. She flung herself on the bed sobbing, 'I can't bear it. If only the door had never been unlocked. I was contented before, at any rate I had accepted my lot. Now I have seen what happiness can be, and I am *never* to have any more.' She sprang up, went to the box, and began rummaging to get the letter.

The gong rang for dinner. Her father hated unpunctuality, and she went downstairs. He was still snubbing at dinner. She began to be sure – she had often suspected it – that, far from comforting, she wearied him, wearied him more than she used to do; she would weary him still more. Her head burned with nervous fear; she felt she could bear it no longer.

Suddenly, for no reason, she was quite happy. She felt her lips breaking into smiles. From a child she had been occasionally seized with what she used to call 'transports of bliss.' They were a counterbalance to her depression. 'Thou shalt also light my candle; the Lord God shall make my darkness to be light.' The words flashed through her mind, and at the same moment the candle went out. But by its light she had become tranquil and able to look at the present with common sense, and leave the future to itself. She owned, when she did so, that her father's irritability, which had sometimes made her almost hopeless, was less, not more; he was growing gentler.

It could not be expected from one of his generation that he would apologize; but he was sorry, and the happy circumstance of his gammoning her three times running made him say pleasantly, 'No one ought to be as unlucky as you, my dear.' Half an hour earlier she could have echoed in the bitterness of her heart, 'No indeed.' She did not feel herself specially unlucky now.

Next day Emma had one of her attacks, about which she always enjoyed consulting Dr King. Her business disposed of with the attention due to the Rectory parlourmaid, he turned to Mary, saying, 'You don't look up to the mark. What have you been doing to yourself?' It was a relief when, on examination, he declared she ought to have a change immediately. 'Go to a bright sunny place, and see plenty of fresh people.'

He made a point of speaking to her father and frightening him about Mary. He and his wife thought of Canon Jocelyn as an ogre father, battening on his daughter's vitality. If Mary had known how much conversation was spent in pitying her, she would have felt much less benevolent towards her neighbours.

When Mary next saw her father he was off his pinnacle, a little fussy and muddled with anxiety. 'Fred had better go over to Cayley *at once* for your prescription,' said he. Fred had been gardener's boy ten years before. 'Or did not some one say Fred had sprained his ankle? What are we to do? I don't quite see what is to be done.'

'Dr King is sending up my medicine this afternoon, Father, thank you, so that there will be no difficulty about that.'

138

'You are sure that will be in time enough? You are not ill, Mary, are you? Why did you not tell me?'

'Oh, not ill in the least, only –' She hesitated. She knew it would not do to say, 'Only one gets run down in the spring,' because he hated any weather, particularly mild weather, upsetting anybody, or 'only influenza,' because there was no such thing as influenza, though affected people pretended there was. 'Only that little cough I had left me rather weak.'

'That cough, yes, I remember your cough. Stay away till you are quite well. Cook and Emma will take very good care of everything.'

His affectionate smile warmed her; for the first time since Mr Herbert's kiss she felt that she might be happy again in her ordinary life.

18

Now was the time to pay that long-promised visit to the Redlands. She wrote proposing herself. An enthusiastic letter from Mildred welcomed her. 'Dora, unluckily, is still away,' ran the letter, 'for,' with the slight note of pity the robust spinster sister feels for the helpless married, 'poor Gertrude is expecting again, so Dora will look after things generally as long as she is wanted. We don't know when we shall get her back.'

To miss Dora was a disappointment, but also a relief.

The little house at Southsea was a hive of good works. Each of the three daughters was busy over something. Linda, a middle one, had, in addition, the charge of 'dear mother' – not an onerous charge. She had always been the placidest, most good-tempered woman; now, in old age, placidity was passing into drowsiness. She smiled as sweetly as ever, and Mary could not but admire the way in which she was content to live in a fuss. Lunch was always late for somebody, tea always early, dinner always turning into cocoa and buttered eggs, because they had to scramble off to a meeting. What were still called 'the girls' were hearty and affectionate, offering cups of tea and hot-water bottles, and Mary was to put her feet up all day long if she liked, though they never put theirs up themselves. And Mildred, the youngest, *made* time by getting up early to take Mary a walk by the sea every morning. Though the household was so busy, there was one place in which it appeared no one did anything. That was the drawing-room. Apparently the main idea in its arrangement – the pictures, sofa, cushions, little tables, ornaments – was to form pyramids and circles, and combinations of pyramids and circles. Implements for all employment were hidden away. It looked a kind of temple dedicated to boredom. But no one was ever bored there. If it was a temple, it was a temple to birthdays and sales of work. Every year there were sales, and all the sisters went to buy presents for each other and dear mother, and out of pity chose the fancy objects that were hanging fire. There were, therefore, all sorts of pieces of needlework, bags, mats, cushions, chairbacks of pink, green, and mauve, faded into greyish-brown by continual washing. The Redlands deserted nothing that was down in the world, not even an antimacassar. There were photographs of cheerful, plain, like-minded friends, and those large portraits of ladies in court-dress, which somehow find their way into many villa drawing-rooms. As to the books, numbers of Christmas anthologies, gems from Wordsworth, Tennyson, Longfellow, Browning, Whittier, Ella Wheeler Wilcox, and Matthew Arnold (with all the doubts expurgated) were planted about in miniature shelves, whose manufacture had been just up to the level of deserving cripple lads. They had little skimpy, home-made curtains hung over them, for Mrs Redland had a feeling against books in the drawing-room. It was odd to think that such a room should be the deliberate choice of people as easy and cheerful as the Redlands.

The evenings, what there were left over from meetings, were always spent there, when four pairs of hands made articles for future bazaars. The fifth member of the party read aloud a novel from the library. As a treat for Mary they read *Bleak House*, and as a treat for Linda they read *The First Violin*; they classed them together as the same sort of book. Linda and Mary were good-humouredly laughed at for liking '*old* books' they had read as school-girls. 'You two are so sentimental.' It seemed there was thought to be an added intellectual aroma in what was new. Here they resembled Brynhilda's set. Mary, on her side, wondered at their taste. Anything did that the girl at the library gave them as long as it was not indecent – they would have hated that – but the American sentiment and the vulgarity! And they in themselves were the absolute reverse of vulgar. Their books seemed as unlike them as their drawing-room. They were ready to take things as they found them; they liked what people round them liked, whereas Mary thought out her own opinions. She might have been happier if she had not. She would have had more in common with her generation.

Mary was vexed that after joining energetically in the hum of life all the first week, the stuffy, noisy clubs and the stuffy, fervent meetings made her head in a whirl. The whirl ended one day in a fainting fit. The doctor had to be called in. He told her to take a fortnight in bed. She would not trespass on her friends' kindness by standing out and making a fuss, though she dreaded rest, for she still dreaded thought. She went to bed, and was surprised to find that she dozed most of the day and slept all night. She was thankful for the peace. Frances nursed her, and nothing pleased her more than plying an invalid with beaten-up egg and glasses of hot milk. Mrs Redland, too, liked stumping heavily upstairs and fussing over Mary. Her bedside tales were of kind landladies, grateful parishioners, devoted cooks. If her mind had not been so sleepy, Mary might have preferred now and then as a treat a tale of moral failure; it was almost too treacly. But Mrs Redland never seemed to have encountered anybody ungrateful or malicious. If they had been once, it was only that their eventual goodness might glow more richly. It was comforting to find this the verdict of a long life. If it was the haziness of old age, might it not be the haziness of a sweet September afternoon, when the sun is shining behind?

When she was allowed to get up, Mary was not yet considered strong enough for meetings; she had to own that she was still very languid. But she could be busy in many other ways. She could take round reports or send them off by post, remind dilatory subscribers of their shillings, prepare garments under Mildred's supervision for the working parties and girls' clubs, number tickets, make lists, enter things on different pages, all cherished occupations of the middle-aged, but *not* copy the text of the sermon into a little black book, or wind skeins of wool, or read aloud from the *Daily Mail* the movements of what newspapers call the 'well known' and the headlines in order of size. These were Mrs Redland's duties, which none in that affectionate household could have borne to take from her.

Mary liked the whole family. If there was a 'but,' a something she wished otherwise, it was that they would not contradict one another, particularly all at once and about such trifles. The hubbub was sometimes bewildering to one accustomed to stillness. She hardly ever contradicted at home, unless goaded past bearing; when she disagreed, she disagreed as sweetly as if she agreed. She knew it was foolish to mind – contradiction was nothing to them; no trace of huffiness entered in. In the height of vociferation they said in the same loud, sure voice, 'Oh, of course it *was* the 12th, not the 14th.'

They all had their jokes against Ella – not good ones. Neither they nor Ella saw that her and their various forms of activity were manifestations of the same spirit – the wonderful desire which is so strong in English spinsters to serve, to help, to be perhaps almost too busy in other people's affairs.

Mary and Mildred had many talks – not interesting talks, which was all the more restful for Mary.

One day Mildred remarked, 'Our nephew and nieces always seem to have something the matter with them. Poor Gertrude, she has rather a poor time. Walter is so selfish. I suppose husbands generally are, but then perhaps I don't do men justice. I have never wanted to marry at all. I shouldn't think Linda or Frances did either, only I never happened to ask them. Dora at one time was rather taken up with your brother Will, I think, but it never came to anything.'

Mary wondered at the isolation in which even sisters can live together. 'Life gets fuller and happier every year, don't you find?' Mildred continued, 'and one does *love* the kiddies so.'

Mary had never felt at all as Mildred did, though she had often envied her comfortableness when she had seen her in girlhood and womanhood. Now there seemed a barrier between them. Her experience gave her – she hated herself for it – a tinge of superiority. It would have been inexplicable to Mildred. Some people might have thought the Redlands' active contentment a pose, or abnormal, but one only had to look at Mildred's clear eyes and round, rosy cheeks to see that she was a lay nun, a wholesome, though not very luscious apple. She was more pleased to love and be useful to other people's children than to have them of her own. She was of those whose friends, or still more fellow-workers, find it necessary to get into corners, and whisper, 'If only she would not be so –' But the difficult things were left for her to do.

Unmarried women often look on men with idealizing romance. The Redlands had, not a low, but a poor opinion of them as incapable, forgetful, tactless, capricious – rather the view of the Cranford ladies. They did not care for men's society. This was fortunate, for, as is usual with spinster households, they saw few. Mrs Redland's verdict was more lenient, so was Ella's. She liked men and wished to penetrate into their domain; the sisters were content to remain as they were. A source of friction on Ella's holiday was her desire to ask men to tea, when the sisters desired to be left to the less taxing society of their own sex.

None of them had the power or wished to enter into the inner mind of themselves or other people. For this Mary was thankful. She existed for them still as the quiet, slightly queer, little Mary Jocelyn they had known so many years ago. They just remembered Dora had mentioned Mary writing a book, and Mildred, the greatest joker, called her Mrs Humphrey Ward once or twice. They did not want to know about her affairs. 'How is your father?' Mrs Redland said the first evening. 'Dora gave us such a nice account of him when she stayed with you. How good he was to my dear husband.'

'Yes, how is the dear old man?' said the daughters, who had a cordial respect for the older generation. Mrs Redland often said, 'Please give your father my kindest, my very kindest regards when you write.'

'And how are the boys?' said Mildred. 'The men, I ought to say. What glorious games of cricket we had with them.'

Otherwise it was talk of classes, cases, and clubs the whole day long.

Mary could not tell why the sharing in their busy, concentrated, narrow present cheered her so much. She felt as if it were the Redlands, not the air, that helped her. She gave them all grateful kisses when she left, to Mildred the warmest of all. Home had recovered its value. She was now not merely ready, but eager to begin her old life – the life before she met Mr Herbert.

The Redlands talked her over; they recognized a certain change.

'Mary Jocelyn is *very* nice, and she has lost that abrupt manner she had when she was a little girl. She has not much in her, but she is just the person for a clergyman's daughter in the country. The Girls' Club was a little much for her.'

19

How fared it meanwhile with Mr Herbert? After he had written his letter to Mary he awaited the answer with uncontrollable excitement. He tore it open; he read it through twice, and put it back in the envelope. He had not expected more. She would not have been the Mary he loved if she had written more. He did not know what he wanted, but if there could have been a word of forgiveness – of understanding – no, he would not even to himself desire it – of longing. But the restlessness to know, to hear more of her was unendurable. If he could see her for one second he would be satisfied. He supposed she despised him beyond forgiveness; he deserved it. She could not despise him more than he despised himself.

In this seething agitation he must write to Kathy. He had determined that it should not be put off a day longer. The task seemed more distasteful than ever. He forced himself to go to his drawer and take out Kathy's love letters. There were not many, the engagement had been so short, and at her most emotional she was halting with a pen.

There was one in answer to his first, written after he came home to Lanchester, mad with joy.

144

'I loved your letter. It *was* idiotic, the most idiotic ever written, I should think. Some day you'll find me out, and then there'll be a drop, and you'll be awfully disappointed. You really had better understand, once for all, I'm *absolutely nothing at all*. Now I've warned you. It won't be my fault.'

He gazed at her radiant photograph, the one he had shown Mary – it stood unnoticed on his study table. He remembered her face at the station. As she had said, it was not her fault, it was all his own. This did not make him love her the more.

As for going out to the Riviera now to restrain Kathy with the thought of his and Mary's kiss weighing on him, he *could* not do it. Nor would he persuade Kathy to come back from pity for his accident. He did not mention it.

But he would do his best. With untold toil he wrote the following: 'The garden and the dogs and cats and Taffy, who would like to take you out hunting, are all asking me when you are coming back. When you do, I will try to make you happier. You have a great deal to forgive. Will you bear with me and let me try to make amends?' When he had written this he felt himself a hypocrite and a scoundrel.

The letter did not have a favourable result. Kathy flushed deeply, as she read it, and threw it over to Lesbia. 'It's awfully flattering to know one's wanted so much,' said she.

'You won't go back, Kathy, will you? It would be frightfully unsporting to throw up your part in the tableaux, not to mention Captain Stokes.'

'No fear, I'm certainly going to stay, only I think husbands are so ripping.'

'Well, my dear child, I did tell you, didn't I? He never was meant for you. You and a padre, it was too priceless.'

Kathy might have said, 'What about Jack being the man for you?' but she would not hit Lesbia's sore spot. 'Nobody's the man for anybody, or the woman for anybody,' said she. 'That's all it comes to. Such is life. It's *le vie*, as that Russian of yours with the infernal scent says. Let's have an ice.'

When they had finished, she went to the hotel, and dashed off the following letter to Mr Herbert:

My Dear Boy – Sorry no prospect of return. Kiss the beasts for me. No need to blame yourself. I'm not cut out for a parson's wife; that's the little difficulty. What I'm cut out for is Monte. So long.   K.

When she had torn Mr Herbert's letter into small fragments and hurled them out of window, she felt relieved. She went downstairs and screamed 'Monte for ever and ever,' rejoicing the heart of a crowd which had been discomposed at her naughty husband wanting her back.

She talked to some Frenchmen very fast and loud, and laughed more than was natural to her. They were fascinated, but thought her *bien Anglaise*, by which they meant outrageously noisy. And she was *bien Anglaise*, though not in their sense. She was suited to her own country and county, and everything in the anglicized cosmopolitan hotel was alien to her, except the food.

The gay brilliance of the landscape, the beauty of its outlines were wasted on her. She was fond of saying, 'I can't be bothered with scenery,' but she loved twilight falling over the English fields, on the way back from hunting. It was connected in her mind with much she could not put into words. Such a twilight might have comforted her a little; the hard flaring sun and sea of the south were pitiless. How *could* she have shown his letter to Lesbia? She did not cry to relieve herself, as Mary might have done. She sat on a hard chair, dug her feet into the floor, and ground her teeth, ejaculating under her breath, for fear Lesbia or Mansfield might overhear, coming to the door, 'You cad, you cad, you ass, you cad.'

She had often felt homesick, and had exclaimed, 'Wasting all the best weeks of the year in this dusty hole.' But now homesickness bound her down to the earth. She longed for small things – Bimbo's licks, Taffy's kisses; she longed for a cloudy sky and the meets. And her husband, if she could have recovered even one moment of what it had been in her first year of marriage! But that would never come back; now most certainly she knew it could never come back.

Her letters and others similar, written at long intervals, made it still harder for Mr Herbert not to think of Mary. He did not waste hours dreaming of her, he did his utmost not to think of her at all, but he lost his temper, and quarrelled with his churchwardens and brother clergy. He became a nuisance, and made difficulties in parish business; he did not smile on the children – that very sweet smile which lighted up his grave face. Superior members of the congregation murmured to one another, 'How depressing the vicar was this morning again.' He did not neglect his duties, but his flock saw the heart was wanting. His sciatica continued violent; his cook wrote privately to old Mrs Herbert asking her to come.

'But why is Katherine not with you?' demanded the old lady, pink with indignation at Kathy's modern behaviour.

'She is not with me,' replied Mr Herbert, 'because it is her obvious duty to remain with her sister-in-law, whose health makes it necessary for her to winter in the Riviera.'

'And what about your health, Robert?'

'Oh, mine. Oh, a touch of sciatica shows a healthy system. No one ever dies of sciatica.'

In his heart he said, 'I wish they did.'

'I think it is most remiss of Katherine,' said Mrs Herbert, looking at the photograph of Kathy as a sparsely-clothed Diana at a fancy ball. Kathy had sent it on purpose to annoy him that morning. 'And she has time for all sorts of very uncomfortable amusements, I see.'

'If Kathy and I are satisfied that her duty lies with her sister-in-law, surely that is sufficient. Kathy does not know of my sciatica, because I have not mentioned the fact to her, neither, I hope, will you. I shall be perfectly right in a few days. I have never been able to see that lamentations do any good to anybody, and I should be very much obliged if we could change the subject. For-give my saying it, Mother, but the affair has nothing whatever to do with you.'

He had never spoken so roughly to her; she trembled. Of course she knew Kathy's duty was a fiction, he did not desire to deceive her. But what was he to tell her? He was the one to blame in the marriage. But Mrs Herbert, both as mother and woman, would lay all on the wife. He would be the victim, unless he told of Mary, and that would break his mother's heart – a tough heart, but it could not have stood that.

He dreaded Kathy's return above all things, but he was

aggrieved that she would not come back, and he felt as sore at the photograph as Kathy hoped he would.

Mrs Herbert tried no more expostulation, but she wrote a letter to Kathy that night. Kathy read no more than the first sentence, made a face, and threw the letter away.

'I wish we could hear that Mrs Hollings was stronger,' said old Mrs Herbert to Dennis the parlour-maid. 'Mrs Herbert doesn't like to leave her, and the winds are very treacherous here still.'

'So they are, 'm. Anybody ought to be very careful, but I'm sorry Mrs Hollings isn't getting on.'

Thus spoke Dennis, in deferential commiseration. Mrs Herbert considered servants very worthy people, always to be treated as children. Information might be infinitely cooked for them, especially of course discreditable information about the family. But Dennis knew much more than Mrs Herbert, for she had a letter from Mansfield in her pocket.

The style was modelled on the ladies' papers and Kathy's conversation. Mansfield had a passion for Kathy.

Dear Little Densykensy – I am having the time of my life here, or would have written before. Everything is a rush, so I haven't had any old time. Poor old Lanchester, it seems *too* funny to think of it. We had a fancy dress dance at our hotel on Wednesday. Some of the dresses were the limit, but she looked a dream. She really is a darling. She has given me that awfully smart navy costume of hers with the gold buttons, and I look rather fetching in it. You always say your Babs has a good opinion of herself. We are a jolly crowd at the valets' table. I don't like the French girls; they're very fast to my mind, but there's an Italian, the chauffeur of an American millionaire, well, *billionaire*, they say, who's a duck. The Cat (Lesbia) is as nosey as ever, but I pay no attention to her; I can't bear her style. I suppose he's as grumpy as usual. All the men here rave about her, particularly one. Kisses from

BABS.

In Mrs Herbert's experience servants' letters were grammatically incorrect, but irreproachably respectful. She had not conceived of their writing any others.

Lesbia had a little regretted her letter to Crab. Above all things, she wanted to stay on with Kathy to the end of the season. She wrote again to Mr Herbert, describing Kathy's passion for a motor-bicycle. Mr Herbert, absorbed in his own difficult concerns, hardly noticed the letter. Kathy made no more references to Captain Stokes. What had been less than nothing when she wrote to Mr Herbert was now occupying her mind seriously.

Captain Stokes was rather worthless, one could see it in his expression. He would have repelled Mary, but was the perfect exemplar of what Kathy liked in masculine appearance. As she was the cynosure of the men's eyes that season, he was the cynosure of the women's. Each was gratified by the admiration of the other.

Kathy had more than once received compromising overtures from men. Mary imagined that there was a ring fence round wives, that they never heard love mentioned except by their husbands. Kathy had checked aspirants with a withering 'Thanks awfully, but I'm not taking any.' These overtures had neither repelled nor flattered her; she merely reflected, 'Some men are like that.'

When Captain Stokes came with his overtures, he received at first the same answer. He persisted; she could easily have daunted his persistency, but after Mr Herbert's letter she had begun to wonder. He wanted to be her secret lover. To that she would never consent, but at length he found she might be persuaded to leave her husband openly and go away with him. He said he was mad about her, but he was calm enough at times to remember that he had no private income. If they went away together, his career in the army would be ruined. At the same time, he wanted her so much that if those were the only terms on which he could have her, he would risk all. He loved her so far as he cared for anybody, but the excitement of subduing the impregnable fortress others were attacking in vain, counted perhaps for more than his love.

At length she answered, 'I don't know, perhaps.' She never loved him, but was very much attracted to him; she thought that he loved her. At times she felt she preferred his love to Mr Herbert's indifference.

'Look here,' said he one day to a friend, Captain Battiscombe,

149

to whom he had confided the excitement of the chase. 'Congratulations.' He threw him a note from Kathy. Captain Battiscombe read, 'All right, I don't mind. – KATHY.'

'I call it rather a freezing way of welcoming your passion,' said he. He was a lazy, clever man, who bore with Captain Stokes because they had known one another all their lives. 'Of course she may resemble the working-classes. I believe it's their most eager form of acceptance.'

'That's Kath all over; she never gushes.'

'Well, I hope when my time comes, whoever it is will be more cordial.'

'Oh, she'll warm up all right.'

'I'm not so sure. Excuse pushing in – I haven't personal experience of these affairs – but I think one wants a woman to be more demonstrative in your line of business than in an ordinary engagement. On the whole, she gains in an engagement, but here she gets nothing but you – no offence, you're a prize, of course – and loses a good deal.'

'Kathy's cold. You can't alter nature.'

'You don't think she's taking you out of pique? I believe she's still hankering after that parson husband. I heard her downing Lesbia one day, when she was attacking the husband, and it wasn't promising for you. Why not go in for Lesbia? She's quite good-looking, and her heart – what there is of it – is to let.'

'I don't want Lesbia,' said Captain Stokes sulkily. 'Who would?' He went on more complacently, 'Of course you don't know Kath. She's not much of a hand at letters, nor am I, but she can be all right when she likes.'

Kathy was sometimes stony, sometimes recklessly inviting. If she had cold fits, so had he. When they definitely decided to go away together, he had more than she. Once they postponed the day. They had meant to tell no one, but Lesbia could always scent out news. She persuaded Kathy to confide in her; then every one knew.

Kathy's mind was distracted at the time with another matter. She had a swelling in her mouth. With the terror of some one who does not know what it is to be ill, she thought it was cancer. It deadened her longing for Mr Herbert and her delight in Captain

Stokes. She told no one. After days of anxiety, she at last went for advice to a shark-like Dr Lovat, the smartest and most expensive of the cosmopolitan doctors that frequented the big hotels. He declared she must have an immediate operation. 'There is nothing whatever to be alarmed about, but there is a small local trouble, which we had better dispose of now, and then you'll have no more bother with it. I'll get you into a pleasant Nursing Home, which I find my patients are rather enthusiastic about. It will be a matter of three or four days or a week at most – quite a trifling thing.'

She and Captain Stokes raged with annoyance to one another. But both were relieved that the plan was again put off. They had a loving scene together before Kathy went to the home.

What the local paper called 'Mrs Herbert's hosts of friends' were assured by the bulletin that 'The operation has been entirely successful. Progress satisfactory.'

But the second most expensive doctor, who had assisted at the operation, remarked to his confrère, 'You've made a most infernal bungle of it, and I don't quite see how you're going to bluff it myself.'

'I should like you to prepare the way tomorrow,' said Dr Lovat to the fashionable nurse. 'You will be careful to keep the atmosphere cheery and optimistic. I shall be coming rather later than usual.'

'You're getting on so splendidly, Mrs Herbert,' said Nurse next day with her smart drawl, 'that I believe I'm going to let you do your own hair. I'm on strike. Of course,' she added, as she brought the hand glass, 'you mustn't be surprised after an operation of this sort – it often happens that – I mean people look rather different at first, just at first, till the muscles settle down. It's nothing to worry about a bit.'

Though she said it was nothing to worry about, she felt her heart beating as she spoke. She nodded reassuringly and withdrew.

When Kathy looked at herself in the glass, she found her mouth was all twisted to one side. She could not believe her eyes. She tried to force her lips straight again and again and again – in vain. Then she ceased her efforts. She felt herself become very cold;

151

she lay quite still, and made no sound. She had not even exclaimed when she first saw her reflection. For one thing she must
be thankful, she had been left to face the shock alone. Nurse
meanwhile listened trembling outside the door. After a discreet
interval she knocked gently. 'I've brought you just a little egg and
brandy, Mrs Herbert; I want you to toss it off.'

'Oh, certainly,' said Kathy. 'I love tippling. Only, why just
now? Is it supposed I shall faint with horror at the sight of my
beautiful face?'

'I know it's a most awful, terrible shock, dawling,' said Nurse,
not looking at Kathy. 'But of course it's very early days yet. The
muscles must settle down – they had to be pulled about during
your op., and really doctors can do anything nowadays.'

'Just bring the rouge here, would you, Nurse?' said Kathy.
With her peerless complexion she had always scorned cosmetics,
but Mansfield could not have held up her head before the other
maids, if her 'lady' had not had all the latest preparations on her
toilet table. Kathy wanted rouge in a desperate attempt to ward
off the doctor's pity.

'I know what you mean,' said Nurse effusively, thankful to have
skated past the terrible topic. 'I always think it's *such* a nice idea
to put a teeny touch on for the doctor. And let me sprinkle your
hanky with that lovely *rose d'amour* Mrs Van Vorst sent you
yesterday. They say it's simply "it" in Paris. All the nice people
are using nothing else.'

'Oh, Lord, no,' said Kathy. 'I hate stinks. You can keep it,
Nurse, if you like, only don't put it on when you come near me.'

'Oh, ta,' said Nurse. 'Now let me make your bed comfy, and
draw the blinds, shall I, and see if you can get a nice little rest
before Dr Lovat comes.'

Kathy got no rest. She lay with her eyes wide open, staring at
the cerise and grey eiderdown, English comfort was the note of the
Nursing Home. She was buoyant by nature, but now she had
little hope.

Dr Lovat looked more sleekly spruce and omnipotent than
ever as he sat by her bedside.

'Now, I'm going to have a little talk with you, Mrs Herbert.
Nurse, I shan't want you just now. I should like to tell you per-

fectly plainly about your operation. It has succeeded magnificently. I think we both feel – Dr Harding and I – that what we wanted done couldn't have been done more thoroughly. But here you must follow me closely; there are certain other consequences, which have not been so favourable. This is not what we call a major operation, we apply that term to the abdominal operations, but it's a tiresome business, very, very tricky. There are always risks attending it.'

'I thought you said it was a little one, and there was nothing to bother about.'

'There was absolutely no danger to life, but it was what I might call a big adventure, and in my opinion all the risks of the big adventure must be borne by the doctor. It must be sunshine and hope for the patient always. Now in a percentages of cases these severances of the muscles do occasionally take place. There is a most complicated network of the nerves and muscles in the particular part we were dealing with, I wish I could explain it to you more fully, but it is too long today. In spite of the greatest care a disturbance of Nature's equilibrium sometimes occurs, and the delicate balance may be destroyed.'

'It often happens, then?'

'Not infrequently.'

'Will it get right?'

'Nature has very wonderful recuperative powers, Mrs Herbert,' said he, shunting on to Nature what Nurse had shunted on to doctors. 'I should advise doing nothing at all for the present. Leave it to her. Later you might consult my friend Dr Warden, he's a very rising Harley Street man.'

'Has anybody ever got well?'

'I think we can hardly look for entire cure.'

'I see.'

He did not notice the pause before Kathy spoke again. She was steeling herself to show nothing in his presence. He was occupied in earnest hope that his explanation might bamboozle her. 'How soon can I travel? I'm due back home.'

He was posted in the gossip of the English set, and had known the very hour Kathy was to have gone with Captain Stokes.

'Of course you must be anxious to be at home. And I want to

get you back to the English spring. Spring in the English country, there's absolutely nothing like it, that soft grey sky and the primroses. I always order it for my patients who have had any nervous tension, and the smallest operation is a strain, you must remember that. This air is too bracing, it irritates.'

The English doctors got rid of patients to the Riviera, the Riviera doctors sent the poor shuttlecocks back to England.

'How soon can I start? Thursday or Friday?'

'We mustn't rush things too much; we must get you up and out first of all, but I promise you it shall be as soon as possible.'

He was as anxious as she for her return to England.

'The pulse isn't very satisfactory, Nurse,' said he outside on the landing. 'Of course it's a bad shock for a smart handsome girl like her.'

'I do think she's the most awfully brave woman,' said Nurse. 'She was joking about it the moment after.'

'Yes, she's got no end of grit. Those kind of hunting people have. But I should watch her. Don't leave her too much alone. Those windows are all right, I suppose? She can't open them?'

Kathy did not mean to kill herself; it was against her ideas. But when she was alone, and Nurse out of earshot, she often said to herself, 'God, do let me die.'

Many thoughts surged through her brain. Dr Lovat had, as it were, pronounced sentence of death; so much in life would be gone. Considering her future, she did not see that anything would be left but the bare routine of existing. One thing must be done, and that immediately. All intercourse with Captain Stokes was ended. 'I'm not going to have any one ruin their career for a scarecrow,' she reflected. In the shipwreck of everything she did not know whether Captain Stokes counted for much.

She wrote to him:

Dear Stocky – It's off. I'm going home. I've had the op.; it's been a bit of a frost. I don't think you'd have liked it really. I'm not seeing *any one*, so will say good-bye now. This is the only intimation, as they say about funerals. No flowers, by request. Good luck.

KATHY.

When Captain Stokes read the letter, he felt the one thing in the world he wanted was Kathy. He rushed to the Nursing Home, and bribed and wheedled Nurse to let him see her. His distress moved her more than the bribe. She was afraid of Kathy, and called up all her impudence to announce, 'Here's a particular friend, who simply *will* see you, Mrs Herbert.'

He came in. When he saw her face, the bunch of roses he carried shook violently and almost dropped from his hands.

'Good God', he said, standing and looking in consternation at her, not coming near the bed. He did not know the expression of horror – almost repulsion – which came into his face at sight of her. She saw it, and cried out blackly, 'I told you *not* to come; it's infernal cheek of you. I suppose you bribed that rotten woman.'

'I felt I must come just to – I brought these,' he said, coming nearer and holding out the roses.

'You can take your damned flowers, and as there isn't a fire, you can just throw them out of window. No, there's a catch, and you can't. Give them here.'

She tore them to pieces, scratching her hands with the thorns as she did it.

'I never thought –' he said. 'But you'll be all right soon, Kath.'

'No, I shan't.'

'Go to some first-rate man.'

'What's the use?'

'Is there anything that I can do for you?'

'Nothing I know of, except clear out.'

'You know how awfully I –'

'Oh, *drop* it.'

He was silent; at last he said, 'Then you're going back to England.'

'I told you so in my letter.'

They were silent again. 'I expect that's the best thing to do.'

More silence.

'I should think perhaps it isn't much use my staying any longer,' he said at length.

'I should think perhaps it isn't.'

'Well, good-bye. This is simply too rotten – I had no idea –'

'No, of course you hadn't. Why should you? Good-bye.'

He came near, and bent over the bed to kiss her.

'*No*,' she said passionately, putting up her hands. He went out of the room, glad it was over.

'Nurse,' said Kathy freezingly, 'you can't have understood that I said I would see no one. Please carry out my orders in future. I expect Mrs Hollings tomorrow, and my maid to pack my things the day after. You are not to let any one else up here.'

Kathy kept Lesbia at arm's length also.

'My poor, poor darling thing,' said Lesbia hysterically, sincerely affected. 'What a *ghastly* business.'

'For God's sake, don't *maul* me, Lesbia. You know how I loathe it. And why should I be kissed now, of all times? Yes, it's hopeless, and we won't refer to it again.'

'How perfectly and utterly scandalous, Kath. You really ought to bring an action, and get damages; you oughtn't to pay him a farthing. You know I said all along that Frenchman would have been better. He's so marvellous.'

'He'd have done just the same,' said Kathy fractiously. 'If it's to be, I'd sooner an Englishman did it than a beastly foreigner. Now about plans. I'm going home on Wednesday. I'll come back to the hotel Monday, just to practise walking before the journey. You'll stay on here, I expect?'

'It seems beastly not to go with you, but you know it's the Cotillon at Princess Nicholas's on Wednesday, and the *Tales of Hoffmann* at the Casino. I don't see that I *could* go with you very well.'

'No, of course not.'

'Don't you think you'd better wait? It's soon to travel.'

'I shall be perfectly all right. If I wasn't, it wouldn't matter to me, or you either.'

'Have you written to Captain Stokes, Kathy?' asked Lesbia pryingly.

'Is that any business of yours? Still there's no reason I shouldn't tell you – that's off.'

'Oh, it's off. I wondered.'

When Kathy arrived at the hotel she found Lesbia had decked her room charmingly with bunches of stocks and lilacs. 'Oh, Lesbia,' she cried, 'do clear all that stuff away. The smell's putrid.' And when Lesbia, hovering about, explained that she had arranged for Kathy's meals to be served upstairs, Kathy answered, 'What rot! They'll think I've turned into a lunatic, and you're my keeper. Of course I'm coming down. That's the point of the hotel, otherwise I might have stayed at the Home.'

She faced looks, averted in kindness and embarrassment, sincere and insincere inquiries, and torturing sympathy with unflinching calmness, as well aware, as if it were addressed to her, of the ceaseless gossip going on about herself and her affairs.

It was only with Mansfield she allowed herself the indulgence of breaking down. 'You silly ass,' she said, patting Mansfield's chic shoulder, while tears ran down her own cheeks. 'Do stop, you'll howl the ceiling down.'

In the two days before her journey Kathy and Lesbia quarrelled without ceasing.

'I was wondering, dear,' said Lesbia. 'Don't think me grabbing, but I simply don't know how I shall manage that head-dress without Mansfield. She just makes it "it"; I can't get the line. I don't know what she does, and Myra's woman is quite useless. I wonder if you could leave her behind. It really is a very simple journey, and you seem so awfully well, it's splendid how you've picked up, and I know the Matthesons are going back on Wednesday. They'll take care of you.'

'Protect me from all the Frenchmen who will be so smitten with my charms,' said Kathy bitterly. 'I see. Yes, you can have Mansfield.'

She dreaded the journey inexpressibly, she who had never been afraid of anything. But she would not confess her weakness before Lesbia. She had once or twice in past days, she never would again.

Later she said to Lesbia, 'Sorry you can't have Mansfield. She's sure "Mother wouldn't like her to be with a lady like Mrs Hollings."'

'How can you let her be so impertinent?' said Lesbia crossly.

'She wasn't impertinent, she was most polite, and said, "Excuse me for mentioning it."'

'Such nonsense. Mansfield's quite hot stuff herself. You should see her with all those waiters at the back there.'

'Mansfield can do what she jolly well likes,' said Kathy.

'What Mansfield means I can't think,' said Lesbia. The dart went on rankling. 'It's so outrageous.'

'How *any one* can care what any one else thinks,' said Kathy. 'And what *Mansfield* thinks.'

Her scorn was of a special, most withering quality. It made Lesbia burn with resentment. When the depths of her spite had been stirred, she was capable of anything. 'And what about you?' cried she. 'It wasn't as if it was only Stokes; you know you tried for Reggie and Lord Gresley, only they weren't taking any. Now that I *do* call going the pace. Poor Crab doesn't realize you're only going back because nobody else would have you.'

'What a lot you know, don't you, Lesbia?'

'I consider Crab ought to know.'

'Hadn't you better tell him, then?'

'Look here, Kathy, I'm *not* going to be talked to as if I was dirt.'

Kathy laughed. 'All right, I'll depart, as I don't seem very welcome.'

Lesbia went off and wrote letters abusing Kathy in a frenzy of rage.

Later she came to herself (what self there was to come to) and said, 'I was a pig, Kath; I'm sorry.'

'Oh no, you aren't,' said Kathy indifferently.

The two women had constantly bickered, but not often quarrelled, because of Kathy's good-natured imperturbability. Now Kathy started quarrels; it was the only thing she seemed interested in.

That same evening Kathy said to Lesbia, 'So you've been writing to Crab and Mrs Herbert.'

'How do you know?'

'You know how thick Mansfield is with André. She saw them in the office, of course.'

'Why shouldn't I write? I wanted to tell them how you were getting on.'

'I see, and that's why you get purple in the face when I mention it. You don't go out of your way to write kind letters, do you?'

Lesbia became redder.

'Oh, well,' said Kathy. 'It doesn't matter. Nothing matters that I know of.'

With all the remorse she was capable of Lesbia regretted the letters, but it did not seem possible to write now and unsay all she had said.

Just before Kathy left she gave Lesbia a cheque for £50.

'I shall only want twopence halfpenny for the future, so you may as well have it, and you can play the giddy goat to the end of the season.'

Nothing quelled Lesbia like Kathy's generosity. It did not come from personal love to her. It rather dropped, not like the gentle rain, but like the sturdy shower beneath.

The tension of the two days at the hotel had been almost unendurable for Kathy.

'You are not to come near me the whole night long,' she said to Mansfield, when she had been arranged in her *coupé lit*.

Mansfield heard her sobbing hour after hour, and wept herself in misery. Kathy cried till she was cold almost with the cold of death, and did not reject the hot tea and hot-water bottle Mansfield ventured to bring when the horrible chill dawn was coming. The only thing that supported her through the journey was the prospect of home and Crab. She felt it must be right when she got back; she had no idea why.

But when she reached London, she changed to terror at the thought of meeting him. She wanted to go to her Aunt – to a hotel – back to the Riviera – anything to avoid him. But the same feeling which made her never ride round by the road, or pick out the easiest jumps, forced her to go on to Lanchester.

20

IT was just when Mary was setting out for Southsea that Mr Herbert received Kathy's post card. 'I shall be back some time this week. Don't meet me, for I can't say exactly which day. I'll taxi from the junction.'

She arrived about six on a stormy, snowy evening. In spite of all desire to the contrary Mr Herbert's feeling was one of *ennui*, annoyance, and dread. He heard the motor, and went to meet her. It was an open car, she had not been able to get a taxi. She sprang out, and ran past him. He followed her into the drawing-room. What he could observe of her face – it was muffled in a motor-veil – looked dead white; the jolly, merry expression in her eyes had changed to one almost of despair.

'Take off those wet things down here,' he said, 'and come to the fire. You must be perished with the cold.'

'Oh, I'm all right,' she answered, turning her back on him. 'Bring my things in here, Mansfield. No, you needn't wait. I can manage. Go and get warm.'

He unfastened her coat and took off her boots; she supported herself with her hand on his shoulder, as he did it, but did not look at him.

'Let me find your shoes, where are they?'

'Oh, somewhere; no, not that thing – the little bag, I think.' She knelt down before the fire without saying anything. He brought her shoes and put them on, and then began taking off her veil.

'No, no, don't bother,' she said. 'I'll do that.'

She put up her hand, but before she could stop him he had got the veil off, and her mouth was revealed. She covered her face with her hands, but took them away at once, saying, 'It doesn't matter. You had to know, only I wanted to tell you something before you found out.'

She looked at him, and saw that he had become deadly pale.

'Oh, don't mind it so much,' she cried.

'What was it?' he said breathlessly. 'What has happened?'

'I had an abscess or something, and they said I must have an operation – quite a slight one – and when I came to, I was like this, and the man said there was nothing more to be done.'

'My poor, poor darling,' he cried, seizing her in his arms.

She felt his tears against her cheek.

'There *must* be something to be done,' he said. 'We'll find out who the man is to go to. I'll telephone to Lawes' (a doctor friend of his) 'after tea.'

'I say,' cried she, with a laugh, 'wonders never cease. Crab condescending to telephone. You can't go to Yeabsley' (the nearest telephone) 'in the snow, Billy.'

'I believe I've been out in the snow before,' he said, smiling.

'It's not so bad seeing your ugly smile again,' said she. 'It won't be any good, you know,' she went on, looking at him mournfully.

'Yes, it will,' he said, clasping her closer.

'You *are* so comforting,' she said at last, breaking down and bursting into tears. Then she seemed to regret speaking so warmly, and continued rather drily, gulping her sobs back resolutely. 'It's awfully nice of you. I'm really not worth it all. The worst of it is, it's the only decent thing about me gone.'

He did not know what she said, but she did not mind his not answering.

'Look here,' she said, extricating herself. 'I didn't mean it to be like this. I've got something to tell you, I meant to tell you at once.'

'You're trembling,' he said. 'Wait and have tea, and get warm.'

'Oh, it's not cold, I'm not in the least cold. Have you heard from Lesbia about me?'

'From Lesbia? No.'

'Well, you will. No, don't keep hold of my hand. The thing is, I wasn't coming back. I knew you didn't much care for me, and it was a failure. I was coming back all right first of all, of course. Then there was that letter, I saw *you* didn't want me, whatever the animals did. There was a man out there, who seemed frightfully keen on me, and he asked me to go away with him. I liked him awfully, and I agreed. When I got like this, I wrote to him that it was off. But he would come to the Nursing Home. When he *did* see me, of course I could see in an instant how jolly lucky he felt he was to be out of it. Look here, you've broken great-great-grandmamma's ring, my very best, go-to-meeting ring. It was all right. What else could you expect? Still, I'm glad I didn't go off with him, and when I told Lesbia I was coming home she wrote to you and your mother that I was only doing it because no one else would have me. I thought you'd have got the letter. There, now you know it all. *Oh*, I do so wish I was dead. Nobody can want me. I know *you* don't.' It was the last thing she had meant to reveal to him, but the cry came up from her heart unawares.

He was on his knees before her, and his arms were clasped round her. When he could speak, which was not at once, he begged for her forgiveness again and again. 'It was my fault you went away, everything has been my fault.'

When she could speak, she said, 'Of course it was always you really, but Lesbia kept on saying how you hated me, and I thought you did. Then I thought at the back of my mind *perhaps* in spite of all his beastliness he does care, and you *do*, you *do*.' She gave two sobs of joy.

Their eyes met; her sad, joyful eyes melted to tenderness he had never seen there before. He loved her as he had not loved her even in the first wonderful bliss of their engagement.

'Crab,' she said suddenly, 'this isn't all out of pity?'

At that instant any thought of Mary was blotted out, and he told her how he loved her. 'Every part of you, and that poor sweet mouth above all.'

'If it had been pity,' said Kathy, 'I don't think I should have gone and drownded myself, that's such a footling thing to do, but I should never have troubled you again.'

'And if you had loved that – that – animal, Stocks,' he began.

'Don't splutter,' she interrupted. 'It's Stokes. He isn't an animal, he was only like everybody else.'

'I should never have troubled you again either.'

She laughed her jolly schoolgirl laugh. He had not heard it for many months, she laughed a different laugh with Lesbia.

Immediately on his words flashed upon him the remembrance of the kiss. How could he look Kathy in the face?

She had made her confession to him, did not he feel it incumbent on him to make a like confession to her? He did, and perhaps if he had been braver, stronger, more pitiless, he might have told her. He had never lacked courage, moral or physical – in dealing with men he had had rather more than enough, but his housekeepers and landladies had always ridden roughshod over him, because he hated to be hard on a woman. To Kathy he had been hard, because nervous irritability knows no mercy; but with her mutilated mouth before him and their arms round one another it was not in him to tell her he had kissed another woman.

'It's no good beginning to say I'm sorry,' whispered Kathy, stroking his cheek, 'so I shan't try.'

When the tea came, there was Lesbia's letter on the tray, it had been delayed in the post. He took it and threw it into the fire. She did not say anything, but her eyes gleamed.

After tea, as she lay against him, she became drowsier and drowsier. At length she opened her eyes, full of sleep and happiness, to smile at him, and say, 'Sorry, I can't be as bright and brainy as usual, but I seem to be going to roost,' and she fell asleep. He carried her in his arms upstairs. Then he came down and sat by the fire and abhorred himself. The thought of his unfaithfulness to her – unfaithful in his heart, which she had never been – weighed on him still more, now that her presence was removed from him. Perhaps of the many heads under which he put his loathing, the principal was that he had complained of her to Mary. How was he to make it up to her? To set himself at ease with himself, to be free from the intolerable position of granting forgiveness when he should implore it, urged him to go upstairs this instant, fall on his knees before her, and tell her all; this relief was not possible for him.

Such intensity of feeling could not last. It was not long before Kathy and Mr Herbert felt ill at ease with each other. Kathy showed her embarrassment by hilarity which, to Mr Herbert's despair, jarred on him just as it had done before. He had supposed nothing could jar again. She, too, had thought the exquisiteness of their meeting must make all easy. Hilarity was the cloak she put on to hide the bitterness of her disappointment. He did not yet understand her; it seemed to him a sort of ingrained levity. If now she had asked him was it pity, he would have found it hard to answer.

She bore the disfigurement with great courage, and went out and showed herself among the village people, rejecting with a laugh Mansfield's tearful proffers of the thickest motor veils. Such strangeness almost shocked Mansfield; she vicariously did what should have been done, stayed indoors, and gave up the miserable satisfaction of mingling tears over Kathy in the choicest homes of Lanchester.

Kathy found the ordeal harder than at Monte Carlo. Then there had been the hope of respite – of more than respite. She felt now her hope had come and gone. It was a relief to her, and to him also, when shortly after her return she had to go to bed with a chill and could be alone with her wretchedness. The chill turned to pleurisy and she was in danger for a few weeks. The visit to the London doctor had to be postponed. She had nurses, but she was always asking for her husband, and was less restless if he sat with her.

When she was convalescent she told him that she was going to have a baby. Her delight was intense, and so was his. She said she did not mind even that the doctor ordered her to lie up for several weeks. The hours, however, were very long to fill. She asked him to read to her. The choice was difficult, for there seemed no common ground, only each was so anxious to please the other.

Her dependence on him, her feebleness and misery, made him feel he could not do enough for her. She felt the change in him. The bitterness and hostility he had shown during Lesbia's visit had vanished. She valued his gentleness and devotion, but she knew it was more than that he had felt the evening of her return. She made up her mind it was to be expected; she had got something, she must be content with that. She did not again ask him if he loved her, for as the poor, proud, humble beauty said to herself, 'He's tried, but of course he can't.' One day she took his hand and said, 'Look here. I'm "taking notice," as they say about babies. You know what I mean. You're *awfully* good to me, and I hope I shall die, and we shall have a nice strong boy, that will be the best plan.' Otherwise they talked of everyday matters. But Kathy was wrong, for, though weak and faithless, it never entered into his mind, consciously or unconsciously, to think less of her because she was no longer beautiful. On the contrary, the mixture of chivalry, of honour, of determination that every thought of his heart should be turned to making up to her for the cruelty of destiny, kindled his never-dead love again. In those long hours of one another's society they drew nearer to one another, and he found out she was neither the ideal beauty to whom he had become engaged nor the smart, vulgar follower of Lesbia who

164

had driven him to despair, but an entirely different person, his own wife Kathy.

He had written to his mother the day after his wife's return saying that she had told him everything. Old Mrs Herbert had burnt Lesbia's letter unanswered. She did not speak of it to Mr Herbert till years afterwards. When she heard a baby was expected, she was very anxious to come and help entertain the invalid. But Kathy refused to have her. She would not hear of Lady Meryton either, and she was equally stout against the ministrations of all cousins or old friends.

21

'LADY MERYTON was here yesterday,' said Canon Jocelyn as they sat at dinner on the evening of Mary's return from Southsea, 'inquiring when you would be back. She tells me that Mrs Herbert has been very ill – some operation, I believe. I thought you might go and inquire at Lanchester tomorrow.'

Mary thought so too. She had determined to avoid no longer a meeting with the Herberts. She was now to take up her old life again, as if there had never been that episode. It was nearly four months since she had schooled herself to restraint.

The shock at the sight of Kathy was very great. She had been Mary's ideal of triumphant loveliness. Mary could not speak for emotion. If she had known the circumstances, she would never have intruded, but Mr Herbert said some easy words, and Kathy joined in about the bright day. Mary had called early to avoid tea; Kathy said she must stay and have coffee at any rate.

Mary met Mr Herbert's eye as little as she could. She saw him once, when he did not see her, smile with intense tenderness at his wife; she saw Kathy's answering smile. She was thinking so much of Kathy she did not feel embarrassed; she could not have believed it would have been so.

After a few inquiries for her father, Mr Herbert rose and said he must see the Inspector.

'Stay here, Crab,' said Kathy.

'If you don't know, Miss Jocelyn, who is familiar with the race, knows that inspectors wait for no man. I mustn't stay.'

'Don't leave me longer than you can help,' said Kathy.

'You know I shan't,' he answered, smiling at her.

'You'll stay, Miss Jocelyn, won't you?' said Kathy.

'I should like to very much,' said Mary, pitying her.

Mr Herbert took Mary's hand. Mary would almost have despised him if in that hour of Kathy's misery he had had one thought of her. But when she remembered their last parting, she could not control a pang; his was the handshake of an acquaintance.

It was difficult to think of anything to say, she and Kathy had only Mr Herbert in common. Apparently the call was not a failure, for when Mary took leave Kathy said, 'Come again soon. You're awfully comfortable.'

In spite of her resolution to meet the Herberts, she would not come again. She made difficulties, she refused almost rudely. But Kathy, having rejected all her old friends, was very lonely when Mr Herbert had to leave her. Her nerves, which had hitherto been so well balanced she had not known she possessed them, were all tender and ajar after the strain of the operation. She wanted company to keep them at bay. When Mary refused, wretched tears she hated and could not control welled up into her eyes. She, whose society had always been courted, humbled herself to entreat.

'I thought perhaps you would,' she said. 'It's jolly lonely sometimes. If you have a free afternoon, you might think of me.'

Who could have resisted her?

Mary had refused because she was ashamed to meet her. She had wronged her, she had hated her. She thought Kathy did not love him, despised him, neglected him. She had been utterly mistaken. As to the kiss, had it all been a dream, a figment of the imagination? In four months he had utterly forgotten her and turned to Mrs Herbert. 'She made a mistake, and I made a mistake,' he had said. Now there was no mistake, but complete understanding. Thus her prayers had been answered. It was astonishing to her that it had never occurred to her that he would solve their difficulties by forgetting her. With Kathy thrown on his compassion, he would not have been the man she loved so ardently if he had not forgotten her. But she believed in a like case she could not have forgotten him.

She had determined, as she drove yesterday from the station, to have a kind of renaissance in her mind, and start again. She was surprised to find on the whole how little effort was required. There was some. At times she, who had no right, grudged him to Kathy, who had every right, and considered herself doubly ill-treated because, from reverence for Kathy's misfortune, she could not indulge herself in hating her. But the absolute end of suspense – it was not hope, it never had been hope – was a great help. Her father's pleasure at her return – she had never known him show his dependence on her so much – an accumulation of village duties, her restored health, all helped too. The struggle in the spring now bore fruit, self-command had become a habit. A very, very slight tendency to think herself attractive to the opposite sex, which had refreshed her for a few months, dried up from henceforth. She had felt herself more confident in society, she returned to what she was before.

She looked back on that experience of her life as bliss, and as a nightmare. She repented much in herself, but not that she had loved him. She was very thankful to have had his love, she was contented, she was glad it was over. While it was burning her up, she had been fit for nothing else. As to blaming him, who was at least as much to blame as she was, she never thought of it. Her love was blind. If she had married him, how she would have spoilt him. She imagined that everyone's love affairs went as deep as her own. When she saw the village boys and girls together, she thought of the nerve-racking rapture they were experiencing. She did not realize that perhaps one in a thousand feels as strongly as she did.

She found herself often going to the Rectory. Each time when she left, Kathy begged her to come again.

'It's an awful fag for you, I know,' said Kathy, 'just talking to me. It's jolly decent of you. I've always liked you, and wanted to know you since we met at Mr Sykes'. Do you remember talking about hearing a fox bark? You said you thought it beastly digging foxes out. So it is – beastly unsporting – and they're such jolly beasts; only, of course, it's always done. I meant to ask you to come over years ago, but then Aunt Edith bored so about you.'

Mary read stories to her of the Redland level, only more vulgar, and rather improper; Kathy did not really care for anything else. Out of gratitude she had tried to string herself up to something high-class to please her husband. Generally she and Mary talked: Mary attracted confidences, particularly sad ones. Kathy in weakness, lying day after day, worn-out in mind and body, turned to her with eagerness.

Mary, however, nearly dried up the possibility of confidence by referring pitifully to Kathy's affliction. She had some of the simplicity of cottage people; it had more than once put her into difficulties with her own class. Every villager would have felt Miss Mary unkind and 'queer' if, in a similar case, nothing had been said. She would have felt it herself. If she had been afflicted, she would rather have been wept over than ignored. In mental anguish she wanted to hide from sight. She did not, and could not, imagine what it was to a great beauty to lose her charms.

Kathy had introduced the subject, calling herself the freak. Mary with ready-springing tears took her hand, and said, 'I can't *tell* you how sorry I am.'

'But you *are* telling me, unluckily,' said Kathy. 'Not much "can't" about it.'

'I'm so very –' began Mary. 'I beg your pardon.'

'All right,' said Kathy. 'Do what you like. Kick me down the stairs, or trample me in the dust, only, for God's sake, don't pity me.'

In their confusion their eyes happened to meet. Mary saw tears rolling down Kathy's cheeks, and her eyes showed the wretchedness she would not speak of. She turned away, but she resolutely faced Mary a second afterwards, and said cheerfully, 'Give the freak some cake, it's hungry.'

If Mrs Herbert had heard Kathy speak about pity, she might have understood her better. The things money buys, though essential in a way, Kathy thought so unimportant that one might take them from an inferior without obligation, paying for them with smiles, but in the spirit one paid a tradesman. Pity, which touched her pride, she could hardly bear from any one. It was the greatest tribute to Mary, and a sign of highly disordered nerves, that in the end she accepted hers.

'Mary,' said Lady Meryton, 'I'm so glad you are seeing Kathy. You know my old Dawson, her niece – such a pretty little thing – is Kathy's maid, and so devoted to her. She tells Dawson you have been several times; it's exactly what I was wanting. Dear Kathy shrinks from all of us. I understood it so well. I felt just like that in my long illness after the children died. I didn't want to see even my sister Eleanor. I had been worrying about Kathy so. But it's wonderful how right everything has come between her and Robert. Mansfield said to Dawson, "It's lovely to see them together," but of course I knew it would.'

People less continuously prosperous than Lady Meryton might not have been quite so certain.

Lady Meryton discussed the neighbourhood very freely with Dawson. Dora Redland would have said with significant nods, 'With maids you *must* be so careful what you say, they might take advantage.' But Lady Meryton was never careful, for no one ever took advantage. As the Redlands were inclined to lump all the working class together, Lady Meryton was inclined to lump all the working and middle class together. She did not realize the indescribable difference between talking to Dawson and talking to Mrs King.

Sometimes Mr Herbert was there when Mary called, but not often. She chose the times when he was most likely to be out, not on his or her account, but because Kathy wanted no one else when she had him. He almost always rose to go immediately.

One day Kathy remarked on this. 'You and Mary are so priceless, you always fly from one another like the plague. *I* think it's rude. She doesn't bite, Robert; she eats out of my hand quite nicely.'

'Miss Jocelyn realizes, which you don't, that there are one or two humble offices for a parson to perform in his parish.'

They laughed. Kathy said no more, but she remarked afterwards, 'It's rather putrid to be a burden. He's awfully good to me, though I'm a heavy trial to him, poor boy. There he is always waiting on me; and he gets nothing for it. I think a woman ought to be good-looking, or ride well to hounds, or have tons of babies –

boys of course, otherwise she'd better drown herself – and I shall never be No. 1 again, and never hunt again, and you bet I shall have ten girls.'

On one or two occasions Mary and Mr Herbert got into some conversation, and they all talked together, or rather she and Mr Herbert talked, and Kathy dropped out and played with Bimbo. They were not personal subjects – old disappearing village words, a poem of George Herbert's. Mary noticed it had become a *tête-à-tête*; it would be an affectation to make anything of what was an unimportant accident. He did not sit with them more than half an hour.

When they were alone, Kathy said wistfully, 'I wish I was more brainy. I might have learnt more – only I had such asses of governesses.' Willing to be generous even to governesses, she added, 'No, it was my own fault really.'

Mary had found her brains cut her off from her neighbours. She answered quickly, 'I shouldn't wish that if I were you.'

Kathy did not listen to answers, she went on. 'I wish I was more like you.' She was feeling very depressed today, a prey to nervous doubts and desires.

'Like *me. You.* You can't mean it. Why?'

'Oh, I don't know,' said Kathy; she never analysed. The entrance of tea and the kitten turned her thoughts elsewhere.

Mary thought over the strange compliment again in bed. Like many things in life, it came 'like pardon after execution.' In the compliment season – eighteen to thirty-three – few had reached her. They would have given her a fillip up, which then would have made a great deal of difference. She knew, before her aunt told her, of her bad carriage, awkward manner, sallow complexion. She did not remember that any one had ever observed anything favourable. Her father remarked before the Archdeacon's garden party, 'I cannot say I like that hat.' She smiled at the recollection. She would not trouble herself whether she had been unkindly treated, but she always went out of the way to admire the Sunday School girls' frocks. It seemed curious to think of vacillating Aunt Lottie as a critic whom she had once been very anxious to conciliate.

The compliment should have at any rate one result. She ob-

170

viously need not continue to be shy of some one who wished to resemble her. She felt her tongue unloosed, and began to talk easily in her admirer's presence. Happily she never knew that as soon as the admirer's nerves were a little better, she was very much tickled at her aberration.

That unloosening of her tongue made them more intimate. It was perhaps a case of misery making strange bedfellows. Mary would never have been Kathy's choice. But now they discussed a variety of things, in some of which Mary, with intellectual arrogance – her one arrogance – had never supposed Kathy could be interested.

Kathy talked freely of her own affairs also, more freely than Mary herself could have done.

'I think Riviera people, English and American, the beastliest cads unhung. The women are only beaten by one thing – that's the men. The women's sympathy when I got like this – *ugh*.'

She told Mary about Captain Stokes. 'He was a frightfully handsome man. I can't quite imagine now how I could ever have agreed. I think a woman ought to run straight' (the excellent truism she enunciated with great simplicity). 'Robert seems so nice now, but he was awfully cutting in our second year, and I simply couldn't bear it.'

So her detestable hope had nearly come true, only frustrated by the terrific intervention of Providence. Mary almost felt she had a share in the destruction of Kathy's beauty.

They often discussed people, and naturally, therefore, people's behaviour. Mary was really staggered, as Mrs Herbert had been, by Kathy's universal tolerance, sincere, simple tolerance, quite different from Mr Worsley's desire to shock. Too many things in Mary's childhood and girlhood had been thought wrong; sometimes she found Kathy's tolerance refreshed her. When Kathy's nerves were troubling her, she could be bitter, but tolerance was her real condition of mind. It was combined with rather a high personal standard. She 'ran straight,' not apparently as the result of effort, but from a healthy spring of natural goodness. Almost anything that anybody did she condoned by 'poor kid.' If the sinner was elderly, she was chivalrously called 'poor girl.' Sometimes Kathy would throw in 'old' to soften the condemnation.

Jack, her unsatisfactory brother, was always 'poor old Jack.' Even Lesbia was 'poor devil.' In general she seemed to consider misbehaviour like the measles, which any one might have the ill-luck to catch. Certain sorts of cruelty, but only certain sorts, and certain sorts of swindling, but only certain sorts, roused her indignation.

She disapproved of women tempting husbands away. 'Lesbia's a disgusting cat, but she's had something to put up with. Of course the reason why Jack took the job in Nigeria was because there's a woman out there. She's a wrong 'un, if ever there was one, and she always goes for the married men; she's done it again and again. It's such a blackleg thing to do. Nobody would mind if she went for the others, but when one knows what all men without exception are –'

Mary hardly knew what impulse made her say, 'Do you think there is ever anything to be said for them, Kathy?'

'Them? Who?'

'The blacklegs.'

'Oh, I don't know; if the wives are wrong 'uns perhaps, but they're a rotten lot. Besides, Lesbia *wasn't* a wrong 'un! She was awfully gone on Jack first of all, poor kid – well, for years she was, until there wasn't much left to be gone on.'

Kathy did not often embark on general reflections, and now she was back at Lesbia, it was not possible to divert her. Whoever talked to Kathy must follow her lead in conversation. If Mary had wanted somehow to plead for herself with Kathy, the chance was gone. Kathy had not noticed the flush, the breathless hesitation. If she had, she would never have connected Mary with blacklegs. In her eyes Mary by her plainness was as cut off from men as a nun by her cloister.

Women have perhaps been considered more spiteful than they are. Certainly Kathy thoroughly enjoyed the beauty and attainments of the girls she knew. She had not a spark of envy in her, and never grudged anybody anything, greeting success cordially with 'lucky kid.' Generosity of mind, which Mary had not attained after years of striving, came quite naturally to her. Generosity towards her circle, that is to say, for Kathy drew with absolute definiteness the aristocratic line of where her sympathy ended.

172

Not of course that it was a line dividing rich and poor, such as the middle class often draws between itself and the working class. The servants, and village, and tradespeople they dealt with, all relations, and her set of friends were warm and cosy inside the circle. It was the foolish people trying to get into it on equal terms who were debarred from sympathy. They were employed if wanted, but Kathy had no compunction in making them feel out of it, when they were not.

> He casts off his friends like a huntsman his pack,
> For he knows when he likes, he can whistle them back.

Mary thought these lines well described Kathy. But Kathy never bothered about whistling people back; they came back. She sometimes seemed very lacking in the scruples of a lady. She really had not the delicacy of mind of Miss Gage. Miss Gage had of course many extra scruples and cares, such as the laying of the afternoon tea cloth diamond-wise, but she *could* not have hurt as Kathy hurt. Kathy had the most strange resemblance to the roughest factory girl, skipping all the grades of society one would have expected to be more like her.

They had become so intimate that one day Mary broached the subject of Kathy's rudeness to her and Dora at the Meryton garden party. It took some time to recall the meeting to Kathy's mind.

'Wait a bit. I think I do remember something. It was the day we settled to try Taffy with the martingale, but it didn't work a *bit*. I never knew such a brute as Taffy. Yes, you were there, and a fair woman with a bit of a lisp. I was rude, do you say? But I was *never* rude to you, old Towzer, was I? I should have been a beast if I was. Of course I remember now, Claudia said she always used to take her mother for Dawson's sister, only it was rough on Dawson's sister. But she was a bit of an outsider. One has to draw the line somewhere, and I used to draw it at parsons' daughters; only if the kid's a girl, I shall make an exception for the Lanchester parson's daughter – Oh, and for you, Mary.'

Mary might have been eloquent on this text, but resentment at their first meeting had worn out. She only said, 'That parson's daughter is my greatest friend.'

'Is she? Oh, I daresay she's all right, then. Good old Claudia,' turning to something which interested her. 'She's the best woman at a gate I ever met. Not a ditch, mind you – Jim-jam's better there – a gate.'

If Mary expected expressions of remorse, she did not get them.

22

KATHY asked Mary to be godmother.

'You're to be godmother to Hugo, won't you. It *shall* be Hugo. If it's Mary, I shan't be able to bear it, because she might grow up like me, and that would be too beastly a fate for any one.'

'Surely you'll ask Mr Herbert's mother,' said Mary.

'I shan't, because it will disappoint her so terrifically, and that's just what I want.'

This was a groundless, nervous animosity for the most part. Mrs Herbert's letter had been mild; Kathy had answered insolently. Then had come Lesbia's letter of accusation.

It had cut old Mrs Herbert to the quick. She had not shown her wretchedness, except by allowing her interesting book on Java to lie unread for half-hours together. She sat in a special armchair, never leaning back. She would not lean back now, but unhappiness made her huddle up into herself. She burnt Lesbia's letter as she had burnt Kathy's. She paid no attention to it, neither answering it nor speaking of it; she merely let fall two remarks. 'I am afraid things are in rather an uncomfortable state,' and 'She seems to be mixed up with a very queer set of people.' From these expressions of opinion, and an apathy in contradiction, her sister-in-law gathered that something was very wrong.

She felt the indignity for him who was her pride even more than her darling. She would have minded only one thing in the world more – the illicit kiss he had given to Mary.

Isabel felt it also. One night Mrs Herbert had a sore throat. She could not read a clerical biography aloud – her custom of a

Sunday after Church and supper. She handed the book to Isabel; Isabel's voice showed signs of tears.

'I am *very* sorry,' she said meekly. 'It seems so *miserable* about dear Robert.'

After twenty years she had not learnt that an apology would make the snub, which was bound to come, still more severe.

'I don't think "blubbering", as my dear mother used to call it when we were children, ever helped anything,' said Mrs Herbert.

But to return to the godmother.

'I shouldn't mind old Isabel,' said Kathy – Isabel had written no letter – 'but she'd funk it. Mother-in-law would have her knife in her for ever.'

'Oh, *do* ask Mrs Herbert,' said Mary persuasively.

' *You're* to be godmother.'

Kathy was difficult to oppose, but Mary answered, 'No, I'd rather not, really.' When the request was backed by a wheedling pinch, Mary still repeated, 'Really.'

Kathy of course laughed at Mary, she laughed at most people, with a kind of rough chaff. Her favourite subject was Mary's spinsterhood. Her good-humoured wonder, tinged with contempt, at a woman who had reached Mary's age, and remained unmarried because she could not help it, was much less aggravating to Mary than it would have been to any one more vain. Mary derived some amusement from it. But one day Kathy exceeded the bounds. She greeted her with 'Cheer up. I hear you made a conquest once, after all.'

She went on, 'My cousin, Milly Grace, motored over yesterday. I wish people wouldn't come and bother one, but they do. She told me all about it. You met her two years ago, didn't you? She said how Maltby was there too, and never left your side. He's a kind of connection of her husband's. He goes the round of hotels. They don't keep him long, they find he's not very fond of paying his bills. I met him at Newquay one year, and we used to call him Ba-bab, because he always came a cropper over his "b's." He wandered about with his tail between his legs when you were gone, and wouldn't be comforted. He said to Milly, "I know I've done for myself, and it's too late now, b-b-but that's the woman I should like to have married. She's not b-b-beautiful, b-b-but b-b-beauty's only skin-deep, and I couldn't expect everything." Wasn't it priceless?'

'I didn't know Mr Maltby got into debt,' said Mary, interrupting Kathy's laughter.

'Oh, rather. Leaves his little b-b-bills about all over the shop. It's b-b-baccarat, you b-b-bet.'

'I must be going,' said Mary, getting up abruptly.

'Oh, must you? I thought you were going to stay hours more. Well, come again soon.'

But Mary could not. 'I believe the county are the vulgarest people in the world,' she said to herself. Worthless as he was, Mr Maltby's feeling for her made her – not exactly grateful, but sensitive. There had been times of thinking herself a failure, when the assurance of even his admiration would have cheered. She resented Kathy's insolence, she imagined the revenge of telling her that it was she, the despised, who had been the first object of the man Kathy adored.

Kathy missed her. She wrote, 'You are *not* to sulk in your hole, Towzer.' (The joke about Towzer was so poor even its author, Kathy, could not remember its point.) 'Come to tea tomorrow and we'll have crumpets.'

She said when they met, 'I don't believe you liked my tale about your one and only. I thought you'd love it. But' (naïvely) 'you haven't very much sense of humour, have you?' It was true that Mary's little rill of fun dried up immediately in Kathy's presence. Very different things amused them.

'I don't think there was anything to laugh at,' said Mary.

'Oh, Milly and I *screamed*,' said Kathy; then seeing Mary's face, she cried, 'I *say*, you don't mean, by any chance, you'd have taken Maltby? I haven't been putting my foot in it?'

'Oh, most *certainly* not,' said Mary.

'Then I believe you've got the hump because you don't go down with men. I shouldn't bother about that,' Kathy went on kindly. 'They're not worth a damn, the whole lot of them, except one.'

She herself would not have cared to go through life without their admiration.

When she said 'except one,' she gave a rapturous smile. That special smile Mary found disarmingly sweet. Both Kathy's vulgarity and her own resentment were blotted out.

At first Mary constantly returned from her visits to Lanchester with the feeling that, admire Kathy as she might, the marriage was very strange. She would have been certain in those few weeks, when each knew what was in the other's mind, that Mr Herbert's fastidiousness would have been greater than her own. Was it pity? When Kathy had trampled on her not unduly sensitive *amour-propre* – that it was always unintentional aggravated the offence – Mary had a spiteful desire that the feeling might be pity. But the more she saw of Kathy – she saw her with all her failings exposed, Kathy was incapable of concealment – the more she came under her sway. There was a curious something in Kathy, impossible to describe, which, if she had sunk down into a pauper or a criminal, would have made her still able to command, not deference, nor honour, nor respect, but a sentiment akin to all three. As to the twisted mouth, Mary felt it simply made no difference at all. At her first call on Kathy she wondered how Mr Herbert could have fallen in love with her. Now she thought the wonder would be not to fall in love with her. If a man was to choose between her and Kathy – even the man who knew her as no one else would ever know her, how could he hesitate? 'And he was right,' she said to herself. 'I'm so small compared to her.'

One morning Mary found Kathy tired and flushed. She remarked on it; Kathy snubbed her with 'Oh no, I'm perfectly fit, I always am.'

She had been worrying herself three-quarters of the night. She was feeling sick and worn out, but she had not known a day's illness before her operation, she could not get accustomed to bad health. She bent down and pulled Bimbo's ears in silence for some time, then she said, 'I wanted to ask you something. You're clever, so you can tell me. You know things went wrong our first year. Once he said something about the way I talked – I don't know what it was – about the words I used, I think, but I only talk like everybody else, don't I? Then there was a song, the sort of song you always hear. He was sick about it. I asked him what was the matter with it, and he wouldn't tell me. There were other things too. I asked him to tell me always, if there was anything he didn't like – of course I'd much rather know, – but he wouldn't I don't know why; I think he might have. I could see his face screw up sometimes, as if he had toothache. At the end, before I went to the Riviera, it seemed to me everything –' She hesitated; Mary could see she was panting, and could hardly get on. She knew that feeling; she thought Kathy would never have known it. It came out at last. 'Everything I did drove him frantic.'

She went on, 'Now, you're the only person I can ask. I hate every one else.' But still she did not ask; she could not bring herself to ask. 'I told Lesbia about it. She was awfully bucked. I know you're not that sort, you'd never crow.'

Mary recollected the whiff of triumph she had felt when Lady Meryton told her of the Herberts' difficulties. She blushed as she said, 'Everything is right now, though.'

'Oh, I don't know. I see him screwing his mouth up. Mary, tell me –' Now, at last, Kathy came to what had troubled her all night. 'I want to know, and tell me what you think without bothering about my feelings. Is it – I expect it is really – just pity? He said it wasn't, when I first came back, but he would say that.'

Mary had always thought Kathy's eyes beautiful, but, like the eyes of a Greek statue benignantly satisfied with itself and the world. Her sufferings had put melancholy and longing into them. Now in Mary's opnion they were irresistible. Pity indeed! Kathy had all Mr. Herbert's heart. If there could but have been one crumb left over for her! She had thought all dead and gone, it blazed up again.

'It was never pity,' she answered brusquely, almost violently.

'Are you sure?'

She answered again, 'Absolutely sure.'

'Thank you, old Mary,' said Kathy. 'You're a brick.'

They both bent forward, almost involuntarily. They kissed one another. Mary felt the tears on Kathy's face, Kathy felt Mary's on hers – tears partly for herself, partly, she could not tell exactly why, since Kathy had everything, in tenderness for Kathy.

'It's merely that I'm rather glad, every idiotic thing makes me

178

howl now,' said Kathy. She did not think of Mary's tears at the time, she remembered them afterwards.

23

IN due time Kathy had twin boys. Both throve, and the parents were engrossed with them. Old Mrs Herbert, one of the god-mothers – Kathy's bark was worse than her bite – was tearfully happy; her many anxieties about the marriage might cease.

It was unfortunate that Kathy chose this season of prosperity to apologize for her rude letters. Prosperity set up Mrs Herbert. It was better for her to be kept low; one should never let oneself be in her power.

The apology was not successfully accepted. The phraseology had grated. 'I am most awfully sorry I have been so thoroughly beastly; those putrid letters, etc., etc. Of course I know Crab's miles too good for me.'

'I think indeed there was need for great sorrow,' said Mrs Herbert, 'and need for watchful care still, isn't there? Though I can see my daughter-in-law, or let me say my daughter, is doing her best. But oh, my dear, why will you call your husband by that stoopid name? I can't say I see any fun in it at all.'

Kathy had determined to eat humble pie, but this was too large a slice. She would not give Mrs Herbert the gratification of answering her.

Mary was walking through the fields to Lanchester one day. She came upon Mr Herbert sitting on the trunk of a tree with his head in his hands. He heard her approach and greeted her. 'This view is particularly delightful,' he remarked in a small-talk manner. 'Our eastern counties at their best, and that best is hard to beat.'

His thoughts were not with the eastern counties; the next moment he said quickly, 'Have you seen Kathy? Has she told you?'

'I'm just on my way to the Vicarage now.'

'We've been up to the London doctor; he can set her face right. He doesn't promise success, it might make matters worse, but we've made up our minds to it; Kathy is anxious for it. She's going to the Nursing Home today.'

He had meant to hide away by himself like the animals in pain, after an evening and a morning of pretended high spirits and assurance of success, but once again in his life he could not resist the comfort of confiding in Mary. In the intensity of his feeling that other confidence was as if it had not been. That was not quite the case with her. But her heart was full of Kathy, as she answered, 'I *am* glad.'

'Yes, I ought to be, it's scandalous not to be. One ought not to mind risking something to bring back what she's lost. But I'm a coward, a detestable coward.' He struck the trunk of the tree in his misery again and again. 'I can't keep back these wretched doubts and fears. Think if it has to be another failure, after all she's gone through. You don't know –' He broke off; he was re-calling the despair on Kathy's face when she came back from the Riviera. He had often woken up at nights, after he had dreamt of it. Kathy had not forgotten her despair, she would never forget it completely, but she did not dwell on it.

'If it was merely myself, I would urge her to let well alone. What does it matter to me what she is? Of course it could make no –' he broke off. He murmured, forgetting her presence, 'She could not be dearer. But I have a notion she is doing it for my sake. Could you sound her, Mary? Of course she's absolutely calm herself.'

He did not know he called her Mary. She noticed it; she was glad. She was glad he turned to her; there was a bitter-sweet satisfaction. He turned to her as he might to a sister, and this time she could do Kathy justice. She answered with a full heart. 'I've never known any one so heroic.'

Rumour in the shape of Mansfield had transported the news to Dawson, and Dawson to Lady Meryton. Lady Meryton had come to Lanchester to sympathize, Jim-jam too had dropped in, and what with her, and Mansfield, and Dawson, and portman-teaux and kisses, hubbub reigned supreme, but for the cause of the hubbub, who was her usual imperturbable self.

'Cheerio,' cried she to Mary. 'Come and join the crowd. We're off to London to have another op. The last man said it was a howling success, and this one says it may fail, so it's rather mixed. I don't quite see how I can be more of a scarecrow than I am, but there seems a chance of it, which would be rough on Crab. Still, he must take the risk, it's so damned hard on him to have me to stare at all day long.'

'Don't think of that now,' said Mary, getting a private word with her under cover of the hubbub. 'I know it makes no difference to him.'

'How do you know?'

'He told me just now.'

'Cheek. Then all I can say is he told a lot of crams when we were engaged.'

'I'll tell you his exact words,' said Mary with eager warmth. 'What does it matter to me what she is? She couldn't be dearer.'

But Kathy was well again, her nerves restored. Now she wanted no outsider's assurance of Mr Herbert's love. She spoke with a touch of dryness.

'Still if Crab doesn't mind, I'd as soon have a straight face as a crooked.'

The Hollings had practised the art of setting people in their place for many generations. Mary felt she had been intruding.

On the eve of the journey, Mary came to bid good-bye, and she received, to her astonishment, a warm hug from Kathy; she was usually cool and boyish in her farewells.

'I shan't forget what a trump you've been,' said she; and Mr Herbert, escorting Mary to the gate, said, with both his hands clasping hers, 'I can't thank you for what you've done for her, and for me.'

She looked at him; she saw the wonderful brightness of his eyes. *How* fond he was of Kathy. She could be touched by it now. The sight of his emotion caused her tears to rise; they made her cut the interview short.

They returned from London; the operation was successful. Kathy's face was restored to what it had been, but some slightest trace was left of the misfortune, which made her beauty less perfect, but more wonderful. She was radiant with health and delight at her babies, on the best of terms with all her friends and relations.

It seemed that, contrary to her parting words, she had forgotten Mary. She welcomed her almost uproariously. Hilarity may create a wide gulf; before the visit was over, Mary felt as shy as on her first call. Kathy was not neglectful or ungrateful. She invited Mary cordially to tennis and bridge parties, and called her Towzer to Jim-jam, Claudia, and Cocky; Mary disliked being called Towzer to Cocky. She did not leave her out more than she could help, when she was surrounded with cheerful contemporaries, all wanting to talk to Kathy, and none to Mary.

Jim-jam took a fancy to her. They discussed High Church matters. Jim-jam did not like bridge, she thought it took the mind off hunting. Under her smart clothes, she had some affinity with Mary, she was not formidable. Captain Wyndham always left Mary out.

Soon after the cure Lesbia proposed herself for a long visit, chiefly because there was nowhere else to go. Her friends knew her too well by this time, and Jack continued in Nigeria. Both thought of divorce now and then; they never quite worked themselves up to the expense.

It was the old business of debts and white-washing that brought her to the Rectory. Even she felt some embarrassment. The first night she said, taking Kathy's hand, and speaking with real emotion:

'Kath, I was an absolute cad about that letter.'

'What letter?' asked Kathy.

'That letter to Crab.'

'What letter to Crab?' said Kathy with unfeigned bewilderment.

'When you left Nice.'

'Oh,' said Kathy. 'That letter. Oh, you needn't bother about that. He never opened it.'

Kathy had forgiven – even forgotten her injuries. Lesbia might have felt it more of a compliment if she had remembered them; forgetfulness showed her her power was gone. Kathy treated her with the same off-hand good-nature as before.

Mr Herbert, however, never either forgave or forgot the letter.

He, the exhorter to Christian forgiveness in Church, struggled with himself before he could bear the thought of having Lesbia under his roof. It did not enter the head of the injured party to refuse her.

Mr Herbert sometimes let loose his irony on Lesbia. She did not like it, but it was less annihilating than Kathy's good-nature. She put as good a face on things as she could. She had the old manner of impertinent condescension. Mary, knowing the circumstances, not from Kathy, but from Jim-jam, almost had it in her heart to pity Lesbia, who above all things loved to be of account.

'Kathy's much too good to her,' said Jim-jam. 'I know, because we've always known the Hollings so well. Mac' (Mary, now one of the initiated, was to know instinctively that Mac was Jim-jam's brother) 'is Kathy's trustee. He won't let her have the money she wants for Lesbia. When he says anything, Kath always says, "The poor beggar has got to live," and he says, "So have a few other poor beggars, you and your children, for instance."'

Mr Herbert was not fond of Cocky. He said irritably one day, 'I wonder why, when there are a number of satisfactory young men in the world, we should have to endure Captain Wyndham's company for hours together. Couldn't you consort with some one else?'

'Oh, poor old Cocky,' said Kathy. 'He's a pal of Jack's, and he's not half a bad shot.'

'I think he's worthless,' said Mr Herbert hotly.

'Crab, I really do believe you're jealous. I shall tell Cocky. He'll be tremendously bucked. I don't think any husband's ever been jealous of him before.'

'Jealous is absolutely the last thing I am,' said Mr Herbert, going out of the room and banging the door.

He came back shortly afterwards. 'I told you what was not true just now,' said he. 'The fact is – is – I am jealous.' He did not enjoy this confession, which he made with solemnity, nor did he care for her hearty laughter.

'How quaint,' said she, beaming with smiles. 'I didn't know a brainy person could be such an ass.' She became serious, and said, looking at him very sweetly, 'You needn't ever bother to be jealous. Understand? You're the only man in the world.'

'I never, never will be,' he said, seizing her in his arms. 'I'm an ass. Don't think brains make one less of an ass; I should think they make one rather more.'

This truth was deep for Kathy. It touched her when he ran himself down; he did it so fervently. She did not want to show any *more* feeling just now. She remarked, laughing, 'It seems a mistake, when there's only one man in the world, he should be such a guy.'

Kathy, in her happiness, looking back on her months of illness, could hardly believe she had passed through them. It seemed like a fever, particularly her openings of the heart to Mary. Her ordinary self liked steady affection for friends and steady love for your husband, without too much talk or confiding about either. She had wished she was like Mary! Now she saw her dispassionately. She would not forget her goodness, but perhaps she would have preferred never to meet her again; she recalled what was hateful. To Mary that time, though bitter, had been sweet. She would fain have brought it back.

She began one day hesitatingly. 'Do you remember you said when you were ill –?'

'I'm thankful to say I remember *nothing*,' broke in Kathy. 'I was completely dotty. Don't let's go back to that time. It's over, thank God.' She went on joyously to something else.

From that moment Mary found the barrier between them was impassable. She felt sore, and inclined to think Kathy deteriorated with prosperity. Perhaps people are less attractive in prosperity; certainly they are more unapproachable.

They never talked intimately again. Mary was disappointed; she had lived too long in the world to be surprised. Because one has once been intimate, one does not remain intimate.

She was not offended with Kathy, but she was hurt that Mr Herbert should talk to her so seldom. Civility in his own house demanded more. He still kept to her instructions, and visited her father only on Thursdays. She asked him to come other days more than once, but he did not come. So it happened that, though she and Kathy met fairly often, she hardly ever saw him. There was not merely no love left, but not a spark of friendliness.

184

'I suppose men are like that always,' she thought. 'They care for a short time, and then it is done with, and they forget entirely.'

24

THE Herberts' was a happy marriage. It was not what the tie with Mary would have been. They did not know what each was going to say before the words were uttered, but presumably not one husband or wife in a million do. Indeed, they were often completely astray as to what the other was driving at. The union was quite unequal intellectually. The language he spoke to her was not the language in which he thought; the life of his mind was apart from hers. He had soon given up reading English classics to her; they laughed now at the recollection.

It was owing to this intellectual disparity that Mr Herbert kept up his old friendships more than is generally the case with men who are happily married. He went now and then for a night or two to Cambridge, and his relish of the talk in the Combination Room after Hall was rather too much the joy of seeing rain after drought. Mary would have been wounded. Kathy would have thought, 'Of course he wants more than I can give him, bless him', regarding intellectual conversation as a sort of rocking-horse for a beloved child.

One sees every day that the unequal marriages, on whichever side the inferiority may be, are as happy as any other, possibly happier. Mary was the one person Mr Herbert had met who was truly akin to him. In their marriage, therefore, something would have been wanting that he had now – high spirits, geniality, light-hearted courage, which neither dreaded troubles before they came nor brooded over them when they were past; a good, tough, reasonable insensitiveness, which sometimes repelled him, but attracted him also, and fortified him. He leaned on the calm and steadfast Kathy. She was more of a mother than Mary would have been, not by any means more tender. While still feeling him above her, she found he required much protecting and looking after.

'You *are* quaint, Crab,' she would say. 'Sometimes you seem as if you'd been in the nursery all your life.'

Her eye detected in an instant the lapses to which the 'brainy' are particularly liable – losing their notes of invitation, looking out the Sunday train when they are travelling on Monday. The efficiency, tempered by sweetness, of Kathy's motherliness was such that Mr Herbert at times was on the verge of being afraid of it.

Few people have a better opinion of themselves than the efficient, successful married woman; but Kathy remained what she had always been, boundlessly proud as a Hollings, but in herself as humble as Mary.

She bore with Mr Herbert's moods, sarcasm, and irritability much better than Mary would have done. Mary would have been too indulgently sympathetic over them, and then would have felt them too much. Kathy often did not observe them, and when she did, disregarded them. Once she was sure Mr Herbert was what she called 'all right inside,' she did not mind them.

When they had to start life together again after her return from the Riviera, both had determined, whatever happened, the marriage must now be a success. During Lesbia's long first visit Kathy had sucked in insinuations continually from her, now here, now there. That was ended for good and all.

Habit helped them. It helped Mr Herbert, for instance, to get on with Kathy's jokes; not to listen to them, but to listen to her ringing laugh, which to his ears was one of the pleasantest sounds in Nature, not musical, but delightful, like the cawing of rooks.

What helped their marriage most was the children. They had another boy when the twins were eighteen months old. Kathy managed her sons – one was fractious and slow in developing – as easily as she managed Bimbo. Her time of trial might come later, when she had a daughter with Mr Herbert's difficult nature, but without his sex to plead for her. In the children's service she gave up hunting and sold Taffy. She was dutiful, though she would have felt uncomfortable if duty had been talked about. She called it 'going hard at one's job.' If there is any unpleasant American phrase for duty, she used that too. After her marriage she did what few of her former set were capable of – grew up.

She continued to like plenty of young men about with whom she could be noisy. Mr Herbert had at first been jealous of them and conscious of his middle age. But Kathy made it clear that to disturb himself about them was a waste of energy. 'I like having somebody to play round with when you have your meetings and things, and I always shall.' There they left it. Mr Herbert thought young men a strange interest. She had young women also. They all made a noise, and gave the village much to talk about. It was rather proud of Kathy's success with the opposite sex. It regarded her in a curious way as a something between a mistress, a mother, and a younger sister, and loved to give advice, coupled with admiration, concerning her management of the Glebe farm.

The husband and wife did not grow like each other, but in process of time Mr Herbert realized that, living in the twentieth century, and having definitely joined the party of the younger generation, it was no good wincing at what he formerly had considered vulgarity. Kathy, though always desiring to please him, continually forgot what points distressed him. She made one sacrifice, she banished the words 'ripping,' 'putrid,' 'damn,' and 'infernal' from her mouth when speaking before the village, servants, or children. It *was* a sacrifice. She thought it 'narrow-minded,' an expression she continued to be fond of.

It was through his wife Mr Herbert got into touch with the village and the village with him. Her beaming kindness smoothed away the resentment sometimes roused by his tart or sarcastic retorts. She regarded his learning and literary work somewhat as he regarded her young men; her forbearance helped his parishioners to bear with them too. For, with the spread of education, they looked upon learning as a waste of time; it did not hold the privileged place it had in Canon Jocelyn's prime. It would have outraged Mary that the high faculties of the mind she so much valued, his wife should smile on indulgently as the pretty tricks of a child. Yet Kathy loved and honoured him with all her powers. He loved her and honoured her also, much more than in the first year of their married life, when he knew nothing about her.

He looked back on a day which revealed his love both to Kathy and to himself. Kathy was driving the little boys and Mansfield, now Nanny, in the new pony-cart. Mansfield had cast aside her bright plumes to take the veil in the form of the smartest of nurse's uniforms, turning her back on the Italian chauffeur and such vain delights all for love of the adored one. The pony was a consolation for the loss of Taffy. Kathy was taking it out for the first time. A sidecar came screeching and surging round a sharp turn on the wrong side of the road. There was only just time to get the pony out of the way. Mansfield screamed, and clutched one of the children so tight that he began to cry. The sidecar rushed on with bursts and explosions, and the pony bolted.

'Shut up,' said Kathy, glaring at Mansfield. Mansfield was cowed instantly into silence.

'Isn't this jolly, kids?' cried Kathy, nodding at the children, whose eyes were growing large with terror. 'Lovely bumps.'

At that moment Mr Herbert came over a stile into the lane. He was horrified to see the cart flying towards him.

'Stop Pixie!' called out Kathy.

He tried, but he had the scholar's bad sight and clumsy fingers; his efforts were vain.

'All right,' cried she, smiling at him gaily.

They were not very likely to meet any one before there was a sharp turn into the high-road, where the motors dashed at topmost speed. Mr Herbert ran after the cart, stumbled, fell, scrambled up, ran after them again, and met Kathy with Pixie restored to composure, trotting quietly towards him. Two of Kathy's adoring farmers had caught and stopped the pony.

'The boys are as right as rain,' cried Kathy. 'We all are.'

He squeezed her hand and clasped the children, who threw themselves on to his knees when he got into the cart.

'Nanny, I shan't take *you* next time we run away,' said Kathy, but her nod softened the sting of reproof. Mr Herbert said his pleasant word to Mansfield also. In a minute or two they were at home. Kathy went to the nursery to see that the children were tranquilly occupied with their Teddy bears under the nursemaid's charge. Then she came down to the study and, to Mr Herbert's surprise, fell into an honest hearty fit of hysterics – as Mansfield was already doing on Dennis's shoulder. When she could get out her words connectedly, she said, 'The children, oh, Crab, can

188

you forgive me? I ought to have waited till I knew Pixie better. I thought we were absolutely done for.'

'The children,' he said; 'I don't believe I ever thought of them. It was *you*.' He held her convulsively. She looked up at him and saw his face.

'Then you really do care frightfully,' she said. 'I couldn't believe you quite did. I knew you did rather, all that was necessary, but not all that. You oughtn't to; it's absurd.'

When they had got to calmer topics he said, 'We'd better get rid of the pony if she's going to misbehave like that.'

'Oh, poor lamb, it was only that infernal cad of a motor hog.'

'But if she's going to object to all motors I am afraid her life won't be worth living, or ours either.'

'No, Crab really; she's a thorough lady. I can see she is. I've thought of a bit Claudia has for Duke that will settle her.'

Kathy did not care about being a lady herself, but she liked her horse to be.

To a 'blood' like Kathy it had been almost as trying to have a loved husband bungle over a horse as for a scholar like Mr Herbert to have a loved wife sing an indecent song. But Kathy was more forbearing than he had been. She had made up her mind to the deficiency when she became engaged, and she never allowed herself to resent it.

Kathy's birthday fell a week after this incident. In the morning he put a poem on her dressingtable, entitled, 'To Kathy.' It described his devotion, but it must have lacked the simplicity of great art, for Kathy hardly understood a word except the title. She flung her arms round his neck, and cried, 'I can't make much of it, but I think it's wonderful, awfully good, and I *do* love you.'

So that Mary's words came true, 'Mistakes sometimes turn out right in the end.'

Being relieved of her fears for the marriage, Mrs Herbert could now venture to criticize her daughter-in-law, and even, in a dignified and elegant manner, to snap, a popular habit in Mrs Herbert's prime. Kathy took the pleasant sting out of snapping by paying no attention to it, nor to Mrs Herbert's suggestions and lamentations about the young men. Still, occasionally the snaps told more than Mrs Herbert would have liked, for she never wanted her snaps to rankle. Kathy was not very fond of her mother-in-law; and the annual discussions and congratulations over her improvement, which she knew went on between Lady Meryton and Mrs Herbert at the September visit to Lanchester, never ceased to annoy her.

25

IT appeared that Mary's life had come full circle back to the emptiness when Ruth first died. There had been Dora, Brynhilda and the hope for her writings, Mr Herbert, and last Kathy. Her heart had been very busy, now there seemed nothing for it to do. Mr Herbert would never want her any more. She had had the satisfaction of serving him through Kathy; Kathy did not want her either. Dora was still away in China, and Brynhilda she had long lost sight of.

>   Change and decay in all around I see.

Hitherto this had seemed an incorrect description of Dedmayne; nothing did change. Now the truth of the line came home to her. But thirty-nine is a less bitter age than thirty-five; she was more able to face loneliness. None the less, it was a red-letter day when she heard from Dora. She was back in England, and her first visit must be to Dedmayne, if they could put her up for two nights next week.

She came. China and all the wonders of the East had left her just where she was, her mind not enlarged, her standard not lowered.

She described her experiences. 'There are numbers of foreigners, you know, Mary. One was really nice – a Frenchman. He played tennis splendidly, and was almost like an Englishman. Gertrude took some time getting into things, but the shops are not bad, and they say Harrod may be starting a branch. The natives are just like children. Walter says they simply don't understand kindness; they get so independent at once. My great friend out there was the wife of a missionary. She was teaching the girls to do lovely drawn-thread work, really as good as one can get in the London shops, and the brown babies are too sweet for anything.'

There she was – her own pleasant, limited self, as palatable to Mary as good country bread.

She, on her side, was delighted to revisit Dedmayne.

'Canon Jocelyn is not a day older,' said she. 'His voice was splendid in that beautiful sermon last night. I wish *you* looked better Mary. We must feed you up. I shall go and talk to cook.'

She always noticed the physical more than the mental, or she might have seen that what had changed most was Mary's expression. Her eyes had always been sad; they were perhaps sadder now, but they had gained that special something which often makes the eyes of the middle-aged more interesting, even more beautiful, than the eyes of youth.

Mary found there was a barrier between them – Mr Herbert's kiss. To open her heart freely had been a need of her warm nature from childhood – a need which had never been satisfied. She had, too, a conscientiousness of repulsion against concealment which was morbid, perhaps, a weakness, but a strength. When Dora said, with the delight in other people's virtues which was one of her characteristics, 'Mary, I *do* think you're the best person I've ever met,' Mary longed to tell her all, to be no longer under false pretences. And it was true. If Dora had known of Mr Herbert, Mary would have forfeited her high place for ever.

They had embarked on one of Dora's stories, long, certainly, and in this case, though not in most cases, painfully interesting. 'And one thought she seemed *so* respectable – dressed so quietly. When she told me there was going to be a baby, I said, "I cannot *think* how you could have done it, Annie," and she said, "He seemed so unhappy, and she did lead him a life." He was married, which made it so much worse. "It was all over in a rush, but I know it was wrong." She wants us to take her back, but we *couldn't*, could we?'

'No,' said Mary, 'I suppose you couldn't, but in a way I wish you would. I feel' – her heart beat, she made a sudden resolution – 'I feel I understand it more now.'

'Understand what more now?'

'I know love isn't everything, not even the most important thing. I used to think it was, but doesn't Shakespeare say it's like a madness? It makes one do the thing one hates most, and yet one would not, no, one would not have had it.'

'What *do* you mean, Mary?'

'Once I – there was a man – I would rather tell you, Dora –'

She became a prey to the incoherence which had exasperated Canon Jocelyn in her girlhood.

'Yes, I am not all you think me. It was before I was ill and came to Southsea. It really was the strain of that –'

In counting up her misfortunes Mary might have included that the narrow, uncomprehending Dora was her only intimate friend, if she had not already mentioned Dora's active sympathy in counting up her advantages. Had Dora not been Dora, she would now have told her all. But she saw Dora's gentle, innocent gaze, benevolent to almost all, particularly benevolent to her, turn to hardness. The resolution which had nerved her failed suddenly. If she had gone on talking all night, she could never have made Dora understand. She shrank into herself and said, 'Never mind, it was nothing, at least nothing I can talk about.'

The secret remained a barrier between them. Mary never felt for Dora what she had felt before. In the close friendship which lasted till death, Mary was never entirely at ease with her again. They sat silent. Dora felt her heart beating. She was convinced that Mary was going out of her mind, and the flushed face, burning eyes, and hurried, stuttering words gave grounds for uneasiness. She braced herself to speak in a few seconds, and said with peculiar gentle cheerfulness, which indicated exactly what was in her mind, 'Seeing Annie in the hospital brought back my old hospital days. You know I trained for some time, don't you, and then my ankles were too weak.' She talked on about hospital as a doctor entertains a patient when his mind is occupied with another case. After the right interval of distraction she said, 'Mary, dearest, you look a little tired, and so am I. What about early bed tonight?'

She did not go to bed herself, but listened long outside Mary's door, and heard her tossing, for Mary's night was broken with questioning of what she ought to have done.

At exactly the right hour for refreshment Dora brought Mary 'a little cup of Benger. I have just been making myself some, and it's so soothing. Let me arrange your bed for you, dear, and your *pillow*. I was wondering whether maltine wouldn't be a good thing in the middle of the morning. Gertrude found it splendid.'

She watched with a careful eye next day, but could see no further sign of the hallucination. She said to Mildred when she went home, 'I think the strain of Canon Jocelyn – he's wonderful, but it *is* a strain – is beginning to tell on dear Mary. She is getting a little neurotic –' She had picked up that favourite nurse's word in hospital. 'I shall go there as often as I can.'

26

EARLY one winter afternoon Mary came into the drawing-room. She found Canon Jocelyn sitting by the fire. It was an unusual time for him to be there.

'I came just now,' said he, 'to get some stamps' – he never would keep stamps in his study, only notepaper – 'and my eye caught this on your table.'

It was a poem Mary had written the night before, and forgotten to put away.

'I must ask your pardon for prying at what does not belong to me, but I took the liberty of reading it. There is a want of finish, an unevenness here and there in the rhythm' (Canon Jocelyn was an authority on metre), 'but there are some striking lines in it. Is it your own composition?'

Mary blushed, and said it was.

'Indeed; I had no idea that your talents turned in that direction. Have you any other specimens? I should like to see them.'

She could not believe her ears. She went upstairs, and brought down a small pile of manuscript. He read it attentively, commenting here and there. She felt she had never sufficiently realized the range and acuteness of his critical powers. He said more than once, 'Your thought was this, I imagine, but you have not made it as limpidly clear as a poet should. I have no poetic gift. You will clothe what I mean in a suitable form, but should there not be so and so?' and he expressed exactly what had been in her mind.

It was easier for him to understand her thoughts than she knew – they were often his own – only all these years they neither would, nor could, speak of them to one another.

'Strange,' he said, 'that you were never a literary character. You had more feeling for scholarship than any of your brothers, and was there not some childish composition which showed promise? but never since then. It was a pity you did not let me see these before.' She remembered her article on education. 'I will write a line to Stephens' (his publisher) 'tonight. He might advise you. I think they should be published.'

At tea he said, 'I have never had any of the higher gifts of the writer – creative power, imagination. What I have been able to do is due to hard work. Minds with creative imagination can do more.' He looked at Mary with a sweet, grave smile of congratulation, and said, 'I think the Almighty has blessed you with this great gift, Mary.' Such an austere life and home as Mary's was not unpropitious soil for the nurture of a poet, but Canon Jocelyn's judgement was today sweetened and softened by approaching decline. He thought her tender woodland poems better than they were. A week ago he would have liked them, but not so well. Some mysterious foreshadowing made him draw near to Mary, and love her writings because they were hers.

Canon Jocelyn talked on for half an hour as he never had before. He spoke of his beginnings in authorship; he discussed the books he had written. Mary noticed that sometimes his sentences were not perfectly coherent, and he took up the poem he had liked best and said, after re-reading it, 'I had not seen that. That is as good as any.'

From time to time, when he was tired, his memory weakened, but Dr King had told her not to be anxious. 'He'll be all right when he's rested,' and hitherto he always had been.

She was summoned by Emma. A woman had sent up for something from the parish medicine chest. As she went out of the room she heard him murmur with a certain bewilderment, but contentedly, 'That's a great comfort about Mary.'

She went upstairs and got what was wanted. On the way down she stood by the landing window. The twilight was disappearing into darkness; there was the wonderful pause which comes between the two. The chestnut tree stood out against the sapphire sky, black, calm, and majestic. Such a winter's twilight is perhaps the most beautiful of all aspects of the year. She had never failed since she was a child to gaze at it on some December or January afternoon. Every year it sent a thrill of inexplicable happiness through her, which she felt at no other season. Today her happiness was increased. She and her father had never been so near to one another. His praise had been nectar to her; his smile was more precious still. The desire of many years was accomplished. But she forgot how frail is any building whose foundations are old age.

When she returned to the drawing-room her father was still there, reading Virgil to himself.

'I think I shall not be working any more today,' he said. 'I feel a little tired.'

Each winter for some years he had had a chill, and was forced to submit to bed and Dr King for three or four days. Such a remark was the general precursor of his chills. Mary was accustomed to it, and knew its harmlessness, but it always made her heart give an unreasonable quake. When the gong rang he said he would not go into the dining-room. 'I will stay quietly here.'

She had his bed prepared, and his fire lighted upstairs.

She said to him, 'I wonder if you would feel more rested in bed?' The annual answer was forthcoming.

'Oh dear, no. I shall do very well here.'

She hastened back from the dining-room. She found he had huddled himself in his greatcoat. She again suggested bed in a casual manner that he might not feel himself fussed. He sent a chill through her by answering, 'I think perhaps I will. I do not feel very well tonight.'

He had never owned such a thing before.

When she had followed him up to bed and attended carelessly

to the fire, as if Emma had forgotten something, she went to the window, where she had looked out so happily two hours ago. She stood with her hands clenched to prevent herself from crying out, 'It has come. Death has come.'

Yet the doctor, when he arrived, and again on his second visit, did not seem anxious.

'One never can tell at his age, and I wish there wasn't this nasty 'flu about, but his pulse is very steady. I think it's the usual thing, and we shall have him out and about in three or four days.'

But it came as no surprise to Mary when Dr King said kindly, his merry face made serious by genuine emotion, for he admired Canon Jocelyn, though he did not understand him, 'He is not holding his own; it's got at his lungs,' and later, 'It is not hopeless, but you had better not hope too much.'

The nursing duties were so easy that Mary did not feel bound to employ a nurse. He would have been a case, and, as a case, not interesting. A nurse might have chaffed him. Mary had felt sorry for working-class old age at the mercy of kind chaff, but her father – So Susan nursed at night, and considered every service to him an honour.

There was no younger generation to send for. Aunt Lottie wrote that the weather was too bad for travelling. Mary was able to have the last hours at peace with him. She had often dreaded them in anticipation, but they were not terrible; she did not even find them sad; she was transported above sadness. The soft, south-wind, silver, winter days, particularly English, and his favourites of the year, did not jar on her as unfeeling in their beauty.

Canon Jocelyn asked that Mr Sykes should give him the Sacrament. After the short service Mary left them together. They were friends of fifty years. Each realized that their next meeting would be beyond the grave. Canon Jocelyn did not break through his customary reserve – he was reserved even with Mr Sykes – but, leaning wearily against the pillow, with languid, halting tones he renewed one of their favourite old conversations – a comparison of the *Æneid* and *Paradise Lost*, and his dying eyes lit up with a spark of pleasure when it could be made clear that Virgil was superior.

The first day or two he listened with interest to his old friend *Guy Mannering*, later he was drowsy and lay silent. Once, when Mary gave him some medicine, he took her hand, saying, 'Thank you, my child, and for everything.' He smiled. He looked feeble, but the smile was more tender than usual; it was also mysterious, as if the soul was already beyond her reach. She was sure he knew he was not going to live, and was saying good-bye. She felt as if she must clasp him in her arms, so that Death should not have him. She pressed his hand gently, and said, 'Dear Father.'

He sometimes broke the silence by murmuring to himself. She heard him whisper, 'Fanny, my beloved, my beloved one.' He had never mentioned her mother's name. Sometimes she imagined he had forgotten her. But his wife had always been far dearer to him than Mary; it was to her his confused mind turned in death. Though she was grudging, Mary did not grudge him to her mother. He smiled to himself. She was astonished to see that he looked young, like the drawing of the handsome, romantic young man who had courted her mother. With occasional words and sighs of unintelligible wandering, his life ebbed away; he passed into lethargy, and slept himself quietly to death.

All the Jocelyns' friends rallied round Mary. Some offered to stay with her, so that she should not be alone in the house. She was touched by their kindness, but it was belated. They might have done much for her in ordinary times; just now they could do nothing. She wanted to be alone. She was accustomed to solitude, and solitude would be her portion in future. Only in solitude could she realize to the full the mysterious feeling that the house was filled with her father. He had been far from her in life, now he was quite near. She knew the feeling was transient, the result of an unnatural tension, which seems to expand the faculties, but she drank it in as a refreshment for the future, when the jog-trot tedium of ordinary life began again. Pity was lavished on her; she did not need it. She felt apart from the ordinary world, above it, as if it was she who should pity it, not it her. The days passed like a dream; outside things did not touch her. But she regretted that the Herberts were away, so that Mr Herbert could not take part in the funeral service.

The business of moving from the Rectory must be started immediately. She wanted to take a small house in the neighbourhood with Cook, where she could keep in touch with Dedmayne without hampering their successors at the Rectory. She had seen a whitewashed house, with a real East Anglian high-peaked, thatched roof, in a spot not too damp for rheumatism and damp enough for luxuriance. But the project was knocked on the head. Aunt Lottie wrote that her old servant, on whom she relied for everything, was to be married immediately, and she had decided to move into a smaller house. The curate of her church appointed to a living at Croydon; she thought she would like to follow him there, and would Mary and Cook go and live with her? Mary said yes. She did not blind herself to the drawbacks. She felt as if her heart would break to leave the neighbourhood, and the flat eastern county itself, to decline on Croydon; but she knew it would not, and Aunt Lottie could turn to no one else. Mary was aware she herself had reached an age when she was fortunate in being wanted.

Aunt Lottie came to the Rectory in a paroxysm of fuss. It was an unfavourable omen. Now Mary accepted Dora's offer of a visit with gratitude. To look through the accumulations and prepare for departure with Aunt Lottie roaming over the house was a staggering task.

Among Canon Jocelyn's papers Mary found a journal, and, reading it over, she grew to understand him more than she had done in life. Most of it was concerned with his views on literary matters, or referred to his literary projects, but there were occasional expressions of regret, of self-abasement, which she might almost have written herself.

A certain passage particularly struck her. It was one of the few references to herself in the journal: beyond 'Mary went – Mary returned.' It was written on the night of Ruth's death. 'I consider that poor afflicted life, the countless sufferings which I have done nothing to mitigate. I was helpless before them. Mary devoted herself actively to the task; she has been both sister and mother. She told me just now with tears of her grief. I feel no grief. How should I? I have not deserved to grieve. The feelings of that moment were very bitter. Mary's nature is infinitely higher than my own; she has much of her mother about her. In the short time that I may be spared, let me endeavour to be more worthy of her.'

And she had never ceased to blame him for his indifference to Ruth. She would not recall that he had shown himself more worthy by continuing to behave exactly as before.

Soon the sublimity of grief left Mary. Its place was taken by an overmastering desire to be rid of Aunt Lottie for ever. The prospect of life at Croydon rose before her: interminable sitting in chilly, stuffy rooms, for Aunt Lottie enjoyed her economies; a trickle of chatter, which she seemed more insistent should be answered than at Broadstairs; makings and unmakings of the mind up twenty times a day; putting on one's things and instantly taking them off; a tracking down of the wind, the rain, the damp, the dust, the glare, the dark, the draught, the fog, the crowds, the motors; a tepid shower of complaints about various people, principally Cook, Mary foresaw, for Aunt Lottie and Cook were already beginning to bicker.

Just now Aunt Lottie did not show her best side. She had left some possessions at Dedmayne years ago; she had never troubled to take them away. The wonder whether they should or should not be sold produced unusual activity of mind. Mary could not forget that, though the wind and the time of year made it impossible for her to come and say good-bye to Canon Jocelyn, they had not interfered when it was a matter of furniture.

Dora's coming was a refreshment. She listened to reminiscences of Canon Jocelyn which would not interest Aunt Lottie, who was already consigning him to the hush of oblivion.

Mary had found in the drawing-room blotting-book a letter Canon Jocelyn had begun to his publisher. She showed it to Dora. 'DEAR STEPHENS,' it ran, 'I am glad you can arrange for the publication of the Tertullian so soon. You speak of further schemes of work. I do not think it is likely that I shall embark on any new undertaking. My time now must be close at hand. I venture, however, to send you the enclosed, which I hope, will hope, will interfere for you –' The sentence wandered, and the letter stopped. There were words scratched out, with others inserted. Mary could see the labour it cost to write. She read the few confused lines many times.

'I shall feel it a charge from him to get my things published now,' said she. 'It is the first thing I shall do after the business is finished. Dora,' she went on, a sudden thought striking her, 'if I died next week – of course I might live forty years longer, but I might die next week – would you arrange it for me? I was going to ask you if you would have my personal things, and do what you like with them. I want to make my will. Of course everything of value must go to Will's children, but I should like you to have the rest. I am very much alone, you know; we have no first cousins.'

'Thank you, Mary,' said Dora, with her usual calm gravity. 'I will certainly do my best about the writings and anything else you like to leave me. But why do you speak of dying next week? You don't feel ill, do you, dear?'

'No, not at all. I wish I did. Death seems so much nearer and more homely than life.'

'I know what it is, Mary, but that goes, and one is almost sorry it goes. Looking back, I think almost the best days of my life were just after Father's death.'

'Yes,' said Mary, 'but I see it would not do for it to last on. I must "Arbeit zurück." I have been thinking of Mignon's Requiem so often lately, but I wish "Arbeit" was not connected with that horrible furniture.'

'I was wondering whether your aunt could not sell the walnut chairs,' said Dora. They went back to the ordinary world again, from which Dora's talk rarely strayed, though her thoughts might.

Mary had many letters. The one she read most often was Mr Sykes', because it had something of Canon Jocelyn in the old-fashioned turn of the sentences; the terseness and jerkiness of modern English was unpleasant to them both. While Mr Sykes lived, she could feel there was still something of her father left on the earth.

My Dear Mary – You know with what a heavy heart I assisted at the sad ceremony this afternoon. When we grow old we do not fear Death as you who are young, because, as Wesley's father said, 'Time has shaken us by the hand, and Death is knocking at the door.' But I have parted with one who was dearer to me than all others, outside the immediate circle of my family. That gap cannot be filled. Time mercifully mitigates every sorrow, and will mitigate yours, but I know that nothing

in this life will ever really make up to you for the loss of your father.
– With my very affectionate remembrances, I remain your old friend,

JAMES SYKES.

There will be much sad business awaiting you in the course of the next few weeks. Could I be of any service, be sure that I will assist you to the utmost of my ability.

This letter was a special comfort to Mary, for some she had received, even from intimate friends, had not quite concealed the writer's private opinion that now she could begin to live. Those who really entered into Mary's grief were the old. They did not have the unconscious feeling of the middle-aged that Canon Jocelyn was a belated traveller; it was time he should be gone.

The task of looking through Canon Jocelyn's precious books was melancholy and unending. The majority were to be sold, but their outsides, if not their insides, were the framework of so much of Mary's past life that she found it hard to part with them. She gave several away to Canon Jocelyn's friends. Among others, she asked Mr Herbert to come over and choose.

He arrived while Dora and Aunt Lottie were still with her. She took him into the study, and left him for half an hour.

He looked up on her return.

'I have taken this volume of Tennyson's early poems,' said he. 'Do you remember your father talking of his admiration for Tennyson the first time he came to Lanchester? And may I have his Virgil also? I have never known any one love Virgil quite as he did. I need not tell you how I shall treasure them both.'

'He was very fond of that copy of Tennyson,' said Mary. 'It was a gift from your father. It is just what he would have wished, that you should have it, and the Virgil too; he was reading it the very afternoon he was taken ill.'

'Will you write my name in them?' he said.

She did so; he looked at other books while she wrote.

'Tea is just ready now,' she said when she had finished. 'Will you come into the drawing-room?'

'Thank you, I must not stay. There's a meeting at Cayley, which I ought not to miss.'

She felt he might have missed the meeting.

'You are leaving the neighbourhood, I hear.'

'Yes. I am going to Croydon with my aunt.'

'We shall all miss you,' he said. 'I hope, after a time, you may find happiness there.'

'Thank you,' she answered. 'It seems impossible at present, but perhaps I may.'

'Will you give my apologies to your aunt for not saying good-bye to her. Thank you again for these and for letting me come.'

They shook hands; as he did so he said with deep feeling, 'God bless you for ever, Mary.'

Until that word she had received his sympathy with calm gratitude, but 'Mary' on his lips roused all the emotion she thought had perished. At that moment she forgot her father entirely. She would not look at Mr Herbert, she would not speak to him. She bit her lips to keep back any words. If they had come they would have been, 'Love me again, if only for one instant I must have your love.'

She controlled herself. Feeling how extraordinary he must think her, she began, 'Mr Herbert, will you –?'

She looked up; he was already gone.

She could not stay in the study. Her senses were all awake that Dora, who could not possibly suspect, might suspect if she were late for tea.

She looked so sad when she came into the dining-room that Dora pressed her hand and whispered, 'I'm afraid it's bad this afternoon?' Mary nodded; Dora must think so.

After this her one desire was to finish with Dedmayne as soon as possible. That solitary lingering over each beloved spot – for Dora and Aunt Lottie both left the Rectory the day after Mr Herbert's call – that farewell visit to each friend, which she had dreaded yet anticipated with melancholy pleasure, should be abandoned. In three short weeks she left Dedmayne for ever.

27

MARY and Aunt Lottie removed to their suburb. They settled in a red-villa road, constructed in the nineties, with all the modern conveniences of that date, considered inconveniences now. Mary made her own room a kind of microcosm of the Rectory; the rest of the house was crowded with Aunt Lottie's little objects, and Mary was always tumbling over the footstools.

At first her exasperation with Aunt Lottie was perpetual. Once it became uncontrollable, and she scolded Aunt Lottie. It had the best possible effect. From henceforth Aunt Lottie was a little afraid of Mary. This suited the old lady; she did best with a master. Annie, her old servant, had been a hard one; Mary was gentle. Aunt Lottie became still fonder of Mary.

The early weeks in the new home seemed to stop still, but before Mary was aware she had settled into a routine; after that time galloped.

It was by no means a solitary routine. The good-natured curate, whom Aunt Lottie had followed to the suburbs, was now a popular vicar. He had the faculty of collecting people about him: children, families, girls, some bachelors, old and young, widows, and, of course, several genial spinsters. They, the spinsters particularly, welcomed Mary as their own, soothed her shyness, shared weekly periodicals with her, made her join a discussion society, took her to matinées, lectures, concerts, and political and philanthropic meetings. As for good works to share in, they were plentiful as blackberries. Her new friends and Dora Redland, and especially Ella Redland, felt that she made an important advance when she was persuaded to sit on committees – even to become a chairman. The working people took her to their hearts at once. They were accustomed to make friends easily with ladies. If they had waited before opening out in the village way, they would have had no friends, for, after three years in one place, suburban people, whatever their layer in society, become restless and want to move on.

It seemed that now, in middle life, Mary had a late blossoming.

She, who had found it so hard to make friends, was suddenly surrounded with many. The social life of a suburb depends much on the clergy. The vicar was Oxford and, or 'but,' as Mr Sykes would have said, an accurate and distinguished scholar. He valued the honourable name of Jocelyn. His influence made the society round him cultivated. If he left, the cultivation would go too; it was not a characteristic of the suburb's own. Now nobody thought Mary 'learned' in an uncomplimentary, only in a complimentary sense. Her qualities were appreciated; she was appealed to and consulted. She stopped being shy; at forty it seemed foolish to be shy.

Her appearance improved. Her dull hair looked better turning grey. The likeness to her father came out, still more the likeness to the distinguished ancestresses. She began to get some Jocelyn dignity; she was talked of as 'that delightful Miss Jocelyn.'

As she expanded, Mary threw off some of her father's belated views. One must be much influenced by one's surroundings. In her new circle there was neither a Canon Jocelyn nor a Mr Herbert. Perhaps she lost some of that individuality, that unlikeness to the ordinary world which had given her a kind of gauche, innocent charm. Perhaps, also, living more in the middle of things, she could no longer have the critical onlooker's sense of proportion. In fact, she gained and she lost.

'It's *wonderful*,' Ella said joyously. 'Mary is getting so much more like other people.'

The Redlands had been sensibly insistent that Mary should not immolate herself for Aunt Lottie, and Aunt Lottie did not grudge her outside interests; she enjoyed the reflected glory of Mary's success. But Ella was vexed that Mary would not go away for a night, because Aunt Lottie had a weak heart.

'I would come and stay whenever you wanted,' said Dora. 'At a moment's notice.'

But Mary was firm. If she went away, she must accept her many invitations to the Merytons and the Herberts; she would rather not go.

She recognized the advantages of her outer life. It was more cheerful, in some ways more congenial, than Dedmayne. What was her inner life?

'We're all so fond of you, Mary,' a new friend said to her. 'But I don't believe you care much for any of us.'

'Yes, I do,' answered Mary, taking her hand. 'But my heart seems like a stone. I have been through a good deal.'

'I *know* you have,' said the friend, not knowing. Mary never revealed what she endured when she first left Dedmayne. She wondered afterwards how she had lived through it. She not only lived through it, but preserved a calm, not unduly sad front to the world. Ella said with surprised satisfaction:

'I think Mary *herself* feels it a release.'

In youth she had resolved not to yield to the luxury of self-pity. That resolution had not been kept. She had yielded at Mr Herbert's engagement, and again after his kiss. The recollection frightened her. She had found self-pity a quagmire in which it was difficult not to be submerged.

Looking back, she could not understand how she had then felt there was nothing left, while she still had her father.

Now all was gone. She lost the sense of her father being near. She was convinced he could never be near, or had been, because he had ceased to be. Christian hope failed her not for hours and days, but for weeks and months. Books, sermons, her longing, the dictates of her reason availed her nothing. She went to the friendly Vicar and said she had doubts; they were not doubts, they were certainties. He talked with sympathetic consolation; he assured her he had no doubts. She came back; she was still more certain. She would confide in no one else. Dora wrote proposing herself – she and Aunt Lottie had become very friendly – 'I have thought of you so often. Do let me come. I know it gets worse and worse in the first few months.' Mary felt that kind Dora's piety would add to her torture. She wanted to be alone, to go through this bitterness alone.

She did not relax even to herself. She had realized it was not wise for a Jocelyn to relax. She wanted this remnant of her life to be worthy of her father and Mr Herbert. She thought of Mr Herbert's words about the chink of light that occasionally came through. She knew now there would be no chink of light; one must walk on without it.

Her solace, sometimes severe, were the duties that sprang up in the little home: the daily winding-up of two clocks, the weekly winding-up of three more; the morning paper, which she read all through to Aunt Lottie and later Aunt Lottie read all through to her, and the evening paper, in which the same news appeared in a still brighter form; the cat and dog, who wanted to be let in, and as soon as they were in to be let out, and as soon as they were out to be let in again; the knitting, which she set ready for Aunt Lottie, undid when she was gone to bed, and knitted up again to be ready for Aunt Lottie next afternoon; the explanations and answers to questions, which must be repeated several times, for Aunt Lottie, though not deaf, was inquisitive and inattentive; the listening to little whining digs of Aunt Lottie against various people, not made in malice, but just a habit, like sniffing. 'And that little inlaid table. I told your father particularly I only *lent* it to your mother, and I wanted it back. I always thought it was *not* very considerate of him, and there were other little things ... about poking the fire ... and I left him so many of my things at the Rectory ... all those books in the spare room were mine.' And though the matter of the inlaid table might seem satis- factorily laid to rest by Mary, it would soon crop up again as robust as ever. Altogether, the Aunt Lottie part of the daily routine had something of a Sisyphus character. Then there was the more exciting, energetic part. Mary showed pleasant interest and gratitude about all her new friends prepared for her to do. They should not realize her mind was elsewhere. She was indiff- erent to their proffered intimacy. There were two people in the world she wanted – her father and Mr Herbert. Nothing besides existed for her. She had felt beyond the verge of feeling; at present she could feel no more.

Sometimes in the morning she shrank at the day's prospect. 'Life hath a load which must be carried on. And safely may.' She said these words, but did not agree with them. To those as near the breaking-point as she was then, there seems no safety. She found the load heaviest in the spring and summer after her father's death. It was then that the suburb looked its crudest – the asphalt paths, the tarred roads, the hoardings, the red and yellow houses with white and chocolate paint, the mustard- coloured privet, the pink may, lilac, copper beech, laburnum, vivid spring green leaves, orange wallflower, and blue forget-me-not, seen under an east-wind mauve sky, made a bright picture, which the inhabitants could not admire enough. Aunt Lottie liked to looke at the picture in the public gardens with the 'summer girls' disporting themselves in their vulgarity.

When Mary was alone, she went to the one field left within reach, and gazed at the haystack, able with the faculty which usually goes with childhood to imagine that the houses partially hidden by the trees were not really there. She was not merely country-bred; the country was part of her. Her heart clung to all its most exasperating characteristics: the stumbling walks in uneven, lumpy fields under feeble starlight, or in black, black darkness; tracts of mud; dank, damp grass; streams of dead leaves in which one can walk ankle deep; shining puddles flowing right across the path; brambles and underwood stretching out their tentacles to catch one; thick, soft, white mist – she loved to stand in it and feel it saturating her; smells of cows and pigs; all the unmusical sounds of animals. Nature did not seem at ease in the suburbs; even her favourite wind was subdued and not himself. Mary wanted to be back in the Dedmayne lanes, where she remembered the snow lying thick and undisturbed. In the early summer she was hungry for the insignificant country flowers – pink, yellow, purple, white – hiding in the grass. Sometimes Mary fancied if she could only be in Dedmayne her numb heart would get warm. But if she saw Mr Herbert it might melt too much.

The soft power of time at length healed her. Autumn came with charm strong enough to transform the suburb. She began to feel again. She remembered the moment that she could say after all life was not over. It was when she heard the small piping song a robin was making to himself, different from the loud chirp with which he greeted his human friends, realizing how deaf and stupid they were. She had heard it and enjoyed it hundreds of times. Now it spoke to her with inexpressible consolation. Another day it was the lovely silvery clouds reposing with majestic tranquillity in the winter sky. It seemed as if Nature drew near Mary in her need. Having done her part of comfort, she retired, and as Mary became more immersed in her present life, Nature withdrew still farther.

Hope had returned. Sometimes it was sudden and transitory, sometimes it lingered. She was able occasionally to experience a mysterious acquiescent joy.

She could think again with happiness of her father. There was a certain hour she kept for him on Sunday evening. With him she thought of Mr Herbert, feeling now, she could not have explained why, that there was nothing which would jar on her father in her remembering them together. She allowed herself to re-read his love-letter, and went over their talks again and again, idealizing perhaps both him and them, as if he were dead also.

Her heart expanded. She could now give something more than dutiful gratitude to her friends; her natural tenderness found many outlets. The interest she had pretended to became genuine. But going on with her outer life she had from henceforth an inner life, and whereas her circle was cheerfully absorbed in the present, she thought much of the past and of the future, feeling the truth of words, which most people find disturbing. 'We have here no continuing city; we seek that which is to come.'

Mary had sent her writings to Canon Jocelyn's publisher before she left Dedmayne. But Mr Stephens was ill abroad, and the younger, smarter partner returned the MS. At the time it had been a very bitter disappointment. She had not the spirit to try elsewhere, and the parcel went back to her drawer; it was replenished now and then in her months of dejection. Later, as her life became busier, she wrote no more.

Kathy more than once made projects for seeing Mary. Besides invitations to Lanchester, she had twice suggested meeting in London, but the plan fell through. The Herberts rarely came to town; neither cared for it. At length Kathy arranged lunch at a restaurant, and a matinée to follow.

'I wanted a good old scream, but I know what you two are,' she explained, beaming on Mary and Mr Herbert, 'so I've fixed on a highbrow show, where you could take dozens of maiden aunts, and none of them turn a hair.'

Mary had supposed unreasonably she should never see Mr Herbert again. She would like to keep that 'God bless you, Mary,' as his last words. Still, she longed to see him, while she dreaded it. But the meeting, when it came, damped any dangerous ardour.

The crude brilliance of the restaurant, the crowd, the bustle, 'the jolly good feed' pressed on them by Kathy – 'Don't let him choose, or we shall get nothing but leg of mutton and tapioca pudding' – brought Mary to earth rather roughly.

There was much old chaff from Kathy, and some new.

'I say, Towzer, you are blooming, quite handsome. I think it's rather a risk having you about with my susceptible husband; I shan't leave you alone together.'

It was fortunate that Kathy's own hearty laugh supplied a comment, for Mary was speechless. That joke cut her. She had never seen Kathy in London clothes before. Smart Kathy must always be, but today she was in rich furs and a plumy hat; she looked a splendid cavalier. Never had Mary felt so much her own insignificance.

They talked a great deal about the children, and gossip of the neighbourhood. They had some general conversation about passing topics. Mary contributed her share. She was more at home in the world's affairs than formerly. It was unreasonable to regret this. Mr Herbert assured himself that she could not have become commonplace, but he wanted her the same; the reality did not seem to correspond to the Mary he mused about. He hardly owned it to himself, but Mary was convinced that he felt a twinge of something, not strong enough to be called disappointment. As for her, she saw him looking well enough, happy enough, almost young enough to match his lovely wife. He seemed to have nothing to do with the Mr Herbert she thought of on Sundays. She was seized with jealousy of him and Kathy – the primal jealousy of an unsuccessful rival. Kathy had him, had children, had everything. If only he could be a little dissatisfied – Mary did not want him to be unhappy – she did not want Kathy to be unhappy, but *why* should he feel her perfection?

In his happy marriage Mr Herbert thought seldom of Mary, but when he found he was to meet her, something came back with irresistible force.

He and Mary had both unconsciously imagined they should meet one another as all that they always had been, and yet sublimated into angels. They had longed too much, and that cruel nervous reaction, which reminds us so pitilessly that we are only mortals, spoilt the reality, and tormented them with criticisms and doubts.

'I must arrange my veil,' said Kathy in the cloakroom after lunch. 'Veils are the deuce, but Lesbia's Polish barber man I went to this morning has got my hair into such a fluff I'm not respectable without a veil. Did I tell you Jack's back? That's why we're up. All merry as a marriage bell so far. I don't suppose that will last long. Well, old thing, it *is* jolly seeing you again, and not changed one bit, except that you're so awfully fit. You haven't told me a thing about yourself. What do you do with yourself all day, without me to see that you don't get into mischief?'

Mary thought of her busy, happy life. She compared it to Kathy's fullness; it seemed starvation.

'I don't think there's much to tell,' said she. 'I only –' She stopped; she felt herself near tears.

'I *say*!' cried Kathy. 'It's nearly the half-hour. We must fly. I loathe being late. And I don't know where Crab won't have wandered off to, not to mention that probably he's forgotten to tip the waiter, though I told him exactly what it was to be. Crab's more responsbility than three children any day.'

Mary had the guest's place between the Herberts at the matinee. During the 'high-brow' play, a sentimental costume melodrama, Mr Herbert sat gazing gloomily at vacancy in transports of boredom, which, man-like, he made no efforts to conceal. He was even provoked because Mary pretended successfully to enjoy herself. Kathy was delighted with the play, as touched by its sentiment and as amused by its jokes as the Cosmopolitan producers, gauging its public well, knew she would be. Mr Herbert allowed his disgust to infect the intervals. He did not take much pains to make himself pleasant. The little time there was, was taken up with matinée talk with Kathy.

Mary had to catch a train immediately after the play. There were cordial and hurried good-byes, and proposals from Kathy of another matinée next time they came to town. But Mary had determined she would never see the Herberts again, and she never did see them again.

It was not at once that Mary could conquer the jealousy she so much despised. It burned again with the fierceness of its first flame after Mr Herbert's engagement.

For some time the remembrance of the matinée took the whole sweetness out of Mary's past. But there is something very romantic about memory. The Mr Herbert of her dreams was reinstated, and the luncheon was blotted out as if it had not been.

28

MARY was stricken with influenza. How long it was after her father's death depends on how one judges of time. Kathy's three boys were well past babyhood, and the delightful years seemed long to her from their fullness. To Mr Sykes, living on alone at Yeabsley, they seemed a few rather melancholy months.

Dora Redland came to help in the nursing and look after Aunt Lottie. Her gentleness awed Nurse into quietness and soothed Aunt Lottie's restless distress. Nurse said to professional friends, 'No one could call Miss Redland *trained*, mind you, though she takes a great deal upon herself. Cottage Hospital – you know the style.'

Mary's mind wandered a little. For the most part she talked confusedly of trifling matters of her present life. She mentioned Ruth, the little sister who had seemed to pass entirely out of her life. In many sentences the word 'he' kept recurring. She had never thought of Mr Herbert as anything but 'he.' 'It's such a strange fancy of dear Mary's,' said Dora to Aunt Lottie. 'She is always talking about her father in the study at Lanchester.'

Once Mary said to Dora drowsily, with a half-whimsical smile, 'Dora, do you think it isn't going to be forty years after all?'

'I wonder,' said Dora, with her sweetest nurse's smile, not in the least understanding what Mary was driving at. 'And now the precocious infant' – the Redlands' pet name for Mary as a little girl (being very ill, Mary was back as a darling child to Dora) –

'must have her Benger's. Cook wants to hear that you've finished every scrap today.'

Though the influenza had not seemed a severe attack first of all, Mary gradually sank, and she died after a three weeks' illness.

Then Dora remembered Mary's words after Canon Jocelyn's death, and she said through her tears, 'Darling Mary, I believe she was glad it wasn't forty years.'

Mary was buried at Dedmayne by her father. Emma was hysterical at the funeral. Cook shed no tears, but she had suddenly grown very small, turned into a little, thin, old woman. Dora gave her a kiss – the last act she could do for Mary. Cook did not cry even then, but said very quietly, 'Oh, miss, I never thought it would be like this. I thought she would have been by me at the end. You feel it, Miss Dora, same almost as me, because you've been about the world just as I've done, and I know ladies, and there never will be any one like her again.'

Dora had felt the harshness, the ingratitude of Death, which would make Mary soon forgotten in the village she had so cherished. But the Jocelyns were not being forgotten yet.

'Ah,' said old Barnes, whom Dora went to visit after the funeral, 'there's terrible changes here with the new Rector.' He was hardly new in point of time, but, as different from the Jocelyns, he and his wife would be new to Dedmayne for years to come.

'I've left the choir,' went on Barnes. 'We was all to turn our faces to the Commandments, same as the congregation, when we says the Creed; he don't seem to know what's the choir's due; and he have cut down the monkey-tree at the Rectory, what was the first monkey-tree planted in the British Isles, so you wouldn't know the old place.'

At tea at the Rectory, Dora saw the reverse side of the shield.

'I know,' said the Rector's wife, who managed to create a feeling of bustle even at a funeral. 'The Jocelyns must have been wonderful, and the people were dreadfully upset when they heard she had passed away, but weren't they rather curious? Fancy no water laid on upstairs. We want to start the Guides here to make it a little brighter, and they say the Canon wouldn't have liked it.

I think country people are most difficult, and we had such a nice congregation at Brixton. No, darling, not now; Mummy's busy.'

The little girl looked as if she might grow into such another as her mother, but when Dora saw her and the baby boy at tea in the old nursery, she felt, although the Rectory had been, as far as possible, turned into a morsel of Brixton, Mary would be content.

Dora's affection urged her to do something with Mary's writings. She wrote to Brynhilda, who still saw Ella from time to time. After hearing from Brynhilda, she sent the packet. Among the papers, unnoticed by Dora, was the envelope containing Mr Herbert's love-letter; with it was Mary's translation from the Spanish. They struck awe into Brynhilda. She felt Mr Herbert and Mary were in a region she never had entered, she never could enter. She showed the poem and letter to Dermott. He read them and threw them into the fire.

'You have shown me what should have been as sacred as a confession,' said he as they watched them burn, 'but I believe I've said before you have no conception what friendship means.'

'One moment,' said Brynhilda musingly, 'I suppose that was all. She had a life so shrivelled it became absurd. She ought to have been married to that man and been happy. People one knows marry, and divorce, and have children, and are bored the whole time. How crazy it all is, and how tragic.'

'Yes, you have all the sentimentality of an atheist,' said Dermott.

'Mary had a pull over us in a way,' said Brynhilda. 'She cared, and we can't care, not much, and never for long, not even for big things, and after a time they aren't big, but quite, quite small.'

'I shan't try and get her things published,' said Dermott. 'I was wrong about them. The average is just the Anglican spinster warbling, but something emerges occasionally – an odd cry from the heart, or whatever there is beyond the heart, and one feels she's curiously complete.'

29

WHEN Mary died Kathy was very sorry. She had too robust a nature to feel remorse that she had not seen more of her; besides it never occurred to her that people would care sufficiently to be disappointed if they did not see her.

Mr. Herbert had been asked to take the funeral service.

'I'll come with you, Crab,' said Kathy, 'not to the house, of course – they won't want me – but just to the church. I should like to be there. She was rather mad, but awfully nice, almost the nicest woman I've ever met.'

'Yes,' he said, 'she was.' His thoughts were elsewhere. Presently he went on, 'Kathy, do you mind not coming?'

'All right. Why?'

'I would rather not tell you today; I will later.'

'You feel it awfully, don't you?' she said, laying her hand on his shoulder. 'I'm so sorry. You liked the old man so much too.'

He nodded his head and went out of the room. He was very sad and silent for weeks afterwards, but when he was depressed – and he was a man given to fits of dejection – his wife never probed him, but left him to find his way back to cheerfulness. She liked his reserve. With her he was reserved; he would not have been with Mary. Kathy would have felt him rather namby-pamby if he had often opened his heart to her.

One afternoon he came to her and said, 'Dearest, I want to tell you something.'

He spoke so solemnly that she looked at him in astonishment. Then, with much hesitation and difficulty, he stammered out to her what he had felt for Mary. During their engagement he had told her that he had a passing fancy for another woman. He had never mentioned the name. Kathy could not believe him.

'You loved Mary, Mary Jocelyn,' she kept repeating, 'and she loved you. Well, I should have thought, after me, you could have found some one not quite so –' 'awfully plain,' she was going to say, but stopped herself.

He was not listening to her.

'You kissed her only once; you are sure it was only once? When was it?'

'It was when you were abroad on the Riviera.'

'I see. Well, you know I don't look back on that time with any satisfaction.'

'At any rate, you can look back on it with more satisfaction than I can. I don't forgive myself –' He broke off. 'I can't talk of it.' This made her laugh.

'But you did care for me when we first married?'

'You know I did.'

'Yes, I know you did. Still, it's a bit confusing. First of all you loved her, and then you loved me, and then you loved her, and then you loved me – a Box and Cox kind of arrangement. Not very complimentary for either of us.'

He frowned in misery.

Another thought struck her.

'Then it *was* pity, just beastly pity, that evening I came back, and you were trying to be kind to me.'

'No,' said he, 'it wasn't; you're wrong; it wasn't pity.'

'Honour bright?' she smiled. 'Well, I'll believe you. Anyhow, it's no use worrying over it *now*.'

'I had Stocky and you had Mary.' She was going to say this, then felt the comparison did not quite suit.

'Never mind, cheer up,' said she, and laughed again. Her mind turned from herself to Mary. 'And she only had one kiss, poor, dear Mary,' she said thoughtfully.

'I wanted to be alone with her this half-hour of her funeral,' he said.

She flushed with jealousy, but she mastered it, and said in a gentler voice than was usual with her, 'Yes, I see.'

'We never met again,' said Mr Herbert, 'till she came to see you when you were ill, and by that time – long before that time, in fact, immediately after I spoke to her, I believe – it was over with her. I have often thought how she must have despised me for what I did.'

'For kissing her? Oh, I don't think *that's* likely,' said Kathy sharply and dryly, partly jealous of Mary, partly ruffling up that any one so plain should dare to despise her husband.

'Don't –' he began.

'All right,' said she, and was silent.

Afterwards she said, 'Crab, I should like to know –' She hesitated. 'Perhaps I'd better not ask you.'

'Ask anything,' he said; 'I want you to know it all.'

'You loved her with real love, not a sort of heavenly thing up in the sky?'

'Yes, I did.'

'You *did*. No, I won't say anything against her. She was good to me when I hated everybody else and was altogether rotten. However, that's all over now.' She waited a moment, thinking; her brain always moved slowly. At last she said, 'You don't wish *now* you'd married her?'

'No, no, that feeling died long ago.'

'And when did you stop loving her?'

'Never,' he said. 'I feel exactly the same to her now.' The lady at the Broadstairs boarding-house was right. It had been Mary's lot to meet the exceptional man in whom she could inspire deep and lasting love. 'But that doesn't make me love you the less, darling,' Mr Herbert went on, trying to take her hand, but she withdrew it.

'Thank you very much,' she said. 'I thought only Mohammedans were supposed to have two wives at the same time.'

'How can you talk in that way?' he said, flushing.

'How else am I to talk when a respectable parson is in love with two people at once? That's quite a different thing from one after another, you know. Which was the chief wife?'

'Don't, for Heaven's sake, speak like that.' She was startled at his vehemence. 'We owe it to her we found one another again.'

'Now you're making matters distinctly worse.'

'It would have been better never to have spoken of it,' he exclaimed bitterly.

'I don't know, only it's rather amusing that when you were welcoming me back as a lost lamb you were just as lost yourself. Of course that cat was never let out of the bag. It was I who did all the going down on my knees. I say, what a cad I am, when it was you who really did go down on your knees.'

Another thought struck her, and she laughed disagreeably.

'After all, when I supposed I don't know what all about you, you were just like all the other men. How quaint.' There was a cynicism in her tone which he had never heard when she spoke to him, only when she spoke to Lesbia.

'I can't speak for other men,' he said, 'but I had never flattered myself that I was no worse than other people. On the contrary, when I–'

'Don't.' She interrupted him roughly. 'Don't gas about it. It's no good talking any more. I shall only say cattish things about Mary. If you go for a walk in one direction, I'll go for a walk in another. I should think it would be better for all parties. We may both feel better and brighter when we meet again.'

She strode along the fields, banging at some thistles with her stick. She, young and beautiful, had been ousted by a plain, middle-aged woman. It was to the plain, middle-aged woman she owed her restored happiness.

'If one is going to be chucked, I'd rather he'd do it with professionals. That's playing the game, and at any any rate they're smart.'

She said this two or three times out of spite, knowing how repelled her husband was when she relapsed into aristocratic coarseness. The thought of old Mrs Herbert's anguish at such a speech added a zest. But her mind was not cheered for long; waves of jealousy kept rushing over her and made her grind her teeth.

She suddenly recollected how she had chaffed Mary because she had had no admirers. Her face became scarlet.

'What a damned fool I made of myself,' she cried. 'How she must have chuckled. No, she wouldn't do that, though; poor old Towzer, she could never chuckle.'

The friendly thought gave way to a bitter one. 'Now one understands why she was always rooting about Lanchester. She had to go and have a scene with him after fluffing round me.'

This she knew to be an unfair charge. Mary's face came before her. She broke into an indignant laugh, but it brought back the hours of nervous misery when Mary had comforted her. She remembered how Mary had at first refused to come. 'I suppose she hated me really.' She remembered, too, asking whether Mr Herbert loved her from pity, and Mary's answer, 'I am sure it was never pity; I am absolutely certain of it.' 'And she knew all the time,' thought Kathy. Then she recollected how Mary had cried when they kissed. She sighed impatiently. 'It's beyond me.' But the memory of those tears made her whisper, 'Poor old Mary,' not that she realized all Mary had suffered.

She was not of a jealous nature – she had so little vanity – and her thick-skinned wholesomeness of disposition stood her in good stead. It was easier for her to be reconciled to Mary than for Mary to be reconciled to her. 'Only, *why* couldn't he have let well alone?' she thought as she made her way home. 'Any other husband would have kept dark about it; still, of course, he's not any other husband. That's where I was wrong; he's not like all the other men.' She smiled; she murmured tenderly, 'He's such a baby, just three and a half.'

Mr Herbert wandered miserably about the lanes. To him there had been anguish in the confession. Her levity over it had scorched him up. He was distracted by her outburst, as if some disturbance of Nature had occurred; she was usually so easy and equable. She was able to talk in an ordinary way at dinner, while he was in a nervous paroxysm of remorse and agonizing irritation.

After dinner she came and sat by him in the study. 'My dear old boy,' said she, 'it's beastly forgiving and that kind of thing, so let's both settle we've done all that. Don't brood about the Mohammedans and the other rotten things I said any more. I'm glad now you told me; I'd rather know. It's no good denying that I did mind, and I do still, and I'm jealous of Mary, which is horrid. I think I shall be pleased in the end that she had anybody like you to love her, and even that you go on loving her. If I am to owe you to anybody, I'd rather it was to Mary, because she was so sweet. You were both awfully good to me, much too good.' She was now in his arms.

'Lesbia said one day she was the sort you ought to have married, and I see now she was right. I wish for you I had died when I came back, and then you could have married Mary. She was better than me.'

'Don't, don't,' he said, shuddering and clasping her tightly.

'Now you've got me, you must put up with me,' she said,

partly laughing, partly sobbing. He did not answer her, because he could not speak. When he could, he said, 'It isn't necessary for us to begin to say what we are to one another at this time of day. You're everything in the world to me, but, dearest, there is a special place in my heart for Mary, and there always will be.'

'All right, old Crab,' said she. 'Go into your Bluebeard's cupboard and lock the door when you like, only don't stay long, because, remember, I *can't* do without you.'

She asked him if he possessed any memento of Mary. He said nothing but one short note. Before his marriage he had thrown Mary's letters away in the general tidying up for the bride. He showed her solemnly the note with the few words, 'Thursday is the day that will suit us best,' which had cost so much to write. Kathy had a schoolboy impulse to laugh at any one cherishing 'Thursday is the day that will suit us best' as a love-letter, but second thoughts made its meaning clearer. She had sometimes chaffed Mary about Thursday and the Infirmary, and she said seriously and almost solemnly, 'I think Mary was a trump.'

'Have you got a photograph of her?' she asked. She wanted, and she did not want, to look a moment on her rival's face.

'No,' said he, rather shyly. 'I never wanted one.'

'No, I remember; she came out almost a freak in a photograph,' said Kathy sympathetically.

But that was not quite the reason, for no photograph, no speaking portrait, could have captured what he loved so much in her – that depth and intensity of feeling which rarely showed itself in her face, or even in her words. He could find it in his county's winds, which she had relished in every part of her. When these winds came, whether the great equinoctial blasts of autumn, or the rough, blustering gales of March, or the hurricanes of August, roaring through the branches bowed down by the heavy late-summer leafage, then Mary came also. She seemed quite close to him, walking by his side again in the garden at Lanchester, where he first began to love her.

MORE ABOUT PENGUINS, PELICANS
AND PUFFINS

For further information about books available from Penguins please write to Dept EP, Penguin Books Ltd, Harmondsworth, Middlesex UB7 0DA.

In the U.S.A.: For a complete list of books available from Penguins in the United States write to Dept DG, Penguin Books, 299 Murray Hill Parkway, East Rutherford, New Jersey 07073.

In Canada: For a complete list of books available from Penguins in Canada write to Penguin Books Canada Ltd, 2801 John Street, Markham, Ontario L3R 1B4.

In Australia: For a complete list of books available from Penguins in Australia write to the Marketing Department, Penguin Books Australia Ltd, P.O. Box 257, Ringwood, Victoria 3134.

In New Zealand: For a complete list of books available from Penguins in New Zealand write to the Marketing Department, Penguin Books (N.Z.) Ltd, P.O. Box 4019, Auckland 10.

In India: For a complete list of books available from Penguins in India write to Penguin Overseas Ltd, 706 Eros Apartments, 56 Nehru Place, New Delhi 110019.

Penguin Modern Classics

THE TRAGIC MUSE

Henry James

Henry James published *The Tragic Muse* in 1890 at the beginning of his intense, but disastrous, flirtation with the theatre. Its themes reflect those preoccupations and, although this is the most 'English' of his novels, James concentrates his debate on the artistic life, in a masterly example of the 'all dramatic, all scenic'.

JOSEPH AND HIS BROTHERS

Thomas Mann

As Germany dissolved into the nightmare of Nazism, Thomas Mann was at work on this novel. This epic recasting of the famous biblical tale is a magnificent reconstruction of the ancient Near East. It stretches back past the days of the patriarchs to the dawn of civilization itself, and constitutes one of Thomas Mann's major achievements.

THE HOUSE OF MIRTH

Edith Wharton

First published in 1905, when it profoundly shocked society, *The House of Mirth* is a novel of manners that helped to carve out for the author an area of social fiction into which not even Henry James could trespass. 'A passionate social prophet' wrote Edmund Wilson, 'is precisely what Edith Wharton became. At her strongest and most characteristic, she is a brilliant example of the writer who relieves an emotional strain by denouncing his generation.'

OUT OF AFRICA
Karen Blixen

After the failure of her coffee farm in Kenya, where she lived from 1913 to 1931, Karen Blixen went home to Denmark and wrote this book which has become a literary classic. Remarkable for its sharp, fine intelligence and its intensely personal – yet detached – judgements as well as its superb prose, it is both a love letter to the people and place she loved so well and a poignant farewell.

THE SPANISH FARM TRILOGY
R. H. Mottram

To the men who came to know the Spanish Farm during the First World War, it offered an oasis of enduring sanity amidst the holocaust and carnage...
The author added three short pieces to connect the novels when the trilogy was published in one volume in 1927: and *The Times Literary Supplement* acclaimed it 'a trilogy of novels which, taken as a whole, is perhaps the most significant work of its kind in English that the War has yet occasioned'.

MORAVAGINE
Blaise Cendrars

Since its first publication in France in 1926, this ferocious and fantastic masterpiece has established itself as a classic of twentieth-century fiction. Narrated by a young French doctor, this semi-autobiographical story is full of tenderness, horror and savage humour, of which Henry Miller wrote 'I was ravished by Cendrars' *Moravagine*'.